PODKAYNE OF MARS

W9-BZP-277

To some readers Poddy is the bestest thing to ever come from Mars. But others find Poddy's self confidence annoying and her wide-eyed little girl teach-me attitude toward spaceship pilots duplicitous as well as cloying. *They* say Poddy must die. So, with the trade publication, we decided to have a contest to let the readers decide.

Did Poddy wind up as the first female starship captain—or just another victim? The readers of the trade edition have already chosen. Heinlein himself wrote it both ways, but as to which becomes the new official ending, the only way to find out it is to buy this newest and only-est mass market edition, complete with the winning essays on why Poddy must die— or live.

See Appendix for details.

Baen Books By Robert A. Heinlein

Glory Road
Podkayne of Mars
Revolt in 2100
Methusaleh's Children
Assignment in Eternity
The Menace From Earth
Sixth Column
The Green Hills of Earth
The Man Who Sold the Moon
Take Back Your Government (*nonfiction*)

ROBERT A. HEINLEIN

PODKAYNE OF MARS

PODKAYNE OF MARS

This is a work of fiction. All the characters and events portrayed in this book are fictional, and any resemblance to real people or incidents is purely coincidental.

Copyright © 1963 by Robert A. Heinlein
Postlude to *Podkayne of Mars*, original version © 1989 by Robert A. & Virginia Heinlein Trust UDT 20 June 1983. "Heinlein on *Podkayne*" was first printed in *Grumbles from the Grave*, edited by Virginia Heinlein and is © 1989 by Robert A. & Virginia Heinlein Trust, UDT 20 June 1983. "We Created a Monster," "The Winners" and "A Final Word" are copyright © 1995 by Jim Baen.

All rights reserved, including the right to reproduce this book or portions thereof in any form.

A Baen Book

Baen Publishing Enterprises
P.O. Box 1403
Riverdale, N.Y. 10471

ISBN: 0-671-87671-6

Cover art by Stephen Hickman

First Baen printing, August 1993
First paperback printing, July 1995

Distributed by
SIMON & SCHUSTER
1230 Avenue of the Americas
New York, N.Y. 10020

Printed in the United States of America

For Gale and Astrid

Printed in the United States of America

I

All my life I've wanted to go to Earth. Not to live, of course—just to see it. As everybody knows, Terra is a wonderful place to visit but not to live. Not truly suited to human habitation.

Personally, I'm not convinced that the human race originated on Earth. I mean to say, how much reliance should you place on the evidence of a few pounds of old bones plus the opinions of anthropologists who usually contradict each other anyhow when what you are being asked to swallow so obviously flies in the face of all common sense?

Think it through— The surface acceleration of Terra is clearly too great for the human structure; it is known to result in flat feet and hernias and heart trouble. The incident solar radiation on Terra will knock down dead an unprotected human in an amazingly short time— and do you know of any other organism which has to be artificially protected from what is alleged to be its own natural environment in order to stay alive? As to Terran ecology—

Never mind. We humans just *couldn't* have originated on Earth. Nor (I admit) on Mars, for that matter—although Mars is certainly as near ideal as you can find in this planetary system today. Possibly the Missing Planet was our first home—even though I think of Mars as "home" and will always want to return to it no matter how far I travel in later years . . . and I intend to travel a long, *long* way.

But I do want to visit Earth as a starter, not only to see how in the world eight billion people manage to live almost sitting in each other's laps (less than half of the land area of Terra is even marginally habitable) but mostly to see oceans . . . from a safe distance. Oceans are not only fantastically unlikely but to me the very thought of them is terrifying. All that unimaginable amount of water, unconfined. And so deep that if you fell into it, it would be over your head. Incredible!

But now we are going there!

Perhaps I should introduce us. The Fries Family, I mean. Myself: Podkayne Fries—"Poddy" to my friends and we might as well start off being friendly. Adolescent female: I'm eight plus a few months, at a point in my development described by my Uncle Tom as "frying size and just short of husband high"—a fair-enough description since a female citizen of Mars may contract plenary marriage without guardian's waiver on her ninth birthday, and I stand 157 centimeters tall in my bare feet and mass 49 kilograms. "Five feet two and eyes of blue" my daddy calls me, but he is a historian and romantic. But I am not romantic and would not consider even a limited marriage on my ninth birthday; I have other plans.

Not that I am opposed to marriage in due time, nor do I expect to have any trouble snagging the male of my choice. In these memoirs I shall be frank rather than modest because they will not be published until I am old and famous, and I will certainly revise them before then. In the meantime I am taking the precaution of writing English in Martian Oldscript—a combination which I'm sure Daddy could puzzle out, only he wouldn't do such a thing unless I invited him to. Daddy is a dear and does not snoopervise me. My brother Clark would pry, but he regards English as a dead language and would never bother his head with Oldscript anyhow.

Perhaps you have seen a book titled: *Eleven Years Old: The Pre-Adolescent Adjustment Crisis in the Male.* I read it, hoping that it would help me to cope with my brother. Clark is just six, but the "Eleven Years" referred to in that title are Terran years because it was written on Earth. If you will apply the conversion factor of 1.8808 to attain real years, you will see that my brother is exactly eleven of those undersized Earth years old.

That book did not help me much. It talks about "cushioning the transition into the social group"—but there is no present indication that Clark ever intends to join the human race. He is more likely to devise a way to blow up the universe just to hear the bang. Since I am responsible for him much of the time and since he has an I.Q. of 160 while mine is only 145, you can readily see that I need all the advantage that greater age and maturity can give me. At present my standing rule with him is: Keep your guard up and *never* offer hostages.

Back to me—I'm colonial mongrel in ancestry, but the Swedish part is dominant in my looks, with Polynesian and Asiatic fractions adding no more than a not-unpleasing exotic flavor. My legs are long for my height, my waist is 48 centimeters and my chest is 90—not all of which is rib cage, I assure you, even though we old colonial families all run to hypertrophied lung development; some of it is burgeoning secondary sex characteristic. Besides that, my hair is pale blond and wavy and I'm pretty. Not beautiful—Praxiteles would not have given me a second look—but real beauty is likely to scare a man off, or else make him quite unmanageable, whereas prettiness, properly handled, is an asset.

Up till a couple of years ago I used to regret not being male (in view of my ambitions), but I at last realized how silly I was being; one might as well wish for wings. As Mother says: "One works with available materials" . . . and I found that the materials available were adequate. In fact I found that I *like* being female; my hormone balance is okay and I'm quite well adjusted to the world and vice versa. I'm smart enough not unnecessarily to show that I am smart; I've got a long upper lip and a short nose, and when I wrinkle my nose and look baffled, a man is usually only too glad to help me, especially if he is about twice my age. There are more ways of computing a ballistic than by counting it on your fingers.

That's me: Poddy Fries, free citizen of Mars, female. Future pilot and someday commander of deep-space exploration parties. Watch for me in the news.

Mother is twice as good-looking as I am and much taller than I ever will be; she looks like a Valkyrie about to gallop off into the sky. She holds a system-wide license as a Master Engineer, Heavy Construction, Surface or Free Fall, and is entitled to wear both the Hoover Medal with cluster and the Christiana Order, Knight Commander, for bossing the rebuilding of Deimos and Phobos. But she's more than just the traditional hairy engineer; she has a social presence which she can switch from warmly charming to frostily intimidating at will, she holds honorary degrees galore, and she publishes popular little gems such as "Design Criteria with Respect to the Effects of Radiation on the Bonding of Pressure-Loaded Sandwich Structures."

It is because Mother is often away from home for professional reasons that I am, from time to time, the reluctant custodian of my younger brother. Still, I suppose it is good practice, for how can I ever expect to command my own ship if I can't tame a six-year-old savage? Mother says that a boss who is forced to part a man's hair with a wrench has failed at some point, so I try to control our junior nihilist without resorting to force. Besides, using force on Clark is very chancy; he masses as much as I do and he fights dirty.

It was the job Mother did on Deimos that accounts for Clark and myself. Mother was determined to meet her construction dates; and Daddy, on leave from Ares U. with a Guggenheim grant, was even more frantically determined to save every scrap of the ancient Martian artifacts no matter how much it delayed construction; this threw them into such intimate and bitter conflict that they got married and for a while Mother had babies.

Daddy and Mother are Jack Spratt and his wife; he is interested in everything that has already happened, she is interested only in what is going to happen, especially if she herself is making it happen. Daddy's title is Van Loon Professor of Terrestrial History but his real love is Martian history, especially if it happened fifty million years ago. But do not think that Daddy is a cloistered don given only to contemplation and study. When he was even younger than I am now, he lost an arm one chilly night in the attack on the Company Offices during the Revolution—and he can still shoot straight and fast with the hand he has left.

The rest of our family is Great-Uncle Tom, Daddy's father's brother. Uncle Tom is a parasite. So he says. It is true that you don't see him work much, but he was an old man before I was born. He is a Revolutionary veteran, same as Daddy, and is a Past Grand Commander of the Martian Legion and a Senator-at-Large of the Republic, but he doesn't seem to spend much time on either sort of politics, Legion or public; instead he hangs out at the Elks Club and plays pinochle with other relics of the past. Uncle Tom is really my closest relative, for he isn't as intense as my parents, nor as busy, and will always take time to talk with me. Furthermore he has a streak of Original Sin which makes him sympathetic to my problems. He says that I have such a streak, too, much wider than his. Concerning this, I reserve my opinion.

That's our family and we are all going to Earth. Wups! I left out three—the infants. But they hardly count now and it is easy to forget them. When Daddy and Mother got married, the PEG Board—Population, Ecology, & Genetics—pegged them at five and would have allowed them seven had they requested it, for, as you may have gathered, my parents are rather high-grade citizens even among planetary colonials all of whom are descended from, or are themselves, highly selected and drastically screened stock.

But Mother told the Board that five was all that she had time for and then had us as fast as possible, while fidgeting at a desk job in the Bureau of Planetary Engineering. Then she popped her babies into deep-freeze as fast as she had them, all but me, since I was the first. Clark spent two years at constant entropy, else he would be almost as old as I am—deep-freeze time doesn't count, of course, and his official birthday is the day he was decanted. I remember how jealous I was—Mother was just back from conditioning Juno and it didn't seem fair to me that she would immediately start raising a baby.

Uncle Tom talked me out of that, with a lot of lap sitting, and I am no longer jealous of Clark—merely wary.

So we've got Gamma, Delta, and Epsilon in the sub-basement of the crèche at Marsopolis, and we'll uncork and name at least one of them as soon as we get back from Earth. Mother is thinking of revivifying Gamma and Epsilon together and raising them as twins (they're girls) and then launching Delta, who is a boy, as soon as the girls are housebroken. Daddy says that is not fair, because Delta is entitled to be older than Epsilon by natural priority of birth date. Mother says that is mere worship of precedent and that she does wish Daddy would learn to leave his reverence for the past on the campus when he comes home in the evening.

Daddy says that Mother has no sentimental feelings—and Mother says she certainly hopes not, at least with any problem requiring rational analysis—and Daddy says let's be rational, then . . . twin older sisters would either break a boy's spirit or else spoil him rotten.

Mother says that is unscientific and unfounded. Daddy says that Mother merely wants to get two chores out of the way at once—whereupon Mother heartily agrees and demands to know why proved production engineering principles should not be applied to domestic economy?

Daddy doesn't answer this. Instead he remarks thoughtfully that he must admit that two little girls dressed just alike would be kind of cute . . . name them "Margret" and "Marguerite" and call them "Peg" and "Meg"—

Clark muttered to me, "Why uncork them at all? Why not just sneak down some night and open the valves and call it an accident?"

I told him to go wash out his mouth with prussic acid and not let Daddy hear him talk that way. Daddy would have walloped him properly. Daddy, although a historian, is devoted to the latest, most progressive theories of child psychology and applies them by canalizing the cortex through pain association whenever he really wants to ensure that a lesson will not be forgotten. As he puts it so neatly: "Spare the rod and spoil the child."

I canalize most readily and learned very early indeed how to predict and avoid incidents which would result in Daddy's applying his theories and his hand. But in Clark's case it is almost necessary to use a club simply to gain his divided attention.

So it is now clearly evident that we are going to have twin baby sisters. But it is no headache of mine, I am happy to say, for Clark is quite enough maturing trauma for one girl's adolescence. By the time the twins are a current problem I expect to be long gone and far away.

Interlude

Hi, Pod.

So you think I can't read your worm tracks.

A lot you know about me! Poddy—oh, excuse me, "Captain" Podkayne Fries, I mean, the famous Space Explorer and Master of Men—Captain Poddy dear, you probably will never read this because it wouldn't occur to you that I not only would break your "code" but also write comments in the big, wide margins you leave.

Just for the record, Sister dear, I read Old Anglish just as readily as I do System Ortho. Anglish isn't all that hard and I learned it as soon as I found out that a lot of books I wanted to read had never been translated. But it doesn't pay to tell everything you know, or somebody comes along and tells you to stop doing whatever it is you are doing. Probably your older sister.

But imagine calling a straight substitution a "code"! Poddy, if you had actually been able to write Old Martian, it would have taken me quite a lot longer. But you can't. Shucks, even Dad can't write it without stewing over it and he probably knows more about Old Martian than anyone else in the System.

But you won't crack my code—because I haven't any.

Try looking at this page under ultraviolet light—a sun lamp, for example.

II

Oh, *Unspeakables*!

Dirty ears! Hangnails! Snel-frockey! *Spit!* WE AREN'T *GOING*!

At first I thought that my brother Clark had managed one of his more charlatanous machinations of malevolent legerdemain. But fortunately (the only fortunate thing about the whole miserable mess) I soon perceived that it was impossible for him to be in fact guilty no matter what devious subversions roil his id. Unless he has managed to invent and build in secret a time machine, which I misdoubt he *would* do if he could ... nor am I prepared to offer odds that he can't. Not since the time he rewired the delivery robot so that it would serve him midnight snacks and charge them to my code number without (so far as anyone could ever prove) disturbing the company's seal on the control box.

We'll never know how he did that one, because, despite the fact that the company offered to Forgive

All and pay a cash bonus to boot if only he would *please* tell them how he managed to beat their unbeatable seal—despite this, Clark looked blank and would not talk. That left only circumstantial evidence, i.e., it was clearly evident to anyone who knew us both (Daddy and Mother, namely) that *I* would never order candy-stripe ice cream smothered in hollandaise sauce, or—no, I can't go on; I feel ill. Whereas Clark is widely known to eat anything which does not eat him first.

Even this clinching psychological evidence would never have convinced the company's adjuster had not their own records proved that two of these obscene feasts had taken place while I was a house guest of friends in Syrtis Major, a thousand kilometers away. Never mind, I simply want to warn all girls not to have a Mad Genius for a baby brother. Pick instead a stupid, stolid, slightly subnormal one who will sit quietly in front of the solly box, mouth agape at cowboy classics, and never wonder what makes the pretty images.

But I have wandered far from my tragic tale.

We aren't going to have twins.

We already have triplets.

Gamma, Delta, and Epsilon, throughout all my former life mere topics of conversation, are now Grace, Duncan, and Elspeth in all too solid flesh—unless Daddy again changes his mind before final registration; they've had three sets of names already. But what's in a name?—they are here, already in our home with a nursery room sealed on to shelter them . . . three helpless unfinished humans about canal-worm pink in color and no features worthy of the name. Their limbs squirm aimlessly, their eyes don't track, and a faint, queasy odor of sour milk permeates every room even when they are freshly bathed. Appalling sounds come from one end of each—in which they heterodyne each other—and even more appalling conditions prevail at the other ends. (I've yet to find all three of them dry at the same time.)

And yet there is something decidedly engaging about the little things; were it not that they are the proximate cause of my tragedy I could easily grow quite fond of them. I'm sure Duncan is beginning to recognize me already.

But, if I am beginning to be reconciled to their presence, Mother's state can only be described as atavistically maternal. Her professional journals pile up unread, she has that soft Madonna look in her eyes, and she seems somehow both shorter and wider than she did a week ago.

First consequence: she won't even discuss going to Earth, with or without the triplets.

Second consequence: Daddy won't go if she won't go—he spoke quite sharply to Clark for even suggesting it.

Third consequence: since they won't go, we *can't* go. Clark and me, I mean. It is conceivably possible that I might have been permitted to travel alone (since Daddy agrees that I am now a "young adult" in maturity and judgment even though my ninth birthday lies still some months in the future), but the question is formal and without content since I am not considered quite old enough to accept full responsible control of my brother with both my parents some millions of kilometers away (nor am I sure that I would wish to, unless armed with something at least as convincing as a morning star) and Daddy is so dismayingly fair with us that he would not even discuss permitting one of us to go and not the other when both of us had been promised the trip.

Fairness is a priceless virtue in a parent—but just at the moment I could stand being spoiled and favored instead.

But the above is why I am sure that Clark does not

have a time machine concealed in his wardrobe. This incredible contretemps, this idiot's dream of interlocking mishaps, is as much to his disadvantage as it is to mine.

How did it happen? Gather ye round— Little did we dream that, when the question of a family trip to Earth was being planned in our household more than a month ago, this disaster was already complete and simply waiting the most hideous moment to unveil itself. The facts are these: the crèche at Marsopolis has thousands of newborn babies marbleized at just short of absolute zero, waiting in perfect safety until their respective parents are ready for them. It is said, and I believe it, that a direct hit with a nuclear bomb would not hurt the consigned infants; a thousand years later a rescue squad could burrow down and find that automatic, self-maintaining machinery had not permitted the tank temperatures to vary a hundredth of a degree.

In consequence, we Marsmen (not "Martians," please!—Martians are a non-human race, now almost extinct)—Marsmen tend to marry early, have a full quota of babies quickly, then rear them later, as money and time permit. It reconciles that discrepancy, so increasingly and glaringly evident ever since the Terran Industrial Revolution, between the best biological age for having children and the best social age for supporting and rearing them.

A couple named Breeze did just that, some ten years ago—married on her ninth birthday and just past his tenth, while he was still a pilot cadet and she was attending Ares U. They applied for three babies, were pegged accordingly, and got them all out of the way while they were both finishing school. Very sensible.

The years roll past, he as a pilot and later as master, she as a finance clerk in his ship and later as purser— a happy life. The spacelines like such an arrangement;

married couples spacing together mean a taut, happy ship.

Captain and Mrs. Breeze serve their ten-and-a-half (twenty Terran) years and put in for half-pay retirement, have it confirmed—and immediately radio the crèche to uncork their babies, all three of them.

The radio order is received, relayed back for confirmation; the crèche accepts it. Five weeks later the happy couple pick up three babies, sign for them, and start the second half of a perfect life.

So they thought—

But what they had deposited was two boys and a girl; what they got was two girls and a boy. Ours.

Believe this you must—it took them the better part of a week to notice it. I will readily concede that the difference between a brand-new boy baby and a brand-new girl baby is, at the time, almost irrelevant. Nevertheless there is a slight difference. Apparently it was a case of too much help—between a mother, a mother-in-law, a temporary nurse, and a helpful neighbor, and much running in and out, it seems unlikely that any one person bathed all three babies as one continuous operation that first week. Certainly Mrs. Breeze had not done so—until the day she did . . . and noticed . . . and fainted—and dropped one of our babies in the bath water, where it would have drowned had not her scream fetched both her husband and the neighbor lady.

So we suddenly had month-old triplets.

The lawyer man from the crèche was very vague about how it happened; he obviously did not want to discuss how their "foolproof" identification system could result in such a mixup. So I don't know myself— but it seems logically certain that, for all their serial numbers, babies' footprints, record machines, et cetera, there is some point in the system where one clerk read aloud "Breeze" from the radioed order and another clerk checked a file, then punched "Fries" into a machine that did the rest.

But the fixer man did not say. He was simply achingly anxious to get Mother and Daddy to settle out of court—accept a check and sign a release under which they agreed not to publicize the error.

They settled for three years of Mother's established professional earning power while the little fixer man gulped and looked relieved.

But nobody offered to pay *me* for the mayhem that had been committed on my life, my hopes, and my ambitions.

Clark did offer a suggestion that was almost a sensible one, for him. He proposed that we swap even with the Breezes, let them keep the warm ones, we could keep the cold ones. Everybody happy—and we all go to Earth.

My brother is far too self-centered to realize it, but the Angel of Death brushed him with its wings at that point. Daddy is a truly noble soul . . . but he had had almost more than he could stand.

And so have I. I had expected today to be actually on my way to Earth, my first space trip farther than Phobos—which was merely a school field trip, our "Class Honeymoon." A nothing thing.

Instead, guess what I'm doing.

Do you have any idea how many times a day *three* babies have to be changed?

III

Hold it! Stop the machines! Wipe the tapes! Cancel all bulletins—

WE ARE GOING TO EARTH *AFTER ALL*!!!!

Well, not *all* of us. Daddy and Mother aren't going, and of course, the triplets are not. But— Never mind; I had better tell it in order.

Yesterday things just got to be Too Much. I had changed them in rotation, only to find as I got the third one dry and fresh that number one again needed service. I had been thinking sadly that just about that moment I should have been entering the dining saloon of S.S. *Wanderlust* to the strains of soft music. Perhaps on the arm of one of the officers . . . perhaps even on the arm of the Captain himself had I the chance to arrange an accidental Happy Encounter, then make judicious use of my "puzzled kitten" expression.

And, as I reached that point in my melancholy day-dream, it was then that I discovered that my chores had started all over again. I thought of the Augean Stables and suddenly it was just Too Much and my eyes got blurry with tears.

Mother came in at that point and I asked if I could *please* have a couple of hours of recess?

She answered, "Why, certainly dear," and didn't even glance at me. I'm sure that she didn't notice that I was crying; she was already doing over, quite unnecessarily, the one that I had just done. She had been tied up on the phone, telling someone firmly that, while it was true as reported that she was not leaving Mars, nevertheless she would not now accept another commission even as a consultant—and no doubt being away from the infants for all of ten minutes had made her uneasy, so she just had to get her hands on one of them.

Mother's behavior had been utterly unbelievable. Her cortex has tripped out of circuit and her primitive instincts are in full charge. She reminds me of a cat we had when I was a little girl—Miss Polka Dot Ma'am and her first litter of kittens. Miss Pokie loved and trusted all of us—except about kittens. If we touched one of them, she was uneasy about it. If a kitten was taken out of her box and placed on the floor to be admired, she herself would hop out, grab the kitten in her teeth and immediately return it to the box, with an indignant waggle to her seat that showed all too plainly what she thought of irresponsible people who didn't know how to handle babies.

Mother is just like that now. She accepts my help simply because there is too much for her to do alone. But she doesn't really believe that I can even pick up a baby without close supervision.

So I left and followed my own blind instincts, which told me to go look up Uncle Tom.

I found him at the Elks Club, which was reasonably certain at that time of day, but I had to wait in the ladies' lounge until he came out of the card room. Which he did in about ten minutes, counting a wad of money as he came. "Sorry to make you wait," he said, "but I was teaching a fellow citizen about the uncertainties in the laws of chance and I had to stay long enough to collect the tuition. How marches it, Podkayne mavourneen?"

I tried to tell him and got all choked up, so he walked me to the park under the city hall and sat me on a bench and bought us both packages of Choklat-pops and I ate mine and most of his and watched the stars on the ceiling and told him all about it and felt better.

He patted my hand. "Cheer up, Flicka. Always remember that, when things seem darkest, they usually get considerably worse." He took his phone out of a pocket and made a call. Presently he said, "Never mind the protocol routine, miss. This is Senator Fries. I want the Director." Then he added in a moment, "Hymie? Tom Fries here. How's Judith? Good, good . . . Hymie, I just called to tell you that I'm coming over to stuff you into one of your own liquid helium tanks. Oh, say about fourteen or a few minutes after. That'll give you time to get out of town. Clearing." He pock-eted his phone. "Let's get some lunch. Never commit suicide on an empty stomach, my dear; it's bad for the digestion."

Uncle Tom took me to the Pioneers Club where I have been only once before and which is even more impressive than I had recalled— It has *real waiters* . . . men so old that they might have been pioneers themselves, unless they met the first ship. Everybody fussed over Uncle Tom and he called them all by their first names and they all called him "Tom" but made it sound like "Your Majesty" and the master of the hostel came over and prepared my sweet himself with about six other people standing around to hand him things, like a famous surgeon operating against the swift onrush of death.

Presently Uncle Tom belched behind his napkin and I thanked everybody as we left while wishing that I had had the forethought to wear my unsuitable gown that Mother won't let me wear until I'm nine and almost made me take back—one doesn't get to the Pioneers Club every day.

We took the James Joyce Fogarty Express Tunnel and Uncle Tom sat down the whole way, so I had to sit, too, although it makes me restless; I prefer to walk in the direction a tunnel is moving and get there a bit sooner. But Uncle Tom says that he gets plenty of exercise watching other people work themselves to death.

I didn't really realize that we were going to the Marsopolis Crèche until we were there, so bemused had I been earlier with my own tumultuous emotions. But when we were there and facing a sign reading: OFFICE OF THE DIRECTOR—PLEASE USE OTHER DOOR, Uncle Tom said, "Hang around somewhere; I'll need you later," and went on in.

The waiting room was crowded and the only magazines not in use were *Kiddie Kapers* and *Modern Homemaker*, so I wandered around a bit and presently found a corridor that led to the Nursery.

The sign on the door said that visiting hours were from 16 to 18.30. Furthermore, it was locked, so I moved on and found another door which seemed much more promising. It was marked: POSITIVELY NO ADMITTANCE—but it didn't say "This Means You" and it wasn't locked, so I went in.

You never saw so many babies in your whole life!

Row upon row upon row, each in its own little transparent cubicle. I could really see only the row nearest me, all of which seemed to be about the same age— and much more finished than the three we had at

home. Little brown dumplings they were, cute as puppies. Most of them were asleep, some were awake and
kicking and cooing and grabbing at dangle toys that
were just in reach. If there had not been a sheet of
glass between me and them I would have grabbed me
a double armful of babies.

There were a lot of girls in the room, too—well,
young women, really. Each of them seemed to be busy
with a baby and they didn't notice me. But shortly one
of the babies nearest me started to cry whereupon a
light came on over its cubicle, and one of the nurse
girls hurried over, slid back the cover, picked it up
and started patting its bottom. It stopped crying.

"Wet?" I inquired.

She looked up, saw me. "Oh, no, the machines take
care of that. Just lonely, so I'm loving it." Her voice
came through clearly in spite of the glass—a hear and
speak circuit, no doubt, although the pickups were not
in evidence. She made soft noises to the baby, then
added, "Are you a new employee? You seem to be
lost."

"Oh, no," I said hastily, "I'm not an employee. I
just—"

"Then you don't belong here, not at this hour.
Unless"—she looked at me rather skeptically—"just
possibly you are looking for the instruction class for
young mothers?"

"Oh, no, no!" I said hastily. "Not yet." Then I added
still more hastily, "I'm a guest of the Director."

Well, it wasn't a fib. Not quite. I was a guest of
a guest of the Director, one who was with him by
appointment. The relationship was certainly concaten-
ative, if not equivalent.

It seemed to reassure her. She asked, "Just what
did you want? Can I help you?"

"Uh, just information. I'm making a sort of a survey.
What goes on in this room?"

"These are age six-month withdrawal contracts," she told me. "All these babies will be going home in a few days." She put the baby, quiet now, back into its private room, adjusted a nursing nipple for it, made some other sort of adjustments on the outside of the cubicle so that the padding inside sort of humped up and held the baby steady against the milk supply, then closed the top, moved on a few meters and picked up another baby. "Personally," she added, "I think the age six-month contract is the best one. A child twelve months old is old enough to notice the transition. But these aren't. They don't care who comes along and pets them when they cry ... but nevertheless six months is long enough to get a baby well started and take the worst of the load off the mother. We know how, we're used to it, we stand our watches in rotation so that we are never exhausted from being 'up with the baby all night' ... and in consequence we aren't short-tempered and we never yell at them—and don't think for a minute that a baby doesn't understand a cross tone of voice simply because he can't talk yet. He knows! And it can start him off so twisted that he may take it out on somebody else, years and years later. There, there, honey," she went on but not to me, "feel better now? Feeling sleepy, huh? Now you just hold still and Martha will keep her hand on you until you are fast asleep."

She watched the baby for a moment longer, then withdrew her hand, closed the box and hurried on to where another light was burning. "A baby has no sense of time," she added as she removed a squalling lump of fury from its crib. "When it needs love, it needs it right now. It can't know that—" An older woman had come up behind her. "Yes, Nurse?"

"Who is this you're chatting with? You know the rules."

"But ... she's a guest of the Director."

The older woman looked at me with a stern no-nonsense look. "The Director sent you in here?"

I was making a split-second choice among three non-responsive answers when I was saved by Fate. A soft voice coming from everywhere at once announced: "Miss Podkayne Fries is requested to come to the office of the Director. Miss Podkayne Fries, please come to the office of the Director."

I tilted my nose in the air and said with dignity, "That is I. Nurse, will you be so kind as to phone the Director and tell him that Miss Fries is on her way?" I exited with deliberate haste.

The Director's office was four times as big and sixteen times as impressive as the principal's office at school. The Director was short and had a dark brown skin and a gray goatee and a harried expression. In addition to him and to Uncle Tom, of course, there was present the little lawyer man who had had a bad time with Daddy a week earlier—and my brother Clark. I couldn't figure out how he got there . . . except that Clark has an infallible homing instinct for trouble.

Clark looked at me with no expression; I nodded. The Director and his legal beagle stood up. Uncle Tom didn't but he said, "Dr. Hyman Schoenstein, Mr. Poon Kwai Yau—my niece Podkayne Fries. Sit down, honey; nobody is going to bite you. The Director has a proposition to offer you."

The lawyer man interrupted. "I don't think—"

"Correct," agreed Uncle Tom. "You don't think. Or it would have occurred to you that ripples spread out from a splash."

"But— Dr. Schoenstein, the release I obtained from Professor Fries explicitly binds him to silence, for separate good and sufficient consideration, over and above damages conceded by us and made good. This is tantamount to blackmail. I—"

Then Uncle Tom did stand up. He seemed twice as tall as usual and was grinning like a fright mask. "What was that last word you used?"

"I?" The lawyer looked startled. "Perhaps I spoke hastily. I simply meant—"

"I heard you," Uncle Tom growled. "And so did three witnesses. Happens to be one of the words a man can be challenged for on this still free planet. But, since I'm getting old and fat, I may just sue you for your shirt instead. Come along, kids."

The Director spoke quickly. "Tom ... sit down, please. Mr. Poon ... please keep quiet unless I ask for your advice. Now, Tom, you know quite well that you can't challenge nor sue over a privileged communication, counsel to client."

"I can do both or either. Question is: will a court sustain me? But I can always find out."

"And thereby drag out into the open the very point you know quite well I can't afford to have dragged out. Simply because my lawyer spoke in an excess of zeal. Mr. Poon?"

"I tried to withdraw it. I do withdraw it."

"Senator?"

Uncle Tom bowed stiffly to Mr. Poon, who returned it. "Accepted, sir. No offense meant and none taken." Then Uncle Tom grinned merrily, let his potbelly slide back down out of his chest, and said in his normal voice, "Okay, Hymie, let's get on with the crime. Your move."

Dr. Schoenstein said carefully, "Young lady, I have just learned that the recent disruption of family planning in your home—which we all deeply regret— caused an additional sharp disappointment to you and your brother."

"It certainly did!" I answered, rather shrilly I'm afraid.

"Yes. As your uncle put it, the ripples spread out.

Another of those ripples could wreck this establishment, make it insolvent as a private business. This is an odd sort of business we are in here, Miss Fries. Superficially we perform a routine engineering function, plus some not unusual boarding nursery services. But in fact what we do touches the most primitive of human emotions. If confidence in our integrity, or in the perfection with which we carry out the service entrusted to us, were to be shaken—" He spread his hands helplessly. "We couldn't last out the year. Now I can show you exactly how the mishap occurred which affected your family, show you how wildly unlikely it was to have it happen even under the methods we did use ... prove to you how utterly impossible it now is and always will be in the future for such a mistake to take place again, under our new procedures. Nevertheless"— he looked helpless again—"if you were to talk, merely tell the simple truth about what did indeed happen once ... you could ruin us."

I felt so sorry for him that I was about to blurt out that I wouldn't even *dream* of talking!—even though they had ruined my life—when Clark cut in. "Watch it, Pod! It's loaded."

So I just gave the Director my Sphinx expression and said nothing. Clark's instinctive self-interest is absolutely reliable.

Dr. Schoenstein motioned Mr. Poon to keep quiet. "But, my dear lady, I am not asking you not to talk. As your uncle the Senator says, you are not here to blackmail and I have nothing with which to bargain. The Marsopolis Crèche Foundation, Limited, always carries out its obligations even when they do not result from formal contract. I asked you to come in here in order to suggest a measure of relief for the damage we have unquestionably—though unwittingly—done you and your brother. Your uncle tells me that he had intended to travel with you and your family ... but that now he intends to go via the next Triangle Line departure. The *Tricorn*, I believe it is, about ten days from now. Would you feel less mistreated if we were to pay first-class fares for your brother and you—round trip, of course—in the Triangle Line?"

Would I! The *Wanderlust* has, as her sole virtue, the fact that she is indeed a spaceship and she was shaping for Earth. But she is an old, slow freighter. Whereas the Triangle Liners, as everyone knows, are utter palaces! I could but nod.

"Good. It is our privilege and we hope you have a wonderful trip. But, uh, young lady . . . do you think it possible that you could give us some assurance, for no consideration and simply out of kindness, that you wouldn't talk about a certain regrettable mishap?"

"Oh? I thought that was part of the deal?"

"There is no deal. As your uncle pointed out to me, we owe you this trip, no matter what."

"Why—why, Doctor, I'm going to be so busy, so utterly rushed, just to get ready in time, that I won't have *time* to talk to anyone about any mishaps that probably weren't your fault anyhow!"

"Thank you." He turned to Clark. "And you, son?"

Clark doesn't like to be called "son" at best. But don't think it affected his answer. He ignored the vocative and said coldly, "What about our expenses?"

Dr. Schoenstein flinched. Uncle Tom guffawed and said, "That's my boy! Doc, I told you he had the simple rapacity of a sand gator. He'll go far—if somebody doesn't poison him."

"Any suggestions?"

"No trouble. Clark. Look me in the eye. Either you stay behind and we weld you into a barrel and feed you through the bunghole so that you *can't* talk—while your sister goes anyhow—or you accept these terms. Say a thousand each—no, fifteen hundred—for travel expenses, and you keep your snapper shut forever about the baby mix-up . . . or I personally, with the aid of four stout, blackhearted accomplices, will cut your tongue out and feed it to the cat. A deal?"

"I ought to get ten percent commission on Sis's fifteen hundred. She didn't have sense enough to ask for it."

"No cumshaw. I ought to be charging *you* commission on the whole transaction. A deal?"

"A deal," Clark agreed.

Uncle Tom stood up. "That does it, Doc. In his own unappetizing way he is as utterly reliable as she is. So relax. You, too, Kwai Yau, you can breathe again. Doc, you can send a check around to me in the morning. Come on, kids."

"Thanks, Tom. If that is the word. I'll have the check over before you get there. Uh . . . just one thing . . ."

"What, Doc?"

"Senator, you were here long before I was born, so I don't know too much about your early life. Just the traditional stories and what it says about you in *Who's Who on Mars*. Just what were you transported for? You *were* transported? Weren't you?"

Mr. Poon looked horror-stricken, and I was. But Uncle Tom didn't seem offended. He laughed heartily and answered, "I was accused of freezing babies for profit. But it was a frameup—I never did no such thing nohow. Come on, kids. Let's get out of this ghouls' nest before they smuggle us down into the sub-basement."

Later that night in bed I was dreamily thinking over the trip. There hadn't even been the least argument with Mother and Daddy; Uncle Tom had settled it all by phone before we got home. I heard a sound from the nursery, got up and paddled in. It was Duncan, the little darling, not even wet but lonely. So I picked him up and cuddled him and he cooed and then he was wet, so I changed him.

I decided that he was just as pretty or prettier than all those other babies, even though he was five months younger and his eyes didn't track. When I put him down again, he was sound asleep; I started back to bed.

And stopped— The Triangle Line gets its name from serving the three leading planets, of course, but which direction a ship makes the Mars-Venus-Earth route depends on just where we all are in our orbits.

But just where were we?

I hurried into the living room and searched for the *Daily War Whoop*—found it, thank goodness, and fed it into the viewer, flipped to the shipping news, found the predicted arrivals and departures.

Yes, yes, *yes*! I am going not only to Earth—but to Venus as well!

Venus! Do you suppose Mother would let me— No, best just say nothing now. Uncle Tom will be more tractable, after we get there.

I'm going to miss Duncan—he's such a little doll.

IV

I haven't had time to write in this journal for *days*. Just getting ready to leave was almost impossible—and would have been truly impossible had it not been that most preparations—all the special Terra inoculations and photographs and passports and such—were mostly done before Everything Came Unstuck. But Mother came out of her atavistic daze and was very helpful. She would even let one of the triplets cry for a few moments rather than leave me half pinned up.

I don't know how Clark got ready or whether he had any preparations to make. He continued to creep around silently, answering in grunts if he answered at all. Nor did Uncle Tom seem to find it difficult. I saw him only twice during those frantic ten days (once to borrow baggage mass from his allowance, which he let me have, the dear!) and both times I had to dig him out of the card room at the Elks Club. I asked him how he managed to get ready for so important a trip and still have time to play cards?

"Nothing to it," he answered. "I bought a new toothbrush. Is there something else I should have done?"

So I hugged him and told him he was an utterly utter beast and he chuckled and mussed my hair. Query: Will I ever become that blasé about space travel? I suppose I must if I am to be an astronaut. But Daddy says that getting ready for a trip is half the fun . . . so perhaps I don't want to become that sophisticated.

Somehow Mother delivered me, complete with baggage and all the myriad pieces of paper—tickets and medical records and passport and universal identification complex and guardians' assignment-and-guarantee and three kinds of money and travelers' cheques and birth record and police certification and security clearance and I don't remember—all checked off, to the city shuttle port. I was juggling one package of things that simply *wouldn't* go into my luggage, and I had one hat on my head and one in my hand; otherwise everything came out even.

(I don't know where that second hat went. Somehow it never got aboard with me. But I haven't missed it.)

Good-bye at the shuttle port was most teary and exciting. Not just with Mother and Daddy, which was to be expected (when Daddy put his arm around me tight, I threw both mine around him and for a dreadful second I didn't want to leave at all), but also because about thirty of my classmates showed up (which I hadn't in the least expected), complete with a banner that two of them were carrying reading:

BON VOYAGE—PODKAYNE

I got kissed enough times to start a fair-sized epidemic if any one of them had had anything, which apparently they didn't. I got kissed by boys who had never even *tried* to, in the past—and I assure you that it is not utterly impossible to kiss me, if the project is approached with confidence and finesse, as I believe that one's instincts should be allowed to develop as well as one's overt cortical behavior.

The corsage Daddy had given me for going away got crushed and I didn't even notice it until we were aboard the shuttle. I suppose it was somewhere about then that I lost that hat, but I'll never know—I would have lost the last-minute package, too, if Uncle Tom had not rescued it. There were photographers, too, but not for me—for Uncle Tom. Then suddenly we had to scoot aboard the shuttle *right now* because a shuttle can't wait; it has to boost on the split second even though Deimos moves so much more slowly than Phobos. A reporter from the *War Whoop* was still trying to get a statement out of Uncle Tom about the forthcoming Three-Planets conference but he just pointed at his throat and whispered, "Laryngitis"— then we were aboard just before they sealed the airlock.

It must have been the shortest case of laryngitis on record; Uncle Tom's voice had been all right until we got to the shuttle port and it was okay again once we were in the shuttle.

One shuttle trip is exactly like another, whether to Phobos or Deimos. Still, that first tremendous *whoosh!* of acceleration is exciting as it pins you down into your couch with so much weight that you can't breathe, much less move—and free fall is always strange and eerie and rather stomach fluttering even if one doesn't tend to be nauseated by it, which, thank you, I don't.

Being on Deimos is just like being in free fall, since neither Deimos nor Phobos has enough surface gravitation for one to feel it. They put suction sandals on us before they unstrapped us so that we could walk, just as they do on Phobos. Nevertheless Deimos is different from Phobos for reasons having nothing to do with natural phenomena. Phobos is, of course, legally a part of Mars; there are no formalities of any sort about visiting it. All that is required is the fare, a free day, and a yen for a picnic in space.

But Deimos is a free port, leased in perpetuity to Three-Planets Treaty Authority. A known criminal, with a price on his head in Marsopolis, could change ships there right under the eyes of our own police—and we couldn't touch him. Instead, we would have to start most complicated legal doings at the Interplanetary High Court on Luna, practically win the case ahead of time and, besides that, prove that the crime was a crime under Three-Planet rules and not just under our own laws . . . and then all that we could do would be to ask the Authority's proctors to arrest the man if he was still around—which doesn't seem likely.

I knew about this, theoretically, because there had been about a half page on it in our school course *Essentials of Martian Government* in the section on "Extraterritoriality." But now I had plenty of time to think about it because, as soon as we left the shuttle, we found ourselves locked up in a room misleadingly called the "Hospitality Room" while we waited until they were ready to "process" us. One wall of the room was glass and I could see lots and lots of people hurrying around in the concourse beyond, doing all manner of interesting and mysterious things. But all we had to do was to wait beside our baggage and grow bored.

I found that I was growing furious by the minute, not at all like my normally sweet and lovable nature. Why, this place had been built by my own mother!—and here I was, caged up in it like white mice in a bio lab.

(Well, I admit that Mother didn't exactly build Deimos; the Martians did that, starting with a spare asteroid that they happened to have handy. But some

millions of years back they grew tired of space travel
and devoted all their time to the whichness of what
and how to unscrew the inscrutable—so when Mother
took over the job, Deimos was pretty run down; she
had to start in from the ground up and rebuild it
completely.)

In any case, it was certain that everything that I
could see through that transparent wall was a product
of Mother's creative, imaginative and hardheaded engineering ability. I began to fume. Clark was off in a
corner, talking privately to some stranger—"stranger"
to me, at least; Clark, for all his antisocial disposition,
always seems to know somebody, or to know somebody
who knows somebody, anywhere we go. I sometimes
wonder if he is a member of some vast underground
secret society; he has such unsavory acquaintances and
never brings any of them home.

Clark is, however, a very satisfactory person to fume
with, because, if he isn't busy, he is always willing to
help a person hate anything that needs hating; he can
even dig up reasons why a situation is even more vilely
unfair than you thought it was. But he was busy, so
that left Uncle Tom. So I explained to him bitterly
how outrageous I thought it was that we should be
penned up like animals—free Mars citizens on one of
Mars' own moons!—simply because a sign read: *Passengers must wait until called—by order of Three-
Planets Treaty Authority*.

"*Politics!*" I said bitterly. "I could run it better
myself."

"I'm sure you could," he agreed gravely, "but,
Flicka, you don't understand."

"I understand all too well!"

"No, honey bun. You understand that there is no
good reason why you should not walk straight through
that door and enjoy yourself by shopping until it is
time to go inboard the *Tricorn*. And you are right

about that, for there is no need at all for you to be locked up in here when you could be out there making some freeport shopkeeper happy by paying him a high price which seems to you a low price. So you say 'Politics!' as if it were a nasty word—and you think that settles it."

He sighed. "But you *don't* understand. Politics is not evil; politics is the human race's most magnificent achievement. When politics is good, it's wonderful . . . and when politics is bad—well, it's still pretty good."

"I guess I don't understand," I said slowly.

"Think about it. Politics is just a name for the way we get things done . . . without fighting. We dicker and compromise and everybody thinks he has received a raw deal, but somehow after a tedious amount of talk we come up with some jury-rigged way to do it without getting anybody's head bashed in. That's politics. The only other way to settle a dispute is by bashing a few heads in . . . and that is what happens when one or both sides is no longer willing to dicker. That's why I say politics is good even when it is bad . . . because the only alternative is force—and somebody gets hurt."

"Uh . . . it seems to me that's a funny way for a revolutionary veteran to talk. From what I've heard, Uncle Tom, you were one of the bloodthirsty ones who started the shooting. Or so Daddy says."

He grinned. "Mostly I ducked. If dickering won't work, then you have to fight. But I think maybe it takes a man who has been shot at to appreciate how much better it is to fumble your way through a political compromise rather than have the top of your head blown off." He frowned and suddenly looked very old. "When to talk and when to fight— That is the most difficult decision to make wisely of all the decisions in life." Then suddenly he smiled and the years dropped away. "Mankind didn't invent fighting; it was here long before we were. But we invented politics. Just think of it, hon— Homo sapiens is the most cruel, the most vicious, the most predatory, and certainly the most deadly of all the animals in this solar system. Yet he invented politics! He figured out a way to let most of us, most of the time, get along well enough so that we usually don't kill each other. So don't let me hear you using 'politics' as a swear word again."

"I'm sorry, Uncle Tom," I said humbly.

"Like fun you are. But if you let that idea soak for twenty or thirty years, you may— Oh, oh! There's your villain, baby girl—the politically appointed bureaucrat who has most unjustly held you in durance vile. So scratch his eyes out. Show him how little you think of his silly rules."

I answered this with dignified silence. It is hard to tell when Uncle Tom is serious because he loves to pull my leg, always hoping that it will come off in his hand. The Three-Planets proctor of whom he was speaking had opened the door to our bullpen and was looking around exactly like a zookeeper inspecting a cage for cleanliness. "Passports!" he called out. "Diplomatic passports first." He looked us over, spotted Uncle Tom. "Senator?"

Uncle Tom shook his head. "I'm a tourist, thanks."

"As you say, sir. Line up, please—reverse alphabetical order"—which put us near the tail of the line instead of near the head. There followed maddening delays for fully two hours—passports, health clearance, outgoing baggage inspection—Mars Republic does not levy duties on exports but just the same there is a whole long list of things you can't export without a license, such as ancient Martian artifacts (the first explorers did their best to gut the place and some of the most priceless are in the British Museum or the Kremlin; I've heard Daddy fume about it), some things you can't export under *any* circumstances, such as certain narcotics, and some things you can take aboard ship only by surrendering them for safekeeping by the purser, such as guns and other weapons.

Clark picked outgoing inspection for some typical abnormal behavior. They had passed down the line copies of a long list of things we must not have in our baggage—a fascinating list; I hadn't known that there were so many things either illegal, immoral, or deadly. When the Fries contingent wearily reached the inspection counter, the inspector said, all in one word: "Nything-t'-d'clare?" He was a Marsman and as he looked up he recognized Uncle Tom. "Oh. Howdy, Senator. Honored to have you with us. Well, I guess we needn't waste time on your baggage. These two young people with you?"

"Better search my kit," Uncle Tom advised. "I'm smuggling guns to an out-planet branch of the Legion. As for the kids, they're my niece and nephew. But I don't vouch for them; they're both subversive characters. Especially the girl. She was soap-boxing revolution just now while we waited."

The inspector smiled and said, "I guess we can allow you a few guns, Senator—you know how to use them. Well, how about it, kids? Anything to declare?"

I said, "Nothing to declare," with icy dignity—when suddenly Clark spoke up.

"Sure!" he piped, his voice cracking. "Two kilos of happy dust! And whose business is it? I paid for it. I'm not going to let it be stolen by a bunch of clerks." His voice was surly as only he can manage and the expression on his face simply ached for a slap.

That did it. The inspector had been just about to glance into one of my bags, a purely formal inspection, I think—when my brattish brother deliberately stirred things up. At the very word "happy dust" four other inspectors closed in. Two were Venusmen, to judge by their accents, and the other two might have been from Earth.

Of course, happy dust doesn't matter to us Marsmen. The Martians use it, have always used it, and it is about as important to them as tobacco is to humans, but apparently without any ill effects. What they get out of it I don't know. Some of the old sand rats among us have picked up the habit from the Martians—but my entire botany class experimented with it under our teacher's supervision and nobody got any thrill out of it and all I got was blocked sinuses that wore off before the day was out. Strictly zero squared.

But with the native Venerians it is another matter— when they can get it. It turns them into murderous maniacs and they'll do anything to get it. The (black market) price on it there is very high indeed ... and possession of it by a human on Venus is at least an automatic life sentence to Saturn's moons.

They buzzed around Clark like angry jetta wasps.

But they did not find what they were looking for. Shortly Uncle Tom spoke up and said, "Inspector? May I make a suggestion?"

"Eh? Certainly, Senator."

"My nephew, I am sorry to say, has caused a disturbance. Why don't you put him aside—chain him up, I would—and let all these other good people go through?"

The inspector blinked. "I think that is an excellent idea."

"And I would appreciate it if you would inspect myself and my niece now. Then we won't hold up the others."

"Oh, that's not necessary." The inspector slapped seals on all of Uncle's bags, closed the one of mine he had started to open, and said, "I don't need to paw through the young lady's pretties. But I think we'll take this smart boy and search him to the skin and X-ray him."

"Do that."

So Uncle and I went on and checked at four or five other desks—fiscal control and migration and reservations and other nonsense—and finally wound up with our baggage at the centrifuge for weighing in. I never did get a chance to shop.

To my chagrin, when I stepped off the merry-go-round the record showed that my baggage and myself were nearly three kilos over my allowance, which didn't seem possible. I hadn't eaten more breakfast than usual—less actually—and I hadn't drunk any water because, while I do not become ill in free fall, drinking in free fall is very tricky; you are likely to get water up your nose or something and set off an embarrassing chain reaction.

So I was about to protest bitterly that the weightmaster had spun the centrifuge too fast and produced a false mass reading. But it occurred to me that I did not know for surely certain that the scales Mother and I had used were perfectly accurate. So I kept quiet.

Uncle Tom just reached for his purse and said, "How much?"

The weightmaster said, "Mmm ... let's spin you first, Senator."

Uncle Tom was almost two kilos under his allowance. The weightmaster shrugged and said, "Forget it, Senator. I'm minus on a couple of other things; I think I can swallow it. If not, I'll leave a memo with the purser. But I'm fairly sure I can."

"Thank you. What did you say your name was?"

"Milo. Miles M. Milo—Aasvogel Lodge number seventy-four. Maybe you saw our crack drill team at the Legion convention two years ago— I was left pivot."

"I certainly did, I certainly did!" They exchanged that secret grip that they think other people don't know and Uncle Tom said, "Well, thanks, Miles. Be seeing you."

"Not at all—Tom. No, don't bother with your baggage." Mr. Milo touched a button and called out, "In the *Tricorn*! Get somebody out here fast for the Senator's baggage."

It occurred to me, as we stopped at the passenger tube sealed to the transfer station to swap our suction sandals for little magnet pads that clipped to our shoes, that we need not have waited for anything at anytime—if only Uncle Tom had been willing to use the special favors he so plainly could demand.

But, even so, it pays to travel with an important person—even though it's just your Uncle Tom whose stomach you used to jump up and down on when you were small enough for such things. Our tickets simply read FIRST CLASS—I'm sure, for I saw all three of them—but where we were placed was in what they call the "Owner's Cabin," which is actually a suite with three bedrooms and a living room. I was dazzled!

But I didn't have time to admire it just then. First they strapped our baggage down, then they strapped us down—to seat couches which were against one wall of the living room. That wall plainly should have been the floor, but it slanted up almost vertically with respect to the tiny, not-quite-nothing weight that we had. The warning sirens were already sounding when someone dragged Clark in and strapped him to one of the couches. He was looking mussed up but cocky.

"Hi, smuggler," Uncle Tom greeted him amiably. "They find it on you?"

"Nothing to find."

"That's what I thought. I trust they gave you a rough time."

"Naah!"

I wasn't sure I believed Clark's answer; I've heard that a skin and person search can be made quite annoying indeed, without doing anything the least bit illegal, if the proctors are feeling unfriendly. A "rough time" would be good for Clark's soul, I am sure—but he certainly did not act as if the experience had caused him any discomfort. I said, "Clark, that was a very foolish remark you made to the inspector. And it was a lie, as well—a silly, useless lie."

"Sign off," he said curtly. "If I'm smuggling anything, it's up to them to find it; that's what they're paid for. 'Any-thing-t'-d'clare?' " he added in a mimicking voice. "What nonsense! As if anybody would declare something he was trying to smuggle."

"Just the same," I went on, "if Daddy had heard you say—"

"Podkayne."

"Yes, Uncle Tom?'"

"Table it. We're about to start. Let's enjoy it."

"But— Yes, Uncle."

There was a slight drop in pressure, then a sudden surge that would have slid us out of our couches if we had not been strapped—but not a strong one, not at all like that giant *whoosh!* with which we had left the surface. It did not last long, then we were truly in free fall for a few moments ... then there started a soft, gentle push in the same direction, which kept on.

Then the room started very slowly to turn around ... almost unnoticeable except for a slight dizziness it gave one.

Gradually, gradually (it took almost twenty minutes) our weight increased, until at last we were back to our proper weight ... at which time the floor, which had been all wrong when we came in, was where it belonged, under us, and almost level. But not quite—

Here is what had happened. The first short boost was made by the rocket tugs of Deimos Port picking up the *Tricorn* and hurling her out into a free orbit of her own. This doesn't take much, because the attraction between even a big ship like the *Tricorn* and a tiny, tiny satellite such as Deimos isn't enough to matter; all that matters is getting the very considerable mass of the ship shoved free.

The second gentle shove, the one that kept up and never went away, was the ship's own main drive—one-tenth of a standard gee. The *Tricorn* is a constant-boost ship; she doesn't dillydally around with economical orbits and weeks and months in free fall. She goes very fast indeed ... because even 0.1 gee adds up awfully fast.

But one-tenth gee is not enough to make comfortable passengers who have been used to more. As soon as the Captain had set her on her course, he started to spin her and kept it up until the centrifugal force and the boost added up (in vector addition, of course) to exactly the surface gravitation of Mars (or 37 percent of a standard gee) at the locus of the first-class staterooms.

But the floors will not be quite level until we approach Earth, because the inside of the ship had been constructed so that the floors would feel perfectly level when the spin and the boost added up to exactly one standard gravity—or Earth-Normal.

Maybe this isn't too clear. Well, it wasn't too clear to me, in school; I didn't see exactly how it worked out until (later) I had a chance to see the controls used to put spin on the ship and how the centrifugal force was calculated. Just remember that the *Tricorn*— and her sisters, the *Trice* and the *Triad* and the *Triangulum* and the *Tricolor* are enormous cylinders. The thrust is straight along the main axis; it has to be. Centrifugal force pushes away from the main axis— how else? The two forces add up to make the ship's "artificial gravity" in passenger country—but, since one force (the boost) is kept constant and the other (the spin) can be varied, there can be only one rate of spin

which will add in with the boost to make those floors
perfectly level.

For the *Tricorn* the spin that will produce level
floors and exactly one Earth gravity in passenger country is 5.42 revolutions per minute—I know because
the Captain told me so . . . and I checked his arithme-
tic and he was right. The floor of our cabin is just over
thirty meters from the main axis of the ship, so it all
comes out even.

As soon as they had the floor back under us and
had announced the "all clear" I unstrapped me and
hurried out. I wanted a quick look at the ship; I didn't
even wait to unpack.

There's a fortune awaiting the man who invents a
really good deodorizer for a spaceship. That's the one
thing you can't fail to notice.

Oh, they try, I grant them that. The air goes through
precipitators each time it is cycled; it is washed, it is
perfumed, a precise fraction of ozone is added, and
the new oxygen that is put in after the carbon dioxide
is distilled out is as pure as a baby's mind; it has to
be, for it is newly released as a by-product of the
photosynthesis of living plants. That air is so pure that
it really ought to be voted a medal by the Society for
the Suppression of Evil Thoughts.

Besides that, a simply amazing amount of the crew's
time is put into cleaning, polishing, washing, steriliz-
ing—oh, they *try*!

But nevertheless, even a new, extra-fare luxury liner
like the *Tricorn* simply reeks of human sweat and
ancient sin, with undefinable overtones of organic
decay and unfortunate accidents and matters best
forgotten. Once I was with Daddy when a Martian
tomb was being unsealed—and I found out why
xenoarchaeologists always have gas masks handy. But
a spaceship smells even worse than that tomb.

It does no good to complain to the purser. He'll listen with professional sympathy and send a crewman around to spray your stateroom with something which (I suspect) merely deadens your nose for a while. But his sympathy is not real, because the poor man simply cannot smell anything wrong himself. He has lived in ships for years; it is literally impossible for him to smell the unmistakable reek of a ship that has been lived in—and, besides, he *knows* that the air is pure; the ship's instruments show it. None of the professional spacers can smell it.

But the purser and all of them are quite used to having passengers complain about the "unbearable stench"—so they pretend sympathy and go through the motions of correcting the matter.

Not that *I* complained. I was looking forward to having this ship eating out of my hand, and you don't accomplish that sort of coup by becoming known first thing as a complainer. But other first-timers did, and I certainly understood why—in fact I began to have a glimmer of a doubt about my ambitions to become skipper of an explorer ship.

But— Well, in about two days it seemed to me that they had managed to clean up the ship quite a bit, and shortly thereafter I stopped thinking about it. I began to understand why the ship's crew can't smell the things the passengers complain about. Their nervous systems simply cancel out the old familiar stinks—like a cybernetic skywatch canceling out and ignoring any object whose predicted orbit has previously been programmed into the machine.

But the odor is still there. I suspect that it sinks right into polished metal and can never be removed, short of scrapping the ship and melting it down. Thank goodness the human nervous system is endlessly adaptable.

*   *   *

But my own nervous system didn't seem too adaptable during that first hasty tour of the *Tricorn;* it is a good thing that I had not eaten much breakfast and had refrained from drinking anything. My stomach did give me a couple of bad moments, but I told it sternly that I was busy—I was very anxious to look over the ship; I simply didn't have time to cater to the weaknesses to which flesh is heir.

Well, the *Tricorn* is lovely all right—every bit as nice as the travel folders say that she is ... except for that dreadful ship's odor. Her ballroom is gorgeous and so big that you can see that the floor curves to match the ship ... only it is not curved when you walk across it. It is level, too—it is the only room in the ship where they jack up the floor to match perfectly with whatever spin is on the ship. There is a lounge with a simulated sky of outer space, or it can be switched to blue sky and fleecy clouds. Some old biddies were already in there, gabbling.

The dining saloon is every bit as fancy, but it seemed hardly big enough—which reminded me of the warning in the travel brochure about first and second tables, so I rushed back to our cabin to urge Uncle Tom to make reservations for us quickly before all the best tables were filled.

He wasn't there. I took a quick look in all the rooms and didn't find him—but I found Clark in *my* room, just closing one of my bags!

"What are you doing?" I demanded.

He jumped and then looked perfectly blank. "I was just looking to see if you had any nausea pills." He said woodenly.

"Well, don't dig into my things! You know better." I came up and felt his cheek; he wasn't feverish. "I don't have any. But I noticed where the surgeon's office is. If you are feeling ill, I'll take you straight there and let him dose you."

He pulled away. "Aw, I'm all right—now."

"Clark Fries, you listen to me. If you—" But he wasn't listening; he slid past me, ducked into his own room and closed the door; I heard the lock click.

I closed the bag he had opened—and noticed something. It was the bag the inspector had been just about to search when Clark had pulled that silly stunt about "happy dust."

My younger brother never does anything without a reason. Never.

His reasons may be, and often are, inscrutable to others. But if you just dig deeply enough, you will always find that his mind is never a random-choice machine, doing things pointlessly. It is as logical as a calculator—and about as cold.

I now knew why he had made what seemed to be entirely unnecessary trouble for himself at outgoing inspection.

I knew why I had been unexpectedly three kilos over my allowance on the centrifuge.

The only thing I didn't know was: *What* had he smuggled aboard in my baggage?

And *why?*

Interlude

Well, Pod, I am glad to see that you've resumed keeping your diary. Not only do I find your girlish viewpoints entertaining but also you sometimes (not often) provide me with useful bits of information.

If I can do anything for you in return, do let me know. Perhaps you would like help in straightening out your grammar? Those incomplete sentences you are so fond of indicate incomplete thinking. You know that, don't you?

For example, let us consider a purely hypothetical case: a delivery robot with an unbeatable seal. Since the seal is in fact unbeatable, thinking about the seal simply leads to frustration. But a complete analysis of the situation leads one to the obvious fact that any cubical or quasi-cubical object has six sides, and that the seal applies to only one of these six sides.

Pursuing this line of thought one may note that, while the quasi cube may not be moved without cutting its connections, the floor under it may be lowered as much as forty-eight centimeters—if one has all afternoon in which to work.

Were this not a hypothetical case I would now suggest the use of a mirror and light on an extension handle and some around-the-corner tools, plus plenty of patience.

That's what you lack, Pod—patience.

I hope this may shed some light on the matter of the hypothetical happy dust—and do feel free to come to me with your little problems.

V

Clark kept his stateroom door locked all the time the first three days we were in the *Tricorn*—I know, because I tried it every time he left the suite.

Then on the fourth day he failed to lock it at a time when it was predictable that he would be gone at least an hour, as he had signed up for a tour of the ship—the parts passengers ordinarily are not allowed in, I mean. I didn't mind missing it myself, for by then I had worked out my own private "Poddy special" escort service. Nor did I have to worry about Uncle Tom; he wasn't making the tour, it would have violated his no-exercise rule, but he had acquired new pinochle cronies and he was safely in the smoking room.

Those stateroom door locks are not impossible to pick—not for a girl equipped with a nail file, some bits of this and that, and *free* run of the purser's office—me, I mean.

But I found I did not have to pick the lock; the catch had not quite caught. I breathed the conventional sigh

of relief, as I figured that the happy accident put me
at least twenty minutes ahead of schedule.

I shan't detail the search, but I flatter myself that
the Criminal Investigation Bureau could not have done
it more logically nor more quickly if limited, as I was,
to bare hands and no equipment. It had to be something forbidden by that list they had given us on
Deimos—and I had carefully kept and studied my
copy. It had to mass slightly over three kilos. It had
to bulk so large and be sufficiently fixed in its shape
and dimensions that Clark was forced to hide it in
baggage—otherwise I am sure he would have concealed it on his person and coldly depended on his
youth and "innocence," plus the chaperonage of Uncle
Tom, to breeze him through the outgoing inspection.
Otherwise he would never have taken the calculated
risk of hiding it in my baggage, since he couldn't be
sure of recovering it without my knowing.

Could he have predicted that I would at once go
sightseeing without waiting to unpack? Well, perhaps
he could, even though I had done so on the spur of
the moment. I must reluctantly admit that Clark can
outguess me with maddening regularity. As an oppo-
nent, he is never to be underrated. But still it was for
him a "calculated risk," albeit a small one.

Very well. Largish, rather massy, forbidden—but I
didn't know what it looked like and I had to assume
that *anything* which met the first two requirements
might be disguised to appear innocent.

Ten minutes later I knew that it had to be in one
of his three bags, which I had left to the last on purpose as the least likely spots. A stateroom aboard ship
has many cover plates, access holes, removable fix-
tures, and the like, but I had done a careful practice
run in my own room; I knew which ones were worth
opening, which ones could not be opened without
power tools, which ones could not be opened without

leaving unmistakable signs of tampering. I checked these all in great haste, then congratulated Clark on having the good sense not to use such obvious hiding places.

Then I checked everything readily accessible—out in the open, in his wardrobe, etc.—using the classic "Purloined Letter" technique, i.e., I never assumed that a book was a book simply because it looked like a book, nor that a jacket on a hanger was simply that and nothing more.

Null, negative, nothing— Reluctantly, I tackled his three pieces of luggage, first noting carefully exactly how they were stacked and in what order.

The first was empty. Oh, the linings could have been tampered with, but the bag was no heavier than it should have been and any false pocket in the linings could not have held anything large enough to meet the specifications.

The second bag was the same—and the bag on the bottom seemed to be the same ... until I found an envelope in a pocket of it. Oh, nothing nearly mass enough, nor gross enough; just an ordinary envelope for a letter—but nevertheless I glanced at it.

And was immediately indignant!

It had printed on it:

> MISS PODKAYNE FRIES
> PASSENGER, S.S. *Tricorn*
> *For delivery in ship*

Why, the little wretch! He had been intercepting my mail! With fingers trembling with rage so badly that I could hardly do so I opened it—and discovered that it had already been opened and was angrier than ever. But, at least, the note was still inside. Shaking, I pulled it out and read it.

Just six words—

Hi, Pod. Snooping again, I see.

—in Clark's handwriting.

I stood there, frozen, for a long moment, while I blushed scarlet and chewed the bitter realization that I had been hoaxed to perfection—*again.*

There are only three people in the world who can make me feel stupid—and Clark is two of them.

I heard a throat-clearing sound behind me and whirled around. Lounging in the open doorway (I had left it closed) was my brother. He smiled at me and said, "Hello, Sis. Looking for something? Need any help?"

I didn't waste time pretending that I didn't have jam all over my face; I simply said, "Clark Fries, what did you smuggle into this ship in my baggage?"

He looked blank—a look of malignant idiocy which has been known to drive well-balanced teachers to their therapists. "What in the world are you talking about, Pod?"

"You know what I'm talking about! Smuggling!"

"Oh!" His face lit up in a sunny smile. "You mean those two kilograms of happy dust. Goodness, Sis, is that still worrying you? There never were any two kilos of happy dust; I was just having my little joke with that stuffy inspector. I thought you knew that."

"I do not mean any 'two kilos of happy dust'! I am talking about at least three kilos of something else that you hid in my baggage!"

He looked worried. "Pod, do you feel well?"

"Ooooooh!—*dandruff!* Clark Fries, you stop that! You know what I mean! When I was centrifuged, my bags and I weighed three kilos over my allowance. Well?"

He looked at me thoughtfully, sympathetically. "It *has* seemed to me that you were getting a bit fat— but I didn't want to mention it. I thought it was all this rich food you've been tucking away here in the ship. You really ought to watch that sort of thing, Pod. After all, if a girl lets her figure go to pieces— Well, she doesn't have much else. So I hear."

Had that envelope been a blunt instrument I would have blunted him. I heard a low growling sound, and realized that I was making it. So I stopped. "Where's the letter that was in this envelope?"

Clark looked surprised. "Why, it's right there, in your other hand."

"This? This is all there was? No letter from somebody else?"

"Why, just that note from me, Sis. Didn't you like it? I thought that it just suited the occasion . . . I knew you would find it your very first chance." He smiled. "Next time you want to paw through my things, let me know and I'll help. Sometimes I have experiments running—and you might get hurt. That can happen to people who aren't very bright and don't look before they leap. I wouldn't want that to happen to *you*, Sis."

I didn't bandy any more words; I brushed past him and went to my own room and locked the door and bawled.

Then I got up and did very careful things to my face. I know when I'm licked; I don't have to have a full set of working drawings. I resolved never to mention the matter to Clark again.

But what was I to do? Go to the Captain? I already knew the Captain pretty well; his imagination extended as far as the next ballistic prediction and no further. Tell him that my brother had been smuggling something, I didn't know what—and that he had better search the entire ship most carefully, because, whatever it was, it was not in my brother's room? Don't be triple silly, Poddy. In the first place, he would laugh at you; in the second place, you don't *want* Clark to be caught— Mother and Daddy wouldn't like it.

Tell Uncle Tom about it? He might be just as unbelieving . . . or, if he did believe me, he might go to the Captain himself—with just as disastrous results.

I decided not to go to Uncle Tom—at least not yet. Instead I would keep my eyes and ears open and try to find an answer myself.

In any case I did not waste much time on Clark's sins (if any, I had to admit in bare honesty); I was in my first real spaceship—halfway to my ambition thereby—and there was much to learn and do.

Those travel brochures are honest enough, I guess— but they do not give you the full picture.

For example, take this phrase right out of the text of the Triangle Line's fancy folder . . . *romantic days in ancient Marsopolis, the city older than time; exotic nights under the hurtling moons of Mars* . . .

Let's rephrase it into everyday language, shall we? Marsopolis is my hometown and I love it—but it is as romantic as bread and butter with no jam. The parts people live in are new and were designed for function, not romance. As for the ruins outside town (which the Martians *never* called "Marsopolis"), a lot of high foreheads including Daddy have seen to it that the best parts are locked off so that tourists will not carve their initials in something that was old when stone axes were the last thing in superweapons. Furthermore, Martian ruins are neither beautiful, nor picturesque, nor impressive, to human eyes. The way to appreciate them is to read a really good book with illustrations, diagrams, and simple explanations—such as Daddy's *Other Paths Than Ours.* (Adv.)

As for those exotic nights, anybody who is outdoors after sundown on Mars other than through sheer necessity needs to have his head examined. It's *chilly* out there. I've seen Deimos and Phobos at night exactly twice, each time through no fault of my own—

and I was so busy keeping from freezing to death that I wasted no thought on "hurtling moons."

This advertising brochure is just as meticulously accurate and just as deceptive in effect—concerning the ships themselves. Oh, the *Tricorn* is a palace; I'll vouch for that. It really is a miracle of engineering that anything so huge, so luxurious, so fantastically adapted to the health and comfort of human beings, should be able to "hurtle" (pardon the word) through space.

But take those pictures—

You know the ones I mean: full color and depth, showing groups of handsome young people of both sexes chatting or playing games in the lounge, dancing gaily in the ballroom—or views of a "typical stateroom."

That "typical stateroom" is not a fake. No, it has simply been photographed from an angle and with a lens that makes it look at least twice as big as it is. As for those handsome, gay, young people—well, they aren't along on the trip I'm making. It's my guess that they are professional models.

In the *Tricorn* this trip the young and handsome passengers like those in the pictures can be counted on the thumb of one hand. The typical passenger we have with us is a great-grandmother, Terran citizenship, widowed, wealthy, making her first trip into space—and probably her last, for she is not sure she likes it.

Honest, I'm not exaggerating; our passengers look like refugees from a geriatrics clinic. I am not scoffing at old age. I understand that it is a condition I will one day attain myself, if I go on breathing in and out enough times—say about 900,000,000 more times, not counting heavy exercise. Old age can be a charming condition, as witness Uncle Tom. But old age is not an accomplishment; it is just something that happens to you despite yourself, like falling downstairs.

And I must say that I am getting a wee bit tired of having youth treated as a punishable offense.

Our typical male passenger is the same sort, only not nearly so numerous. He differs from his wife primarily in that, instead of looking down his nose at me, he is sometimes inclined to pat me in a "fatherly" way that I do not find fatherly, don't like, avoid if humanly possible—and which nevertheless gets me talked about.

I suppose I should not have been surprised to find the *Tricorn* a super-deluxe old folks' home, but (I may as well admit it) my experience is still limited and I was not aware of some of the economic facts of life.

The *Tricorn* is expensive. It is *very* expensive. Clark and I would not be in it at all if Uncle Tom had not twisted Dr. Schoenstein's arm in our behalf. Oh, I suppose Uncle Tom can afford it, but, by age group though not by temperament, he fits the defined category. But Daddy and Mother had intended to take us in the *Wanderlust*, a low-fare, economy-orbit freighter. Daddy and Mother are not poor, but they are not rich—and after they finish raising and educating five children it is unlikely that they will ever be rich.

Who can afford to travel in luxury liners? Ans.: Rich old widows, wealthy retired couples, high-priced executives whose time is so valuable that their corporations gladly send them by the fastest ships—and an occasional rare exception of some other sort.

Clark and I are such exceptions. We have one other exception in the ship, Miss—well, I'll call her Miss Girdle Fitz-Snugglie, because if I used her right name and perchance anybody ever sees this, it would be all too easily recognizable. I think Girdie is a good sort. I don't care what the gossips in this ship say. She doesn't act jealous of me even though it appears that the younger officers in the ship were all her personal property until I boarded—all the trip out from Earth,

I mean. I've cut into her monopoly quite a bit, but she isn't catty to me; she treats me warmly woman-to-woman, and I've learned quite a lot about Life and Men from her ... more than Mother ever taught me.

(It is just possible that Mother is slightly naïve on subjects that Girdie knows best. A woman who tackles engineering and undertakes to beat men at their own game might have had a fairly limited social life, wouldn't you think? I must study this seriously ... because it seems possible that much the same might happen to a female space pilot and it is no part of my Master Plan to become a soured old maid.)

Girdie is about twice my age, which makes her awfully young in this company; nevertheless it may be that I cause her to look just a bit wrinkled around the eyes. Contrariwise, my somewhat unfinished look may make her more mature contours appear even more Helen-of-Troyish. As may be, it is certain that my presence has relieved the pressure on her by giving the gossips two targets instead of one.

And gossip they do. I heard one of them say about her: "She's been in more laps than a napkin!"

If so, I hope she had fun.

Those gay ship's dances in the mammoth ballroom! Like this: they happen every Tuesday and Saturday night, when the ship is spacing. The music starts at 20.30 and the Ladies' Society for Moral Rectitude is seated around the edge of the floor, as if for a wake. Uncle Tom is there, as a concession to me, and very proudsome and distinguished he looks in evening formal. I am there in a party dress which is not quite as girlish as it was when Mother helped me pick it out, in consequence of some *very* careful retailoring I have done with my door locked. Even Clark attends because there is nothing else going on and he's afraid he might miss something—and looking so nice I'm proud of him, because he has to climb into his own monkey suit or he can't come to the ball.

Over by the punch bowl are half a dozen of the ship's junior officers, dressed in mess jacket uniforms and looking faintly uncomfortable.

The Captain, by some process known only to him, selects one of the widows and asks her to dance. Two husbands dance with their wives. Uncle Tom offers me his arm and leads me to the floor. Two or three of the junior officers follow the Captain's example. Clark takes advantage of the breathless excitement to raid the punch bowl.

But *nobody* asks Girdie to dance.

This is no accident. The Captain has given the Word (I have this intelligence with utter certainty through My Spies) that no ship's officer shall dance with Miss Fitz-Snugglie until he has danced at least two dances with other partners—and I am not an "other partner," because the proscription, since leaving Mars, has been extended to me.

This should be proof to anyone that a captain of a ship is, in sober fact, the Last of the Absolute Monarchs.

There are now six or seven couples on the floor and the fun is at its riotous height. The floor will never again be so crowded. Nevertheless nine-tenths of the chairs are still occupied and you could ride a bicycle around the floor without endangering the dancers. The spectators look as if they were knitting at the tumbrels. The proper finishing touch would be a guillotine in the empty space in the middle of the floor.

The music stops; Uncle Tom takes me back to my chair, then asks Girdie to dance—since he is a Cash Customer, the Captain has not attempted to make him toe the mark. But I am still out of bounds, so I walk over to the punch bowl, take a cup out of Clark's hands, finish it, and say, "Come on, Clark. I'll let you practice on me."

"Aw, it's a waltz!" (Or a "flea hop," or a "chassé," or "five step"—but whatever it is, it is just too utterly impossible.)

"Do it—or I'll tell Madame Grew that you want to dance with her, only you're too shy to ask her."

"You do and I'll trip her! I'll stumble and trip her."

However, Clark is weakening, so I move in fast. "Look, Bub, you either take me out there and walk on my feet for a while—or I'll see to it that Girdie doesn't dance with you at all."

That does it. Clark is in the throes of his first case of puppy love, and Girdie is such a gent that she treats him as an equal and accepts his attentions with warm courtesy. So Clark dances with me. Actually he is quite a good dancer and I have to lead him only a tiny bit. He likes to dance—but he wouldn't want anyone, especially me, to think that he likes to dance with his sister. We don't look too badly matched, since I am short. In the meantime Girdie is looking very good indeed with Uncle Tom, which is quite an accomplishment, as Uncle Tom dances with great enthusiasm and no rhythm. But Girdie can follow anyone—if her partner broke his leg, she would follow, fracturing her own at the same spot. But the crowd is thinning out now; husbands that danced the first dance are too tired for the second and no one has replaced them.

Oh, we have gay times in the luxury liner *Tricorn*!

Truthfully we *do* have gay times. Starting with the third dance Girdie and I have our pick of the ship's officers, most of whom are good dancers, or at least have had plenty of practice. About twenty-two o'clock the Captain goes to bed and shortly after that the chaperones start putting away their whetstones and fading, one by one. By midnight there is just Girdie and myself and half a dozen of the younger officers—

and the Purser, who has dutifully danced with every woman and now feels that he owes himself the rest of the night. He is quite a good dancer, for an old man.

Oh, and there is usually Mrs. Grew, too—but she isn't one of the chaperones and she is always nice to Girdie. She is a fat old woman, full of sin and chuckles. She doesn't expect anyone to dance with her but she likes to watch—and the officers who aren't dancing at the moment like to sit with her; she's fun.

About one o'clock Uncle Tom sends Clark to tell me to come to bed or he'll lock me out. He wouldn't but I do—my feet are tired.

Good old *Tricorn*!

VI

The Captain is slowly increasing the spin of the ship to make the fake gravity match the surface gravitation of Venus, which is 84 percent of one standard gravity or more than twice as much as I have been used to all my life. So, when I am not busy studying astrogation or ship handling, I spend much of my time in the ship's gymnasium, hardening myself for what is coming, for I have no intention of being at a disadvantage on Venus in either strength or agility.

If I can adjust to an acceleration of 0.84 gee, the later transition to the full Earth-normal of one gee should be sugar pie with chocolate frosting. So I think.

I usually have the gymnasium all to myself. Most of the passengers are Earthmen or Venusmen who feel no need to prepare for the heavy gravitation of Venus. Of the dozen-odd Marsmen I am the only one who seems to take seriously the coming burden—and the handful of aliens in the ship we never see; each remains in his specially conditioned stateroom. The ship's officers do use the gym; some of them are quite fanatic about keeping fit. But they use it mostly at hours when passengers are not likely to use it.

So, on this day (Ceres thirteenth actually but the *Tricorn* uses Earth dates and time, which made it March ninth—I don't mind the strange dates but the short Earth day is costing me a half-hour's sleep each night)—on Ceres thirteenth I went charging into the gym, so angry I could spit venom and intending to derive a double benefit by working off my mad (at least to the point where I would not be clapped in irons for assault), and by strengthening my muscles, too.

And found Clark inside, dressed in shorts and with a massy barbell.

I stopped short and blurted out, "What are *you* doing here?"

He grunted, "Weakening my mind."

Well, I had asked for it; there is no ship's regulation forbidding Clark to use the gym. His answer made sense to one schooled in his devious logic, which I certainly should be. I changed the subject, tossed aside my robe, and started limbering exercises to warm up. "How massy?" I asked.

"Sixty kilos."

I glanced at a weight meter on the wall, a loaded spring scale marked to read in fractions of standard gee; it read 52%. I did a fast rough in my mind—fifty-two thirty-sevenths of sixty—or unit sum, plus nine hundred over thirty-seven, so add about a ninth, top and bottom for a thousand over forty, to yield twenty-five—or call it the same as lifting eighty-five kilos back home on Mars. "Then why are you sweating?"

"I am not sweating!" He put the barbell down. "Let's see *you* lift it."

"All right." As he moved I squatted down to raise the barbell—and changed my mind.

Now, believe me, I work out regularly with ninety kilos at home and I had been checking that weight meter on the wall each day and loading that same barbell to match the weight I use at home, plus a bit extra each day. My objective (hopeless, it is beginning to seem) is eventually to lift as much mass under Venus conditions as I had been accustomed to lifting at home.

So I was certain I could lift sixty kilos at 52 percent of standard gee.

But it is a mistake for a girl to beat a male at any test of physical strength ... even when it's your brother. Most especially when it's your brother and he has a fiendish disposition and you've suddenly had a glimmering of a way to put his fiendish proclivities to work. As I have said, if you're in a mood to hate something or somebody, Clark is the perfect partner.

So I grunted and strained, making a good show, got it up to my chest, started it on up—and squeaked, "Help me!"

Clark gave a one-handed push at the center of the bar and we got it all the way up. Then I said, "Catch for me," through clenched teeth, and he eased it down. I sighed. "Gee, Clark, you must be getting awful strong."

"Doing all right."

It works; Clark was now as mellow as his nature permits. I suggested companion tumbling—if he didn't mind being the bottom half of the team?—because I wasn't sure I could hold him, not at point-five-two gee ... did he mind?

He didn't mind at all; it gave him another chance to be muscular and masculine—and I was certain he could lift me; I massed eleven kilos less than the barbell he had just been lifting. When he was smaller, we used to do quite a bit of it, with me lifting him—it was a way to keep him quiet when I was in charge of him. Now that he is as big as I am (and stronger, I fear), we still tumble a little, but taking turns at the ground-and-air parts—back home, I mean.

But with my weight almost half again what it ought to be I didn't risk any fancy capers. Presently, when he had me in a simple handstand over his head, I broached the subject on my mind. "Clark, is Mrs. Royer any special friend of yours?"

"Her?" He snorted and added a rude noise. "Why?"

"I just wondered. She—Mmm, perhaps I shouldn't repeat it."

He said, "Look, Pod, you want me to leave you standing on the ceiling?"

"Don't you dare!"

"Then don't start to say something and not finish it."

"All right. But steady while I swing my feet down to your shoulders." He let me do so, then I hopped down to the floor. The worst part about high acceleration is not how much you weigh, though that is bad enough, but how *fast* you fall—and I suspected that Clark was quite capable of leaving me head downwards high in the air if I annoyed him.

"What's this about Mrs. Royer?" he asked.

"Oh, nothing much. She thinks Marsmen are trash, that's all."

"She does, huh? That makes it mutual."

"Yes. She thinks it's disgraceful that the Line allows us to travel first class—and the Captain certainly ought not to allow us to eat in the same mess with decent people."

"Tell me more."

"Nothing to tell. We're riffraff, that's all. Convicts. You know."

"Interesting. Very, very interesting."

"And her friend Mrs. Garcia agrees with her. But I

suppose I shouldn't have repeated it. After all, they are entitled to their own opinions. Aren't they?"

Clark didn't answer, which is a very bad sign. Shortly thereafter he left without a word. In a sudden panic that I might have started more than I intended to, I called after him but he just kept going. Clark is not hard of hearing but he can be very hard of listening.

Well, it was too late now. So I put on a weight harness, then loaded myself down all over until I weighed as much as I would on Venus and started trotting on the treadmill until I was covered with sweat and ready for a bath and a change.

Actually I did not really care what bad luck overtook those two harpies; I simply hoped that Clark's sleight-of-hand would be up to its usual high standards so that it could not possibly be traced back to him. Nor even guessed at. For I had not told Clark half of what was said.

Believe you me, I had never guessed, until we were in the *Tricorn*, that anyone could despise other persons simply over their ancestry or where they lived. Oh, I had encountered tourists from Earth whose manners left something to be desired—but Daddy had told me that all tourists, everywhere, seem obnoxious simply because tourists are strangers who do not know local customs . . . and I believed it, because Daddy is never wrong. Certainly the occasional visiting professor that Daddy brought home for dinner was always charming, which proves that Earthmen do not have to have bad manners.

I had noticed that the passengers in the *Tricorn* seemed a little bit stand-offish when we first boarded, but I did not think anything of it. After all, strangers do not run up and kiss you, even on Mars—and we Marsmen are fairly informal, I suppose; we're still a frontier society. Besides that, most passengers had been in the ship at least from Earth; they had already formed their friendships and cliques. We were like new kids in a strange school.

But I said "Good morning!" to anyone I met in the passageway and if I was not answered I just checked it off to hard-of-hearing—so many of them obviously *could* be hard of hearing. Anyhow, I wasn't terribly interested in getting chummy with passengers; I wanted to get acquainted with the ship's officers, pilot officers especially, so that I could get some practical experience to chink in what I already knew from reading. It's not easy for a girl to get accepted for pilot training; she has to be about four times as good as a male candidate—and every little bit helps.

I got a wonderful break right away. We were seated at the Captain's table!

Uncle Tom, of course. I am not conceited enough to think that "Miss Podkayne Fries, Marsopolis" means anything on a ship's passenger list (but wait ten years!)—whereas Uncle Tom, even though he is just my pinochle-playing, easygoing oldest relative, is nevertheless senior Senator-at-Large of the Republic, and it is certain that the Marsopolis General Agent for the Triangle Line knows this and no doubt the agent would see to it that the Purser of the *Tricorn* would know it if he didn't already.

As may be—I am not one to scorn gifts from heaven, no matter how they arrive. At our very first meal I started working on Captain Darling. That really is his name, Barrington Babcock Darling—and does his wife call him "Baby Darling"?

But of course a captain does not have a name aboard ship; he is "the Captain," "the Master," "the Skipper," or even "the Old Man" if it is a member of the ship's company speaking not in his august presence. But never a name—simply a majestic figure of impersonal authority.

(I wonder if I will someday be called "the Old

Woman" when I am not in earshot? Somehow it doesn't sound quite the same.)

But Captain Darling is not too majestic or impersonal with *me*. I set out to impress him with the idea that I was awfully sweet, even younger than I am, terribly impressed by him and overawed . . . and not too bright. It does not do to let a male of any age know that one has brains, not on first acquaintance; intelligence in a woman is likely to make a man suspicious and uneasy, much like Caesar's fear of Cassius' "lean and hungry look." Get a man solidly on your side first; after that it is fairly safe to let him become gradually aware of your intellect. He may even feel unconsciously that it rubbed off from his own.

So I set out to make him feel that it was a shame that I was not his daughter. (Fortunately he only has sons.) Before that first meal was over I confided in him my great yearning to take pilot training . . . suppressing, of course, any higher ambition.

Both Uncle Tom and Clark could see what I was up to. But Uncle Tom would never give me away and Clark just looked bored and contemptuous and said nothing, because Clark would not bother to interfere with Armageddon unless there was ten percent in it for him.

But I do not mind what my relatives think of my tactics; they work. Captain Darling was obviously amused at my grandiose and "impossible" ambition . . . but he offered to show me the control room.

Round one to Poddy, on points.

I am now the unofficial ship's mascot, with free run of the control room—and I am almost as privileged in the engineering department. Of course the Captain does not really want to spend hours teaching me the practical side of astrogation. He did show me through the control room and gave me a kindergarten explanation of the work—which I followed with wide-eyed awe—but his interest in me is purely social. He wants to not-quite hold me in his lap (he is much too practical and too discreet to do anything of the sort!), so I not-quite let him and make it a point to keep up my social relations with him, listening with my best astonished-kitten look to his anecdotes while he feeds me liters of tea. I really am a good listener because you never can tell when you will pick up something useful—and all in the world any woman has to do to be considered "charming" by men is to listen while they talk.

But Captain Darling is not the only astrogator in the ship.

He gave me the run of the control room; I did the rest. The second officer, Mr. Savvonavong, thinks it is simply amazing how fast I pick up mathematics. You see, he thinks he taught me differential equations. Well, he did, when it comes to those awfully complicated ones used in correcting the vector of a constant-boost ship, but if I hadn't worked hard in the supplementary course I was allowed to take last semester, I wouldn't know what he was talking about. Now he is showing me how to program a ballistic computer.

The junior third, Mr. Clancy, is still studying for his unlimited license, so he has all the study tapes and reference books I need and is just as helpful. He is near enough my age to develop groping hands . . . but only a very stupid male will make even an indirect pass unless a girl manages to let him know that it won't be resented, and Mr. Clancy is not stupid and I am very careful to offer neither invitation nor opportunity.

I may kiss him—two minutes before I leave the ship for the last time. Not sooner.

They are all very helpful and they think it is cute of me to be so dead serious about it. But, in truth, practical astrogation is *much* harder than I had ever dreamed.

* * *

I had guessed that part of the resentment I sensed—
resentment that I could not fail to notice despite my
cheery "Good mornings!"—lay in the fact that we were
at the Captain's table. To be sure, the *Welcome in the
Tricorn!* booklet in each stateroom states plainly that
new seating arrangements are made at each port and
that it is the ship's custom to change the guests at the
Captain's table each time, making the selections from
the new passengers.

But I don't suppose that warning makes it any plea-
santer to be bumped, because I don't expect to like it
when I'm bumped off the Captain's table at Venus.

But that is only part—

Only three of the passengers were really friendly to
me: Mrs. Grew, Girdie, and Mrs. Royer. Mrs. Royer
I met first and at first I thought that I was going to
like her, in a bored sort of way, as she was awfully
friendly and I have great capacity for enduring bore-
dom if it suits my purpose. I met her in the lounge
the first day and she immediately caught my eye,
smiled, invited me to sit by her, and quizzed me about
myself.

I answered her questions, mostly. I told her that
Daddy was a teacher and that Mother was raising
babies and that my brother and I were traveling with
our uncle. I didn't boast about our family; boasting is
not polite and it often is not believed—far better to
let people find out nice things on their own and hope
they won't notice any unnice things. Not that there is
anything unnice about Daddy and Mother.

I told her that my name was Poddy Fries.

" 'Poddy'?" she said. "I thought I saw something else
on the passenger list."

"Oh. It's really 'Podkayne,' " I explained. "For the
Martian saint, you know."

But she didn't know. She answered, "It seems very odd to give a girl a man's name."

Well, my name *is* odd, even among Marsmen. But not for that reason. "Possibly," I agreed. "But with Martians gender is rather a matter of opinion, wouldn't you say?"

She blinked. "You're jesting."

I started to explain—how a Martian doesn't select which of three sexes to be until just before it matures ... and how, even so, the decision is operative only during a relatively short period of its life.

But I gave up, as I could see that I was talking to a blank wall. Mrs. Royer simply could not imagine any pattern other than her own. So I shifted quickly. "Saint Podkayne lived a very *long* time ago. Nobody actually knows whether the saint was male or female. There are just traditions."

Of course the traditions are pretty explicit and many living Martians claim descent from Saint Podkayne. Daddy says that we know Martian history of millions of years ago much more accurately than we know human history a mere two thousand years ago. In any case, most Martians include "Podkayne" in their long lists of names (practically genealogies in synopsis) because of the tradition that anyone named for Saint Podkayne can call on him (or "her"—or "it") in time of trouble.

As I have said, Daddy is romantic and he thought it would be nice to give a baby the luck, if any, that is attached to the saint's name. I am neither romantic nor superstitious, but it suits me just fine to have a name that belongs to me and to no other human. I like being Podkayne "Poddy" Fries— It's better than being one of a multitude of Elizabeths, or Dorothys, or such.

But I could see that it simply puzzled Mrs. Royer, so we passed to other matters, speaking from her seniority as an "old space hand," based on her one just-completed trip out from Earth, she told me a great many things about ships and space travel, most of which weren't so, but I indulged her. She introduced me to a number of people and handed me a large quantity of gossip about passengers, ship's officers, et cetera. Between times she filled me in on her aches, pains, and symptoms, what an important executive her son was, what a very important person her late husband had been, and how, when I reached Earth, she really must see to it that I met the Right People. "Perhaps such things don't matter in an outpost like Mars, my dear child, but it is Terribly Important to get Started Right in New York."

I tabbed her as garrulous, stupid, and well intentioned.

But I soon found that I couldn't get rid of her. If I passed through the lounge—which I had to do in order to reach the control room—she would snag me and I couldn't get away short of abrupt rudeness or flat lies.

She quickly started using me for chores. "Podkayne darling, would you mind just slipping around to my stateroom and fetching my mauve wrap? I feel a tiny chill. It's on the bed, I think—or perhaps in the wardrobe—that's a dear." Or, "Poddy child, I've rung and I've rung and the stewardess simply *won't* answer. Would you get my book and my knitting? Oh, and while you're at it, you might bring me a nice cup of tea from the pantry."

Those things aren't too bad; she is probably creaky in the knees and I'm not. But it went on endlessly . . . and shortly, in addition to being her personal stewardess, I was her private nurse. First she asked me to read her to sleep. "Such a blinding headache and your voice is so soothing, my sweet."

I read to her for an hour and then found myself rubbing her head and temples for almost as long. Oh

well, a person ought to manage a little kindness now
and then, just for practice—and Mother sometimes has
dreadful headaches when she has been working too
hard; I know that a rub does help.

That time she tried to tip me. I refused it. She
insisted. "Now, now, child, don't argue with your Aunt
Flossie."

I said, "No, really, Mrs. Royer. If you want to give
it to the fund for disabled spacemen as a thank-you,
that's all right. But I can't take it."

She said pish and tosh and tried to shove it into my
pocket. So I slid out and went to bed.

I didn't see her at breakfast; she always has a tray
in her room. But about midmorning a stewardess told
me that Mrs. Royer wanted to see me in her room. I
was hardly gruntled at the summons, as Mr. Savvonavong had told me that if I showed up just before ten
during his watch, I could watch the whole process of
a ballistic correction and he would explain the steps
to me. If she wasted more than five minutes of my
time, I would be late.

But I called on her. She was as cheery as ever. "Oh,
there you are, darling! I've been waiting ever so long!
That stupid stewardess— Poddy dear, you did such
wonders for my head last night . . . and this morning
I find that I'm positively *crippled* with my back. You
can't imagine, dear; it's *ghastly!* Now if you'll just be
an angel and give me a few minutes massage—oh, say
a half hour—I'm sure it'll do wonders for me. You'll
find the cream for it over there on the dressing table,
I think . . . And now, if you'll just help me slide out
of this robe . . ."

"Mrs. Royer—"

"Yes, dear? The cream is in that big pink tube. Use
just—"

"Mrs. Royer, I can't do it. I have an appointment."

"What, dear? Oh, tosh, let them wait. No one is

ever on time aboard ship. Perhaps you had better
warm your hands before—"

"Mrs. Royer, I am not going to do it. If something
is wrong with your back, I shouldn't touch it; I might
injure you. But I'll take a message to the Surgeon if
you like and ask him to come see you."

Suddenly she wasn't at all cheery. "You mean you
won't do it!"

"Have it your way. Shall I tell the Surgeon?"

"Why, you impertinent—*Get out of here!*"

I got.

I met her in a passageway on my way to lunch. She
stared straight through me, so I didn't speak either.
She was walking as nimbly as I was; I guess her back
had taken a turn for the better. I saw her twice more
that day and twice more she simply couldn't see me.

The following morning I was using the viewer in the
lounge to scan one of Mr. Clancy's study tapes, one
on radar approach and contact. The viewer is off in a
corner, behind a screen of fake potted palms, and perhaps they didn't notice me. Or perhaps they didn't
care.

I stopped the scan to give my eyes and ears a rest,
and heard Mrs. Garcia talking to Mrs. Royer.

". . . that I simply can't stand about Mars is that it
is so *commercialized*. Why couldn't they have left it
primitive and beautiful?"

MRS. ROYER: "What can you expect? Those *dreadful* people!"

The ship's official language is Ortho but many passengers talk English among themselves—and often act
as if no one else could possibly understand it. These
two weren't keeping their voices down. I went on
listening.

MRS. GARCIA: "Just what I was saying to Mrs.
Rimski. After all, they're all *criminals*."

MRS. ROYER: "Or worse. Have you noticed that

little Martian girl? The niece—or so they claim—of that big black savage?"

I counted ten backwards in Old Martian and reminded myself of the penalty for murder. I didn't mind being called a "Martian." They didn't know any better, and anyhow, it's no insult; the Martians were civilized before humans learned to walk. But "big black savage"!— Uncle Tom is as dark as I am blond; his Maori blood and desert tan make him the color of beautiful old leather . . . and I love the way he looks. As for the rest—he is learned and civilized and gentle . . . and highly honored wherever he goes.

MRS. GARCIA: "I've seen her. Common, I would say. Flashy but cheap. A type that attracts a certain sort of man."

MRS. ROYER: "My dear, you don't know the half of it. I've tried to help her—I really felt sorry for her, and I always believe in being gracious, especially to one's social inferiors."

MRS. GARCIA: "Of course, dear."

MRS. ROYER: "I tried to give her a few hints as to proper conduct among gentle people. Why, I was even *paying* her for little trifles, so that she wouldn't be uneasy among her betters. But she's an utterly ungrateful little snip—she thought she could squeeze more money out of me. She was rude about it, so rude that I feared for my safety. I had to order her out of my room, actually."

MRS. GARCIA: "You were wise to drop her. Blood will tell—bad blood or good blood—blood will always tell. And mixed blood is the Very Worst Sort. Criminals to start with . . . and then that Shameless Mixing of Races. You can see it right in that family. The boy doesn't look a bit like his sister, and as for the uncle— *hmmm*— My dear, you halfway hinted at something.

Do you suppose that she is not his niece but something, shall we say, a bit *closer*?"

MRS. ROYER: "I wouldn't put it past one of them!"

MRS. GARCIA: "Oh, come, 'fess up, Flossie. Tell me what you found out."

MRS. ROYER: "I didn't say a word. But I have eyes—and so have you."

MRS. GARCIA: "Right in front of everyone!"

MRS. ROYER: "What I *can't* understand is why the Line permits *them* to mix with *us*. Perhaps they have to sell them passage—treaties or some such nonsense—but we shouldn't be forced to associate with them . . . and certainly not to *eat* with them!"

MRS. GARCIA: "I know. I'm going to write a very strong letter about it as soon as I get home. There are limits. You know, I had thought that Captain Darling was a gentleman . . . but when I saw those *creatures* actually seated at the Captain's table . . . well, I didn't believe my eyes. I thought I would faint."

MRS. ROYER: "I know. But after all, the Captain does come from Venus."

MRS. GARCIA: "Yes, but Venus was never a *prison* colony. That boy . . . he sits in the very chair I used to sit in, right across from the Captain."

(I made a mental note to ask the Chief Steward for a different chair for Clark; I didn't want him contaminated.)

After that they dropped us "Martians" and started dissecting Girdie and complaining about the food and the service, and even stuck pins in some of their shipboard coven who weren't present. But I didn't listen: I simply kept quiet and prayed for strength to go on doing so, because if I had made my presence known I feel sure that I would have stabbed them both with their own knitting needles.

Eventually they left—to rest a while to fortify themselves for lunch—and I rushed out and changed into my gym suit and hurried to the gymnasium to work up a good sweat instead of engaging in violent crime.

It was there that I found Clark and told him just enough—or maybe too much.

VII

Mr. Savvonavong tells me that we are likely to have a radiation storm almost any time now and that we'll have an emergency drill today to practice for it. The solar weather station on Mercury reports that "flare" weather is shaping up and has warned all ships in space and all manned satellites to be ready for it. The flares are expected to continue for about—

Wups! The emergency alarm caught me in the middle of a sentence. We've had our drill and I think the Captain has all the passengers properly scared now. Some ignored the alarm, or tried to, whereupon crewmen in heavy armor fetched them. Clark got fetched. He was the very last they tracked down, and Captain Darling gave him a public scolding that was a work of art and finished by warning Clark that if he failed to be the first passenger to reach shelter the next time the alarm sounded, Clark could expect to spend the rest of the trip *in* the shelter, twenty-four hours of the day, instead of having free run of passenger country.

Clark took it with his usual wooden face, but I think it hit home, especially the threat to confine him. I'm sure the speech impressed the other passengers; it was the sort that raises blisters at twenty paces. Perhaps the Captain intended it mostly for their benefit.

Then the Captain changed his tone to that of a patient teacher and explained in simple words what we could expect, why it was necessary to reach shelter *at once* even if one were taking a bath, why we would be perfectly safe if we did.

The solar flares trigger radiation, he told us, quite ordinary radiation, much like X-rays ("and other sorts," I mentally added), the sort of radiation which is found in space at all times. But the intensity reaches levels from a thousand to ten thousand times as high as "normal" space radiation—and, since we are already inside the orbit of Earth, this is bad medicine indeed; it would kill an unprotected man about as quickly as shooting him through the head.

Then he explained why we would not require a thousand to ten thousand times as much shielding in order to be safe. It's the cascade principle. The outer hull stops over 90 percent of any radiation; then comes the "cofferdam" (cargo holds and water tanks) which absorbs some more; then comes the inner hull which is actually the floor of the cylinder which is first-class passenger country.

This much shielding is plenty for all normal conditions; the radiation level in our staterooms is lower than it is at home, quite a lot lower than it is most places on Earth, especially in the mountains. (I'm looking forward to seeing real mountains. Scary!)

Then one day comes a really *bad* storm on the Sun and the radiation level jumps suddenly to 10,000 times normal—and you could get a killing dose right in your own bed and wake up dying.

No trouble. The emergency shelter is at the center of the ship, four shells farther in, each of which stops more than 90 percent of what hits it. Like this:

10,000
  1,000 (after the first inner shell, the ceiling of passenger country.)
    100 (after the second inner shell)
     10 (third)
      1 (fourth—and you're inside the shelter)

But actually the shielding is better than that and it is safer to be in the ship's shelter during a bad solar storm than it is to be in Marsopolis.

The only trouble is—and no small matter—the shelter space is the geometrical core of the ship, just abaft the control room and not a whole lot bigger; passengers and crew are stacked into it about as intimately as puppies in a basket. My billet is a shelf space half a meter wide, half a meter deep, and just a trifle longer than I am—with other females brushing my elbows on each side of me. I am not a claustrophobe, but a coffin would be roomier.

Rations are canned ones, kept there against emergencies; sanitary facilities can only be described as "dreadful." I hope this storm is only a solar squall and is followed by good weather on the Sun. To finish the trip to Venus in the shelter would turn a wonderful experience into a nightmare.

The Captain finished by saying, "We will probably have five to ten minutes' warning from Hermes Station. But don't take five minutes getting here. The instant the alarm sounds *head for the shelter at once* as fast as possible. If you are not dressed, be sure you have clothes ready to grab—and dress when you get here. If you stop to worry about *anything*, it may kill you.

"Crewmen will search all passenger spaces the moment the alarm sounds—and each one is *ordered* to use force to send to shelter any passenger who fails to move fast. He won't argue with you—he'll hit you, kick you, drag you—and I'll back him up.

"One last word. Some of you have not been wearing your personal radiation meters. The law permits me to levy a stiff fine for such failure. Ordinarily I overlook such technical offenses—it's your health, not mine. But during this emergency, this regulation will be enforced. Fresh personal meters are now being passed out to each of you; old ones will be turned over to the Surgeon, examined, and exposures entered in your records for future guidance."

He gave the "all clear" order then and we all went back down to passenger country, sweaty and mussed—at least I was. I was just washing my face when the alarm sounded *again*, and I swarmed up those four decks like a frightened cat.

But I was only a close second. Clark passed me on the way.

It was just another drill. This time all passengers were in the shelter within four minutes. The Captain seemed pleased.

I've been sleeping raw but I'm going to wear pajamas tonight and all nights until this is over, and leave a robe where I can grab it. Captain Darling is a darling but I think he means exactly what he says—and I won't play Lady Godiva; there isn't a horse in the whole ship.

Neither Mrs. Royer nor Mrs. Garcia were at dinner this evening, although they were both amazingly agile both times the alarm sounded. They weren't in the lounge after dinner; their doors are closed, and I saw the Surgeon coming out of Mrs. Garcia's room.

I wonder. Surely Clark wouldn't poison them? Or would he? I don't dare ask him because of the remote possibility that he might tell me.

I don't want to ask the Surgeon, either, because it might attract attention to the Fries family. But I surely would like to have ESP sight (if there truly is such a thing) long enough to find out what is behind those two closed doors.

I hope Clark hasn't let his talents run away with him. Oh, I'm as angry at those two as ever . . . because there is just enough truth in the nasty things they said to make it hurt. I *am* of mixed races and I know that some people think that is bad, even though there is no bias against it on Mars. I *do* have "convicts" among my ancestors—but I've never been ashamed of it. Or not much, although I suppose I'm inclined to dwell more on the highly selected ones. But a "convict" is not always a criminal. Admittedly there was that period in the early history of Mars when the commissars were running things on Earth, and Mars was used as a penal colony; everybody knows that and we don't try to hide it.

But the vast majority of the transportees were political prisoners—"counterrevolutionists," "enemies of the people." Is this bad?

In any case there was the much longer period, involving fifty times as many colonists, when every new Marsman was selected as carefully as a bride selects her wedding gown and much more scientifically. And finally, there is the current period, since our Revolution and Independence, when we dropped all bars to immigration and welcome anyone who is healthy and has normal intelligence.

No, I'm not ashamed of my ancestors or my people, whatever their skin shades or backgrounds; I'm proud of them. It makes me boiling mad to hear anyone sneer at them. Why, I'll bet those two couldn't qualify for permanent visa even under our present "open door" policy! Feeble-minded—

But I do hope Clark hasn't done anything too drastic. I wouldn't want Clark to have to spend the rest of his life on Titan; I love the little wretch.

Sort of.

VIII

We've had that radiation storm. I prefer hives. I don't mean the storm itself; it wasn't too bad. Radiation jumped to about 1500 times normal for where we are now—about eight-tenths of an astronomical unit from the Sun, say 120,000,000 kilometers in units you can get your teeth in. Mr. Savvonavong says that we would have been all right if the first-class passengers had simply gone up one deck to second-class passenger country—which certainly would have been more comfortable than stuffing all the passengers and crew into that maximum-safety mausoleum at the center of the ship. Second-class accommodations are cramped and cheerless, and as for third class, I would rather be shipped as freight. But either one would be a picnic compared with spending eighteen hours in the radiation shelter.

For the first time I envied the half-dozen aliens aboard. They don't take shelter; they simply remain locked in their specially conditioned staterooms as usual. No, they aren't allowed to fry; those X-numbered rooms are almost at the center of the ship anyhow, in officers' and crew's country, and they have their own extra layer of shielding, because you can't expect a Martian, for example, to leave the pressure and humidity he requires and join us humans in the shelter; it would be equivalent to dunking him in a bathtub and holding his head under. If he had a head, I mean.

Still, I suppose eighteen hours of discomfort is better than being sealed into one small room for the whole trip. A Martian can simply contemplate the subtle difference between zero and nothing for that long or longer and a Venerian just estivates. But not me. I need unrest oftener than I need rest—or my circuits get tangled and smoke pours out of my ears.

But Captain Darling couldn't know ahead of time that the storm would be short and relatively mild; he had to assume the worst and protect his passengers and crew. Eleven minutes would have been long enough for us to be in the shelter, as shown later by instrument records. But that is hindsight . . . and a captain doesn't save his ship and the lives depending on him by hindsight.

I am beginning to realize that being a captain isn't all glorious adventure and being saluted and wearing four gold stripes on your shoulders. Captain Darling is younger than Daddy and yet he has worry lines that make him look years older.

QUERY: Poddy, are you *sure* you have what it takes to captain an explorer ship?

ANSWERS: What did Columbus have that you don't? Aside from Isabella, I mean. *Semper toujours,* girl!

I spent a lot of time before the storm in the control room. Hermes Solar Weather Station doesn't actually

warn us when the storm is coming; what they do is
fail to warn us that the storm is *not* coming. That
sounds silly but here is how it works:

The weathermen at Hermes are perfectly safe, as
they are underground on the dark side of Mercury.
Their instruments peek cautiously over the horizon in
the twilight zone, gather data about Solar weather
including running telephotos at several wave lengths.

But the Sun takes about twenty-five days to turn
around, so Hermes Station can't watch all of it all the
time. Worse yet. Mercury is going around the Sun in
the same direction that the Sun rotates, taking eighty-
eight days for one lap, so when the Sun again faces
where Mercury was, Mercury has moved on. What this
adds up to is that Hermes Station faces exactly the
same face of the Sun about every seven weeks.

Which is obviously not good enough for weather-
predicting storms that can gather in a day or two, peak
in a few minutes, and kill you dead in seconds or less.

So the Solar weather is watched from Earth's Luna
and from Venus' satellite station as well, plus some
help from Deimos. But there is speed-of-light lag in
getting information from these more distant stations
back to the main station on Mercury. Maybe fifteen
minutes for Luna and as high as a thousand seconds
for Deimos ... not good when seconds count.

But the season of bad storms is only a small part of
the Sun's cycle as a variable star—say about a year out
of each six. (Real years, I mean—Martian years. The
Sun's cycle is about eleven of those Earth years that
astronomers still insist on using.)

That makes things a lot easier; five years out of six
a ship stands very little chance of being hit by a radiation storm.

But during the stormy season a careful skipper (the
only sort who lives to draw a pension) will plan his
orbit so that he is in the worst danger zone, say inside

the orbit of Earth, only during such time as Mercury lies between him and the Sun, so that Hermes Station can always warn him of coming trouble. That is exactly what Captain Darling had done; the *Tricorn* waited at Deimos nearly three weeks longer than the guaranteed sightseeing time on Mars called for by the Triangle Line's advertising, in order to place his approach to Venus so that Hermes Station could observe and warn—because we are right in the middle of the stormy season.

I suppose the Line's business office hates these expensive delays. Maybe they lose money during the stormy season. But three weeks' delay is better than losing a whole shipload of passengers.

But when the storm does start, radio communication goes all to pieces at once—Hermes Station can't warn the ships in the sky.

Stalemate? Not quite. Hermes Station can see a storm shaping up; they can spot the conditions on the Sun which are almost certainly going to produce a radiation storm very shortly. So they send out a storm warning—and the *Tricorn* and other ships hold radiation-shelter drills. Then we wait. One day, two days, or a whole week, and the storm either fails to develop, or it builds up and starts shooting nasty stuff in great quantities.

All during this time the space guard radio station on the dark side of Mercury sends a continuous storm warning, never an instant's break, giving a running account of how the weather looks on the Sun.

. . . and suddenly it stops.

Maybe it's a power failure and the stand-by transmitter will cut in. Maybe it's just a "fade" and the storm hasn't broken yet and transmission will resume with reassuring words.

But it may be that the first blast of the storm has hit Mercury with the speed of light, no last-minute warning at all, and the station's eyes are knocked out and its voice is swallowed up in enormously more powerful radiation.

The officer-of-the-watch in the control room can't be sure and he dare not take a chance. The instant he loses Hermes Station he slaps a switch that starts a big clock with just a second hand. When that clock has ticked off a certain number of seconds—and Hermes Station is *still* silent—the general alarm sounds. The exact number of seconds depends on where the ship is, how far from the Sun, how much longer it will take the first blast to reach the ship after it has already hit Hermes Station.

Now here is where a captain bites his nails and gets gray hair and earns his high pay ... because *he* has to decide how many seconds to set that clock for. Actually, if the first and worst blast is at the speed of light, he hasn't any warning time at *all* because the break in the radio signal from Hermes and that first wave front from the Sun will reach him at the same instant. Or, if the angle is unfavorable, perhaps it is his own radio reception that has been clobbered, and Hermes Station is still trying to reach him with a last-moment warning. He doesn't know.

But he does know that if he sounds the alarm and chases everybody to shelter every time the radio fades for a few seconds, he will get people so worn out and disgusted from his crying "Wolf!" that when the trouble really comes they may not move fast enough.

He knows, too, that the outer hull of his ship will stop almost anything in the electromagnetic spectrum. Among photons (and nothing else travels at speed-of-light) only the hardest X-radiation will get through to passenger country and not much of that. But traveling along behind, falling just a little behind each second, is the really dangerous stuff—big particles, little particles, middle-sized particles, all the debris of nuclear explosion. This stuff is moving very fast but not quite at speed-of-light. He has to get his people safe before it hits.

Captain Darling picked a delay of twenty-five seconds, for where we were and what he expected from the weather reports. I asked him how he picked it and he just grinned without looking happy and said, "I asked my grandfather's ghost."

Five times while I was in the control room the officer of the watch started that clock . . . and five times contact with Hermes Station was picked up again before time ran out and the switch was opened.

The sixth time the seconds trickled away while all of us held our breaths . . . and contact with Hermes wasn't picked up again and the alarm sounded like the wakeful trump of doom.

The Captain looked stony-faced and turned to duck down the hatch into the radiation shelter. I didn't move, because I expected to be allowed to remain in the control room. Strictly speaking, the control room is part of the radiation shelter, since it is just above it and is enclosed by the same layers of cascade shielding.

(It's amazing how many people think that a captain controls his ship by peering out a port as if he were driving a sand wagon. But he doesn't, of course. The control room is inside, where he can watch things much more accurately and conveniently by displays and instruments. The only viewport in the *Tricorn* is one at the top end of the main axis, to allow passengers to look out at the stars. But we have never been headed so that the mass of the ship would protect that sightseeing room from solar radiation, so it has been locked off this whole trip.)

I knew I was safe where I was, so I hung back, intending to take advantage of being "teacher's pet"— for I certainly didn't want to spend hours or days stretched out on a shelf with gabbling and maybe hysterical women crowding me on both sides.

I should have known. The Captain hesitated a split second as he started down the hatch and snapped, "Come along, Miss Fries."

I came. He *always* calls me "Poddy"—and his voice had spank in it.

Third-class passengers were already pouring in, since they have the shortest distance to go, and crew members were mustering them into their billets. The crew has been on emergency routine ever since we first were warned by Hermes Station, with their usual one watch in three replaced by four hours on and four hours off. Part of the crew had been staying dressed in radiation armor (which must be *very* uncomfortable) and simply hanging around passenger country. They can't take that heavy armor off for any reason at all until their reliefs show up, dressed also in armor. These crewmen are the "chasers" who bet their lives that they can check every passenger space, root out stragglers, and still reach the shelter fast enough not to accumulate radiation poisoning. They are all volunteers and the chasers on duty when the alarm sounds get a big bonus and the other half of them who were lucky enough not to be on duty get a little bonus.

The Chief Officer is in charge of the first section of chasers and the Purser is in charge of the second—but they don't get any bonus even though the one on duty when the alarm sounds is by tradition and law the last man to enter the safety of the shelter. This hardly seems fair . . . but it is considered their honor as well as their duty.

Other crewmen take turns in the radiation shelter and are equipped with mustering lists and billeting diagrams.

Naturally, service has been pretty skimpy of late, with so many of the crew pulled off their regular duties in order to do just one thing and do it *fast* at the first jangle of the alarm. Most of these emergency-duty assignments have to be made from the stewards and clerks; engineers and communicators and such usually can't be spared. So staterooms may not be made up until late afternoon—unless you make your own bed and tidy your room yourself, as I had been doing—and serving meals takes about twice as long as usual, and lounge service is almost non-existent.

But of course the passengers realize the necessity for this temporary mild austerity and are grateful because it is all done for safety.

You think so? My dear, if you believe that, you will believe anything. You haven't Seen Life until you've seen a rich, elderly Earthman deprived of something he feels is his rightful due, because he figures he paid for it in the price of his ticket. I saw one man, perhaps as old as Uncle Tom and certainly old enough to know better, almost have a stroke. He turned purple, really purple and gibbered—all because the bar steward didn't show up on the bounce to fetch him a new deck of playing cards.

The bar steward was in armor at the time and couldn't leave his assigned area, and the lounge steward was trying to be three places at once and answer stateroom rings as well. This didn't mean anything to our jolly shipmate; he was threatening to sue the Line and all its directors, when his speech became incoherent.

Not everybody is that way, of course. Mrs. Grew, fat as she is, has been making her own bed and she is never impatient. Some others who are ordinarily inclined to demand lots of service have lately been making a cheerful best of things.

But some of them act like children with tantrums—which isn't pretty in children and is even uglier in grandparents.

The instant I followed the Captain into the radiation shelter I discovered just how efficient *Tricorn* service can be when it really matters. I was snatched—snatched like a ball, right out of the air—and passed from hand to hand. Of course I don't weigh much at one-tenth gravity, all there is at the main axis; but it is rather breath-taking. Some more hands shoved me into my billet, already stretched out, as casually and impersonally as a housewife stows clean laundry, and a voice called out, "Fries, Podkayne!" and another voice answered, "Check."

The spaces around me, and above and below and across from me, filled up awfully fast, with the crewmen working with the unhurried efficiency of automatic machinery sorting mail capsules. Somewhere a baby was crying and through it I heard the Captain saying, "Is that the last?"

"Last one, Captain," I heard the Purser answer. "How's the time?"

"Two minutes thirty-seven seconds—and your boys can start figuring their payoff, because this one is no drill."

"I didn't think it was, Skipper—and I've won a small bet from the Mate myself." Then the Purser walked past my billet carrying someone, and I tried to sit up and bumped my head and my eyes bugged out.

The passenger he was carrying had fainted; her head lolled loosely over the crook of his arm. At first I couldn't tell who it was, as the face was a bright, bright red. And then I recognized her and *I* almost fainted. Mrs. Royer—

Of course the first symptom of any bad radiation exposure is erythema. Even with a sunburn, or just carelessness with an ultraviolet lamp, the first thing you see is the skin turning pink or bright red.

But was it possible that Mrs. Royer had been hit with such extremely sharp radiation in so very little time that her skin had *already* turned red in the worst "sunburn" imaginable? Just from being last man in?

In that case she hadn't fainted; she was dead.

And if that was true, then it was equally true that the passengers who were last to reach the shelter must all have received several times the lethal dosage. They might not feel ill for hours yet; they might not die for days. But they were just as dead as if they were already stretched out still and cold.

How many? I had no way of guessing. Possibly—*probably* I corrected myself—all the first-class passengers; they had the farthest to go and were most exposed to start with.

Uncle Tom and Clark—

I felt sudden sick sorrow and wished that I had not been in the control room. If my brother and Uncle Tom were dying, I didn't want to be alive myself.

I don't think I wasted any sympathy on Mrs. Royer. I did feel a shock of horror when I saw that flaming red face, but truthfully, I didn't like her, I thought she was a parasite with contemptible opinions, and if she had died of heart failure instead, I can't honestly say that it would have affected my appetite. None of us goes around sobbing over the millions and billions of people who have died in the past . . . nor over those still living and yet to be born whose single certain heritage is death (including Podkayne Fries herself). So why should you cry foolish tears simply because you happen to be in the neighborhood when someone you don't like—despise, in fact—comes to the end of her string?

In any case, I did not have time to feel sorrow for Mrs. Royer; my heart was filled with grief over my brother and my uncle. I was sorry that I hadn't been sweeter to Uncle Tom, instead of imposing on him and expecting him always to drop whatever he was doing to help me with my silly problems. I regretted all the many times I had fought with my brother. After all, he was a child and I am a woman; I should have made allowances.

Tears were welling out of my eyes and I almost missed the Captain's first words:

"Shipmates," he said, in a voice firm and very soothing, "my crew and our guests aboard ... this is not a drill; this is indeed a radiation storm.

"Do not be alarmed; we are all, each and every one of us, perfectly safe. The Surgeon has examined the personal radiation exposure meter of the very last one to reach the shelter. It is well within safe limits. Even if it were added to the accumulated exposure of the most exposed person aboard—who is not a passenger, by the way, but one of the ship's company—the total would still be inside the conservative maximum for personal health and genetic hygiene.

"Let me say it again. No one has been hurt, no one is going to be hurt. We are simply going to suffer a mild inconvenience. I wish I could tell you how long we will have to remain here in the safety of the shelter. But I do not know. It might be a few hours, it might be several days. The longest radiation storm of record lasted less than a week. We hope that Old Sol is not that bad-tempered this time. But until we receive word from Hermes Station that the storm is over, we will all have to stay inside here. Once we know a storm is over it usually does not take too long to check the ship and make sure that your usual comfortable quarters are safe. Until then, be patient and be patient with each other."

I started to feel better as soon as the Captain started to talk. His voice was almost hypnotic; it had the soothing all-better-now effect of a mother reassuring a child. I relaxed and was simply weak with the aftereffects of my fears.

But presently I began to wonder. Would Captain

Darling tell us that everything was all right when really everything was All Wrong simply because it was too late and nothing could be done about it?

I thought over everything I had ever learned about radiation poisoning, from the simple hygiene they teach in kindergarten to a tape belonging to Mr. Clancy that I had scanned only that week.

And I decided that the Captain had been telling the truth.

Why? Because, even if my very worst fears had been correct, and we had been hit as hard and unexpectedly as if a nuclear weapon had exploded by us, neverthe-less something can *always* be done about it. There would be three groups of us—those who hadn't been hurt at all and were not going to die (certainly every-body who was in the control room or in the shelter when it happened, plus all or almost all the third-class passengers if they had moved fast), a second group so terribly exposed that they were certain to die, no mat-ter what (let's say everybody in first class country), and a third group, no telling how large, which had been dangerously exposed but could be saved by quick and drastic treatment.

In which case that quick and drastic action would be going on.

They would be checking our exposure meters and reshuffling us—sorting out the ones in danger who required rapid treatment, giving morphine shots to the ones who were going to die anyhow and moving them off by themselves, stacking those of us who were safe by ourselves to keep us from getting in the way, or drafting us to help nurse the ones who could be helped.

That was certain. But there was nothing going on, nothing at all—just some babies crying and a murmur of voices. Why, they hadn't even looked at the expo-sure meters of most of us; it seemed likely that the

Surgeon had checked only the last few stragglers to reach the shelter.

Therefore the Captain had told us the simple, heart-warming truth.

I felt so good that I forgot to wonder why Mrs. Royer had looked like a ripe tomato. I relaxed and soaked in the warm and happy fact that darling Uncle Tom wasn't going to die and that my kid brother would live to cause me lots more homey grief. I almost went to sleep . . .

. . . and was yanked out of it by the woman on my right starting to scream: "Let me out of here! *Let me out of here!*"

Then I did see some fast and drastic emergency action.

Two crewmen swarmed up to our shelf and grabbed her; a stewardess was right behind them. She slapped a gag over the woman's mouth and gave her a shot in the arm, all in one motion. Then they held her until she stopped struggling. When she was quiet, one of the crewmen picked her up and took her somewhere.

Shortly thereafter a stewardess showed up who was collecting exposure meters and passing out sleeping pills. Most people took them but I resisted—I don't like pills at best and I certainly won't take one to knock me out so that I won't know what is going on. The stewardess was insistent but I can be awfully stubborn, so she shrugged and went away. After that there were three or four more cases of galloping claustrophobia or maybe just plain screaming funk; I wouldn't know. Each was taken care of promptly with no fuss and shortly the shelter was quiet except for snores, a few voices, and fairly continuous sounds of babies crying.

There aren't any babies in first class and not many children of any age. Second class has quite a few kids, but third class is swarming with them and every family seems to have at least one young baby. It's why they are there, of course; almost all of third class are Earth people emigrating to Venus. With Earth so crowded, a man with a big family can easily reach the point where emigration to Venus looks like the best way out of an impossible situation, so he signs a labor contract and Venus Corporation pays for their tickets as an advance against his wages.

I suppose it's all right. They need to get away and Venus needs all the people they can get. But I'm glad Mars Republic doesn't subsidize immigration, or we would be swamped. We take immigrants but they have to pay their own way and have to deposit return tickets with the PEG board, tickets they can't cash in for two of our years.

A good thing, too. At least a third of the immigrants who come to Mars just can't adjust. They get homesick and despondent and use those return tickets to go back to Earth. I can't understand anyone's not *liking* Mars, but if they don't then it's better if they don't stay.

I lay there, thinking about such things, a little bit excited and a little bit bored, and mostly wondering why somebody didn't do something about those poor babies.

The lights had been dimmed and when somebody came up to my shelf I didn't see who it was at first. "Poddy?" came Girdie's voice, softly but clearly. "Are you in there?"

"I think so. What's up, Girdie?" I tried to keep my voice down too.

"Do you know how to change a baby?"

"I certainly do!" Suddenly I wondered how Duncan was doing ... and realized that I hadn't really thought about him in *days*. Had he forgotten me? Would he know Grandmaw Poddy the next time he saw her?

"Then come along, chum. There's work to be done."

There certainly was! The lowest part of the shelter, four catwalks below my billet and just over the engineering spaces, was cut like a pie into four quarters—sanitary units, two sick bays, for men and for women and both crowded—and jammed into a little corner between the infirmaries was a sorry pretense for a nursery, not more than two meters in any dimension. On three walls of it babies were stacked high in canvas crib baskets snap-hooked to the walls, and more overflowed into the women's sick bay. A sweeping majority of those babies were crying.

In the crowded middle of this pandemonium two harassed stewardesses were changing babies, working on a barely big enough shelf let down out of one wall. Girdie tapped one of them on the shoulder. "All right, girls, reinforcements have landed. So get some rest and a bite to eat."

The older one protested feebly, but they were awfully glad to take a break; they backed out and Girdie and I moved in and took over. I don't know how long we worked, as we never had time to think about it—there was always more than we could do and we never quite got caught up. But it was better than lying on a shelf and staring at another shelf just centimeters above your nose. The worst of it was that there simply wasn't enough room. I worked with both elbows held in close, to keep from bumping Girdie on one side and a basket crib that was nudging me on the other side.

But I'm not complaining about that. The engineer who designed that shelter into the *Tricorn* had been forced to plan as many people as possible into the smallest possible space; there wasn't any other way to do it and still give us all enough levels of shielding during a storm. I doubt if he worried much about getting babies changed and dry; he had enough to do just worrying about how to keep them alive.

But you can't tell that to a baby.

Girdie worked with an easy, no-lost-motions efficiency

that surprised me; I would never have guessed that she had ever had her hands on a baby. But she knew what she was doing and was faster than I was. "Where are their mothers?" I asked, meaning: "Why aren't those lazy slobs down here helping instead of leaving it to the stewardesses and some volunteers?"

Girdie understood me. "Most of them—all of them, maybe—have other small children to keep quiet; they have their hands full. A couple of them went to pieces themselves; they're in there sleeping it off." She jerked her head toward the sick bay.

I shut up, as it made sense. You couldn't possibly take care of an infant properly in one of those shallow niches the passengers were stacked in, and if each mother tried to bring her own baby down here each time, the traffic jam would be indescribable. No, this assembly-line system was necessary. I said, "We're running out of Disposies."

"Stacked in a cupboard behind you. Did you see what happened to Mrs. Garcia's face?"

"Huh?" I squatted and got out more supplies. "You mean Mrs. Royer, don't you?"

"I mean both of them. But I saw milady Garcia first and got a better look at her, while they were quieting her down. You didn't see her?"

"No."

"Sneak a look into the women's ward first chance you get. Her face is the brightest, most amazing chrome yellow I've ever seen in a paint pot, much less on a human face."

I gasped. "Gracious! I did see Mrs. Royer—bright red instead of yellow. Girdie—what in the world happened to them?"

"I'm fairly sure I know what happened," Girdie answered slowly, "but no one can figure out *how* it happened."

"I don't follow you."

"The colors tell the story. Those are the exact shades of two of the water-activated dyes used in photography. Know anything about photography, hon?"

"Not much," I answered. I wasn't going to admit what little I did know, because Clark is a very accomplished amateur photographer. And I wasn't going to mention *that*, either!

"Well, surely you've seen someone taking snapshots. You pull out the tab and there is your picture—only there's no picture as yet. Clear as glass. So you dip it in water and slosh it around for about thirty seconds. Still no picture. Then you lay it anywhere in the light and the picture starts to show . . . and when the colors are bright enough to suit you, you cover it up and let it finish drying in darkness, so that the colors won't get too garish." Girdie suppressed a chuckle. "From the results, I would say that they didn't cover their faces in time to stop the process. They probably tried to scrub it off and made it worse."

I said, in a puzzled tone—and I *was* puzzled, about part of it—"I still don't see how it could happen."

"Neither does anybody else. But the Surgeon has a theory. Somebody booby-trapped their washcloths."

"Huh?"

"Somebody in the ship must have a supply of the pure dyes. That somebody soaked two washcloths in the inactive dyes—colorless, I mean—and dried them carefully, all in total darkness. Then that same somebody sneaked those two prepared washcloths into those two staterooms and substituted them for washcloths they found there on the stateroom wash trays. That last part wouldn't be hard for anyone with cool nerves—service in the staterooms has been pretty haphazard the last day or two, what with this flap over the radiation storm. Maybe a fresh washcloth appears in your room, maybe it doesn't—and all the ship's washcloths and towels are the same pattern. You just wouldn't know."

I certainly hope not! I said to myself—and added aloud, "I suppose not."

"Certainly not. It could be one of the stewardesses—or any of the passengers. But the real mystery is: where did the dyes come from? The ship's shop doesn't carry them . . . just the rolls of prepared film . . . and the Surgeon says that he knows enough about chemistry to be willing to stake his life that no one but a master chemist, using a special laboratory, could possibly separate out pure dyes from a roll of film. He thinks, too, that since the dyes aren't even manufactured on Mars, this somebody must be somebody who came aboard at Earth." Girdie glanced at me and smiled. "So you're not a suspect, Poddy. But I am."

"Why are you a suspect?" (And if I'm not a suspect then my brother isn't a suspect!) "Why, that's silly!"

"Yes, it is . . . because I wouldn't have known how even if I'd had the dyes. But it isn't, inasmuch as I could have bought them before I left Earth, and I don't have reason to like either of those women."

"I've never heard you say a word against them."

"No, but they've said a few thousand words about me—and other people have ears. So I'm a hot suspect, Poddy. But don't fret about it. I didn't do it, so there is no possible way to show that I did." She chuckled. "And I hope they never catch the somebody who did!"

I didn't even answer, "Me, too!" I could think of one person who might figure out a way to get pure dyes out of a roll of film without a complete chemistry laboratory, and I was checking quickly through my mind every item I had seen when I searched Clark's room.

There hadn't been *anything* in Clark's room which could have been photographic dyes. No, not even film. Which proves precisely nothing where Clark is

concerned. I just hope that he was careful about
fingerprints.

Two other stewardesses came in presently and we
fed all the babies, and then Girdie and I managed a
sort of a washup and had a snack standing up, and
then I went back up to my assigned shelf and surprised
myself by falling asleep.

I must have slept three or four hours, because I
missed the happenings when Mrs. Dirkson had her
baby. She is one of the Terran emigrants to Venus and
she shouldn't have had her baby until long after we
reach Venus—I suppose the excitement stirred things
up. Anyhow, when she started to groan they carried
her down to that dinky infirmary, and Dr. Torland took
one look at her and ordered her carried up into the
control room because the control room was the only
place inside the radiation-safe space roomy enough to
let him do what needed to be done.

So that's where the baby was born, on the deck of
the control room, right between the chart tank and
the computer. Dr. Torland and Captain Darling are
godfathers and the senior stewardess is godmother and
the baby's name is "Radiant," which is a poor pun but
rather pretty.

They jury-rigged an incubator for Radiant right
there in the control room before they moved Mrs.
Dirkson back to the infirmary and gave her something
to make her sleep. The baby was still there when I
woke up and heard about it.

I decided to take a chance that the Captain was
feeling more mellow now, and sneaked up to the control room and stuck my head in. "Could I please see
the baby?"

The Captain looked annoyed, then he barely smiled
and said, "All right, Poddy. Take a quick look and get
out."

So I did. Radiant masses about a kilo and, frankly, she looks like cat meat, not worth saving. But Dr. Torland says that she is doing well and that she will grow up to be a fine, healthy girl—prettier than I am. I suppose he knows what he is talking about, but if she is ever going to be prettier than I am, she has lots of kilometers to go. She is almost the color of Mrs. Royer and she's mostly wrinkles.

But no doubt she'll outgrow it, because she looks like one of the pictures toward the end of the series in a rather goody-goody schoolbook called *The Miracle of Life*—and the earlier pictures in that series were even less appetizing. It is probably just as well that we can't possibly see babies until they are ready to make their debut, or the human race would lose interest and die out.

It would probably be still better to lay eggs. Human engineering isn't all that it might be, especially for us female types.

I went back down where the more mature babies were to see if they needed me. They didn't, not right then, as the babies had been fed again and a stewardess and a young woman I had never met were on duty and claimed that they had been working only a few minutes. I hung around anyhow, rather than go back up to my shelf. Soon I was pretending to be useful by reaching past the two who really were working and checking the babies, then handing down the ones who needed servicing as quickly as shelf space was cleared.

It speeded things up a little. Presently I pulled a little wiggler out of his basket and was cuddling him; the stewardess looked up and said, "I'm ready for him."

"Oh, he's not wet," I answered. "Or 'she' as the case may be. Just lonely and needs loving."

"We haven't time for that."

"I wonder." The worst thing about the midget nursery was the high noise level. The babies woke each other and egged each other on and the decibels were something fierce. No doubt they were all lonely and probably frightened—I'm sure I would be. "Most of the babies need loving more than they need anything else."

"They've all had their bottles."

"A bottle can't cuddle."

She didn't answer, just started checking the other infants. But I didn't think what I had said was silly. A baby can't understand your words and he doesn't know where he is if you put him in a strange place, nor what has happened. So he cries. Then he needs to be soothed.

Girdie showed up just then. "Can I help?"

"You certainly can. Here . . . hold this one."

In a few minutes I rounded up three girls about my age and I ran across Clark prowling around the catwalks instead of staying quietly in his assigned billet so I drafted him, too. He wasn't exactly eager to volunteer, but doing anything was slightly better than doing nothing; he came along.

I couldn't use any more help as standing room was almost nonexistent. We worked it only by having two baby-cuddlers sort of back into each of the infirmaries with the mistress of ceremonies (me) standing in the little space at the bottom of the ladder, ready to scrunch in any direction to let people get in and out of the washrooms and up and down the ladder—and with Girdie, because she was tallest, standing back of the two at the changing shelf and dealing out babies, the loudest back to me for further assignment and the wet ones down for service—and vice versa: dry ones back to their baskets unless they started to yell; ones that had fallen asleep from being held and cuddled.

At least seven babies could receive personal

attention at once, and sometimes as high as ten or eleven, because at one-tenth gee your feet never get tired and a baby doesn't weigh anything at all worth mentioning; it was possible to hold one in each arm and sometimes we did.

In ten minutes we had that racket quieted down to an occasional whimper, quickly soothed. I didn't think Clark would stick it out, but he did—probably because Girdie was part of the team. With a look of grim nobility on his face, the like of which I have never before seen there, he cuddled babies and presently was saying "Kitchy-koo kitchy-koo!" and "There, there, honey bun," as if he had been doing it all his life. Furthermore, the babies seemed to like him; he could soothe one down and put it to sleep quickest of any of us. Hypnotism, maybe?

This went on for several hours, with volunteers moving in and tired ones moving out and positions rotating. I was relieved once and had another snatched meal and then stretched out on my shelf for about an hour before going back on duty.

I was back at the changing shelf when the Captain called us all by speaker: "Attention, please. In five minutes power will be cut and the ship will be in free fall while a repair is made outside the ship. All passengers strap down. All crew members observe precautions for free fall."

I went right on changing the baby under my hands; you can't walk off on a baby. In the meantime, babies that had been being cuddled were handed back and stowed, and the cuddling team was chased back to their shelves to strap down—and spin was being taken off the ship. One rotation every twelve seconds you simply don't notice at the center of the ship, but you do notice when the *unspinning* starts. The stewardess with me on the changing bench said, "Poddy, go up and strap down. Hurry."

I said, "Don't be silly, Bergitta, there's work to be done," and popped the baby I had just dried into its basket and fastened the zipper.

"You're a passenger. That's an order—*please!*"

"Who's going to check all these babies? You? And how about those four in on the floor of the women's sick bay?"

Bergitta looked startled and hurried to fetch them. All the other stewardesses were busy checking on strap-down; she didn't bother me any more with That's-an-order; she was too busy hooking up the changing shelf and fastening baby baskets to the space. I was checking all the others and almost all of them had been left unzipped—logical enough while we were working with them, but zipping the cover on a baby basket is the same as strapping down for a grown-up. It holds them firmly but comfortably with just their heads free.

I still hadn't finished when the siren sounded and the Captain cut the power.

Oh, brother! Pandemonium. The siren woke the babies who were asleep and scared any who were awake, and every single one of those squirmy little worms started to cry at the top of its lungs—and one I hadn't zipped yet popped right out of its basket and floated out into the middle of the space and I snagged it by one leg and was loose myself, and the baby and I bumped gently against the baskets on one wall—only it wasn't a wall any longer, it was just an obstacle to further progress. Free fall can be very confusing when you are not used to it, which I admit I am not. Or wasn't.

The stewardess grabbed us both and shoved the elusive little darling back into her straitjacket and zipped it while I hung onto a handhold. And by then two more were loose.

I did better this time—snagged one without letting

go and just kept it captive while Bergitta took care of
the other one. Bergitta really knew how to handle herself in zero gravity, with unabrupt graceful movements
like a dancer in a slow-motion solly. I made a mental
note that this was a skill I must acquire.

I thought the emergency was over; I was wrong.
Babies don't like free fall; it frightens them. It also
makes their sphincters most erratic. Most of the latter
we could ignore—but Disposies don't catch everything; regrettably some six or seven of them had been
fed in the last hour.

I know now why stewardesses are all graduate
nurses; we kept five babies from choking to death in
the next few minutes. That is, Bergitta cleared the
throat of the first one that upchucked its milk and,
seeing what she had done, I worked on the second
one in trouble while she grabbed the third. And so on.

Then we were very busy trying to clear the air with
clean Disposies because— Listen, dear, if you think
you've had it tough because your baby brother threw
up all over your new party dress, then you should try
somewhat-used baby formula in free fall, where it
doesn't settle anywhere in particular but just floats
around like smoke until you either get it or it gets you.

From six babies. In a small compartment.

By the time we had that mess cleaned up, or 95
percent or so anyway, we were both mostly sour milk
from hair part to ankle and the Captain was warning
us to stand by for acceleration, which came almost at
once to my great relief. The Chief Stewardess showed
up and was horrified that I had not strapped down
and I told her in a ladylike way to go to hell, using a
more polite idiom suitable to my age and sex—and
asked her what Captain Darling would think about a
baby passenger choking to death simply because I had
strapped down all regulation-like and according to
orders? And Bergitta backed me up and told her that

I had cleared choke from at least two and maybe more—she had been too busy to count.

Mrs. Peal, the C.S., changed her tune in a hurry and was sorry and thanked me, and sighed and wiped her forehead and trembled and you could see that she was dead on her feet. But nevertheless, she checked all the babies herself and hurried out. Pretty quickly we were relieved and Bergitta and I crowded into the women's washroom and tried to clean up some. Not much good, as we didn't have any clean clothes to change into.

The "All Clear" felt like a reprieve from purgatory, and a hot bath was heaven itself with the Angels singing. "A" deck had already been checked for radiation level and pronounced safe while the repair outside the ship was being made. The repair itself, I learned, was routine. Some of the antennas and receptors and things outside the ship can't take a flare storm; they burn out—so immediately after a storm, men go outside in armored space suits and replace them. This is normal and unavoidable, like replacing lighting tubes at home. But the men who do it get the same radiation bonus that the passenger chasers get, because old Sol could burn them down with one tiny little afterthought.

I soaked in warm, clean water and thought how miserable an eighteen hours it had been. Then I decided that it hadn't been so bad after all.

It's lots better to be miserable than to be bored.

IX

I am now twenty-seven years old.

Venus years, of course, but it sounds so much better. All is relative.

Not that I would stay here on Venus even if guaranteed the Perfect Age for a thousand years. Venusberg is sort of an organized nervous breakdown and the country outside the city is even worse. What little I've seen of it. And I don't want to see much of it. Why they ever named this dreary, smog-ridden place for the Goddess of Love and Beauty I'll never know. This planet appears to have been put together from the scrap left over after the rest of the Solar System was finished.

I don't think I would go outside Venusberg at all except that I've just got to see fairies in flight. The only one I've seen so far is in the lobby of the hilton we are staying in and is stuffed.

Actually I'm just marking time until we shape for Earth, because Venus is a Grave Disappointment—

and now I'm keeping my fingers crossed that Earth will not be a G.D., too. But I don't see how it can be; there is something deliciously *primitive* about the very thought of a planet where one can go outdoors without any special preparations. Why, Uncle Tom tells me that there are places along the Mediterranean (that's an ocean in La Belle France) where the natives bathe in the ocean itself without any clothing of any sort, much less insulasuits or masks.

I wouldn't like that. Not that I'm body proud; I enjoy a good sauna sweat-out as well as the next Marsman. But it would scare me cross-eyed to bathe in an ocean; I don't ever intend to get wet all over in anything larger than a bathtub. I saw a man fished out of the Grand Canal once, in early spring. They had to thaw him before they could cremate him.

But it is alleged that, along the Mediterranean shore, the air in the summertime is often blood temperature and the water not much cooler. As may be. Podkayne is not going to take any silly chances.

Nevertheless I am terribly eager to see Earth, in all its fantastic unlikeliness. It occurs to me that my most vivid conceptions of Earth come from the Oz stories—and when you come right down to it, I suppose that isn't too reliable a source. I mean, Dorothy's conversations with the Wizard are instructive—but about *what*? When I was a child I believed every word of my Oz tapes; but now I am no longer a child and I do not truly suppose that a whirlwind is a reliable means of transportation, nor that one is likely to encounter a Tin Woodman on a road of yellow brick.

Tik-Tok, yes—because we have Tik-Toks in Marsopolis for the simpler and more tedious work. Not precisely like Tik-Tok of Oz, of course, and not called "Tik-Toks" by anyone but children, but near enough, near enough, quite sufficient to show that the Oz stories are founded on fact if *not* precisely historical.

And I believe in the Hungry Tiger, too, in the most practical way possible, because there was one in the municipal zoo when I was a child, a gift from the Calcutta Kiwanis Klub to Marsopolis Kiwanians. It always looked at me as if it were sizing me up as an appetizer. It died when I was about five and I didn't know whether to be sorry or glad. It was beautiful . . . and so *very* Hungry.

But Earth is still many weeks away and, in the meantime, Venus does have some points of interest for the newcomer, such as I.

In traveling I strongly recommend traveling with my Uncle Tom. On arriving here, there were no silly waits in "Hospitality" (!) rooms; we were given the "courtesy of the port" at once—to the *extreme* chagrin of Mrs. Royer. "Courtesy of the port" means that your baggage isn't examined and that nobody bothers to look at that bulky mass of documents—passport and health record and security clearance and solvency proof and birth certificate and I.D.s, and nineteen other silly forms. Instead we were whisked from satellite station to spaceport in the private yacht of the Chairman of the Board and were met there by the Chairman himself!— and popped into his Rolls and wafted royally to Hilton Tannhäuser.

We were invited to stay at his official residence (his "cottage," that being the Venus word for a palace) but I don't think he really expected us to accept, because Uncle Tom just cocked his left or satirical eyebrow and, "Mr. Chairman, I don't think you would want me to appear to be bribed even if you manage it."

And the Chairman didn't seem offended at all; he just chuckled till his belly shook like Saint Nicholas' (whom he strongly resembles even to the beard and the red cheeks, although his eyes are cold even when he laughs, which is frequently).

"Senator," he said, "you know me better than that.

My attempt to bribe you will be much more subtle. Perhaps through this young lady. Miss Podkayne, are you fond of jewelry?"

I told him honestly that I wasn't, very, because I always lose it. So he blinked and said to Clark, "How about you, son?"

Clark said, "I prefer cash."

The Chairman blinked again and said nothing.

Nor had he said anything to his driver when Uncle Tom declined the offer of his roof; nevertheless we flew straight to our hilton—which is why I don't think he ever expected us to stay with him.

But I am beginning to realize that this is not entirely a pleasure trip for Uncle Tom . . . and to grasp emotionally a fact known only intellectually in the past, i.e., Uncle Tom is not merely the best pinochle player in Marsopolis, he sometimes plays other games for higher stakes. I must confess that the what or why lies outside my admittedly youthful horizon—save that everyone knows that the Three-Planets conference is coming up.

Query: Could U.T. conceivably be involved in this? As a consultant or something? I hope not, as it might keep him tied up for weeks on Luna and I have no wish to waste time on a dreary ball of slag while the Wonders of Terra await me—and Uncle Tom just *might* be difficult about letting me go down to Earth without him.

But I wish still more strongly that Clark had not answered the Chairman truthfully.

Still, Clark would not sell out his own uncle for mere money.

On the other hand, Clark does not regard money as "mere." I must think about this—

But it is some comfort to realize that anyone who handed Clark a bribe would find that Clark had not only taken the bribe but the hand as well.

* * *

Possibly our suite at the Tannhäuser is intended as a bribe, too. Are we paying for it? I'm almost afraid to ask Uncle Tom, but I do know this: the servants that come with it won't accept tips. Not any. Although I very carefully studied up on the subject of tipping, both for Venus and Earth, so that I would know what to do when the time came—and it had been my understanding that *anyone* on Venus *always* accepts tips, even ushers in churches and bank tellers.

But not the servants assigned to us. I have two tiny little amber dolls, identical twins, who shadow me and would bathe me if I let them. They speak Portuguese but not Ortho—and at present my Portuguese is limited to "gobble-gobble" (which means "Thank you") and I have trouble explaining to them that I can dress and undress myself and I'm not too sure about their names—they both answer to "Maria."

Or at least I don't *think* they speak Ortho. I must think about this, too.

Venus is officially bilingual, Ortho and Portuguese, but I'll bet I heard at least twenty other languages the first hour we were down. German sounds like a man being choked to death, French sounds like a cat fight, while Spanish sounds like molasses gurgling gently out of a jug. Cantonese— Well, think of a man trying to vocalize Bach who doesn't like Bach very much to start with.

Fortunately almost everybody understands Ortho as well. Except Maria and Maria. If true.

I could live a long time without the luxury of personal maids but I must admit that this hilton suite is quite a treat to a plain-living, wholesome Mars girl, namely me. Especially as I am in it quite a lot of the time and will be for a while yet. The ship's Surgeon, Dr. Torland, gave me many of the special inoculations needed for Venus on the trip here—an unpleasant subject I chose not to mention—but there still remain many more before it will be safe for me to go outside the city, or even very much into the city. As soon as we reached our suite a physician appeared and played chess on my back with scratches, red to move and mate in five moves—and three hours later I had several tens of welts, with something horrid that must be done about each of them.

Clark ducked out and didn't get his scratch tests until the next morning and I misdoubt he will die of Purple Itch or some such, were it not that his karma is so clearly reserving him for hanging. Uncle Tom refused the tests. He was through all this routine more than twenty years ago, and anyhow he claims that the too, too mortal flesh is merely a figment of the imagination.

So I am more or less limited for a few days to lavish living here in the Tannhäuser. If I got out, I must wear gloves and a mask even in the city. But one whole wall of the suite's salon becomes a stereo stage simply by voice request, either taped or piped live from any theater or club in Venusberg—and some of the "entertainment" has widened my sophistication unbelievably, especially when Uncle Tom is not around. I am beginning to realize that Mars is an essentially puritanical culture. Of course Venus doesn't actually have laws, just company regulations, none of which seems to be concerned with personal conduct. But I had been brought up to believe that Mars Republic is a free society—and I suppose it is. However, there is "freedom" and "freedom."

Here the Venus Corporation owns everything worth owning and runs everything that shows a profit, all in a fashion that would make Marsmen swoon. But I guess Venusmen would swoon at how straitlaced *we* are. I know this Mars girl blushed for the first time in I don't know when and switched off a show that I didn't really believe.

But the solly screen is far from being the only astonishing feature of this suite. It is so big that one should carry food and water when exploring it, and the salon is so huge that local storms appear distinctly possible. My private bath is a suite in itself, with so many gadgets in it that I ought to have an advanced degree in engineering before risking washing my hands. But I've learned how to use them all and purely love them! I had never dreamed that I had been limping along all my life without Utter Necessities.

Up to now my top ambition along these lines has been not to have to share a washstand with Clark, because it has never been safe to reach for my own Christmas-present cologne without checking to see that it is not nitric acid or worse! Clark regards a bathroom as an auxiliary chemistry lab; he's not much interested in staying clean.

But the most astonishing thing in our suite is the piano. No, no, dear, I don't mean a keyboard hooked into the sound system; I mean a *real* piano. Three legs. Made out of wood. Enormous. That odd awkward-graceful curved shape that doesn't fit anything else and can't be put in a corner. A top that opens up and lets you see that it really does have a harp inside and very complex machinery for making it work.

I think that there are just four real pianos on all of Mars, the one in the Museum that nobody plays and probably doesn't work, the one in Lowell Academy that no longer has a harp inside it, just wiring connections that make it really the same as any other piano, the one in the Rose House (as if any President ever had time to play a piano!), and the one in the Beaux Arts Hall that actually is played sometimes by visiting artists although I've never heard it. I don't think there can be another one, or it would have been banner-lined in the news, wouldn't you think?

This one was made by a man named Steinway and it must have taken him a lifetime. I played Chopsticks on it (that being the best opus in my limited reper-toire) until Uncle asked me to stop. Then I closed it up, keyboard and top, because I had seen Clark eying the machinery inside, and warned him sweetly but firmly that if he touched one finger to it I would break all his fingers while he was asleep. He wasn't listening but he knows I mean it. That piano is Sacred to the Muses and is not to be taken apart by our Young Archimedes.

I don't care what the electronics engineers say; there is a vast difference between a "piano" and a *real* piano. No matter if their silly oscilloscopes "prove" that the sound is identical. It is like the difference between being warmly clothed—or climbing up in your Daddy's lap and getting *really* warm.

I haven't been under house arrest all the time; I've been to the casinos, with Girdie and with Dexter Cunha, Dexter being the son of Mr. Chairman of the Board Kurt Cunha. Girdie is leaving us here, going to stay on Venus, and it makes me sad.

I asked her, "Why?"

We were sitting alone in our palatial salon. Girdie is staying in this same hilton, in a room not very differ-ent nor much larger than her cabin in the *Tricorn,* and I guess I'm just mean enough that I wanted her to see the swank we were enjoying. But my excuse was to have her help me dress. For now I am wearing (Shudder!) *support* garments. Arch supports in my shoes and tight things here and there intended to keep me from spreading out like an amoeba—and I won't say what Clark calls them because Clark is rude, crude, unrefined, and barbaric.

I hate them. But at 84 percent of one standard gee,

I need them despite all that exercise I took aboard ship. This alone is reason enough not to live on Venus, or on Earth, even if they were as delightful as Mars.

Girdie did help me—she had bought them for me in the first place—but she also made me change my makeup, one which I had most carefully copied out of the latest issue of *Aphrodite*. She looked at me and said, "Go wash your face, Poddy. Then we'll start over."

I pouted out my lip and said, "Won't!" The one thing I had noticed most and quickest was that *every* female on Venus wears paint like a Red Indian shooting at the Good Guys in the sollies—even Maria and Maria wear three times as much makeup just to work in as Mother wears to a formal reception—and Mother doesn't wear any when working.

"Poddy, Poddy! Be a good girl."

"I *am* being a good girl. I learned that when I was just a child. And look at yourself in the mirror!" Girdie was wearing as High-styled a Venusberg face-do as any in that magazine.

"I know what I look like. But I am more than twice your age and no one even suspects me of being young and sweet and innocent. Always be what you are, Poddy. Never pretend. Look at Mrs. Grew. She's a comfortable fat old woman. She isn't kittenish, she's just nice to be around."

"You want me to look like a hick tourist!"

"I want you to look like Poddy. Come, dear, we'll find a happy medium. I grant you that even the girls your age here wear more makeup than grown-up women do on Mars—so we'll compromise. Instead of painting you like a Venusberg trollop, we'll make you a young lady of good family and gentle breeding, one who is widely traveled and used to all sorts of customs and manners, and so calmly sure of herself that she knows what is best for her—totally uninfluenced by local fads."

Girdie is an artist, I must admit. She started with a blank canvas and worked on me for more than an hour—and when she got through, you couldn't see that I was wearing any makeup at all.

But here is what you could see: I was at least two years older (real years, Mars years, or about six Venus years); my face was thinner and my nose not pug at all and I looked ever so slightly world-weary in a sweet and tolerant way. My eyes were enormous.

"Satisfied?" she asked.

"I'm *beautiful!*"

"Yes, you are. Because you are still Poddy. All I've done is make a picture of Poddy the way she is going to be. Before long."

My eyes filled with tears and we had to blot them up very hastily and she repaired the damage. "Now," she said briskly, "all we need is a club. And your mask."

"What's the club for? And I won't wear a mask, not on top of this."

"The club is to beat off wealthy stockholders who will throw themselves at your feet. And you will wear your mask, or else we won't go."

We compromised. I wore the mask until we got there and Girdie promised to repair any damage to my face—and promised that she would coach me as many times as necessary until I could put on that lovely, lying face myself. The casinos are safe, or supposed to be—the air not merely filtered and conditioned but freshly regenerated, free of any trace of pollen, virus, colloidal suspension or whatever. This is because lots of tourists don't like to take all the long list of immunizations necessary actually to *live* on Venus; but the Corporation wouldn't think of letting a tourist get away unbled. So the hiltons are safe and the casinos are safe and a tourist can buy a health insurance policy from the Corporation for a very modest premium. Then he finds that he can cash his policy back in for gambling chips any time he wants to. I understand that the Corporation hasn't had to pay off on one of these policies very often.

Venusberg assaults the eye and ear even from inside a taxi. I believe in free enterprise; all Marsmen do, it's an article of faith and the main reason we *won't* federate with Earth (and be outvoted five hundred to one). But free enterprise is not enough excuse to blare in your ears and glare in your eyes every time you leave your own roof. The shops never close (I don't think anything ever closes in Venusberg) and full color and stereo ads climb right inside your taxi and sit in your lap and shout in your ear.

Don't ask me how this horrid illusion is produced. The engineer who invented it probably flew off on his own broom. This red devil about a meter high appeared between us and the partition separating us from the driver (there wasn't a sign of a solly receiver) and started jabbing at us with a pitchfork. "Get the Hi-Ho Habit!" it shrieked. "Everybody drinks Hi-Ho! Soothing, Habit-Forming. *Deelishus!* Get High with Hi-Ho!"

I shrank back against the cushions.

Girdie phoned the driver. "Please shut that thing off."

It faded down to just a pink ghost and the commercial dropped to a whisper while the driver answered, "Can't, madam. They rent the concession." Devil and noise came back on full blast.

And I learned something about tipping. Girdie took money from her purse, displayed one note. Nothing happened and she added a second; noise and image faded down again. She passed them through a slot to the driver and we weren't bothered any more. Oh, the transparent ghost of the red devil remained and a nagging whisper of his voice, until both were replaced by another and just as faint—but we could talk. The giant ads in the street outside were noisier and more dazzling; I didn't see how the driver could see or hear to drive, especially as traffic was unbelievably thick and heart-stoppingly fast and frantic and he kept cutting in and out of lanes and up and down in levels as if he were trying utmostly to beat Death to a hospital.

By the time we slammed to a stop on the roof of Dom Pedro Casino I figure Death wasn't more than half a lap behind.

I learned later why they drive like that. The hackie is an employee of the Corporation, like most everybody—but he is an "enterprise-employee," not on wages. Each day he has to take in a certain amount in fares to "make his nut"—the Corporation gets all of this. After he has rolled up that fixed number of paid kilometers, he splits the take with the Corporation on all other fares the rest of the day. So he drives like mad to pay off the nut as fast as possible and start making some money himself—then keeps on driving fast because he's got to get his while the getting is good.

Uncle Tom says that most people on Earth have much the same deal, except it's done by the year and they call it income tax.

> *In Xanadu did Kubla Khan*
> *A stately pleasure dome decree—*

Dom Pedro Casino is like that. Lavish. Beautiful. Exotic. The arch over the entrance proclaims EVERY DIVERSION IN THE KNOWN UNIVERSE, and from what I hear this may well be true. However, all Girdie and I visited were the gaming rooms.

I never saw so much money in my whole life!

A sign outside the gambling sector read:

HELLO, SUCKER!
All Games Are Honest
All Games Have a House Percentage
YOU CAN'T WIN!
So Come On In and Have Fun—
(While We Prove It)
Checks Accepted. All Credit
Cards Honored. Free Breakfast
and a Ride to Your Hilton When
You Go Broke. Your Host,

DOM PEDRO

I said, "Girdie, there really is somebody named Dom Pedro?"

She shrugged. "He's an employee and that's not his real name. But he does look like an emperor. I'll point him out. You can meet him if you like and he'll kiss your hand. If you like that sort of thing. Come on."

She headed for the roulette tables while I tried to see everything at once. It was like being on the inside of a kaleidoscope. People beautifully dressed (employees mostly), people dressed every sort of way, from formal evening wear to sports shorts (tourists mostly), bright lights, staccato music, click and tinkle and shuffle and snap, rich hangings, armed guards in comic-opera uniforms, trays of drinks and food, nervous excitement, and money everywhere—

I stopped suddenly, so Girdie stopped. My brother Clark. Seated at a crescent-shaped table at which a beautiful lady was dealing cards. In front of him several tall stacks of chips and an imposing pile of paper money.

I should not have been startled. If you think that a six-year-old boy (or eighteen-year-old boy if you use their years) wouldn't be allowed to gamble in Venusberg, then you haven't been to Venus. Never mind what we do in Marsopolis, here there are just two requirements to gamble: a) you have to be alive; b) you have to have money. You don't have to be able to talk Portuguese or Ortho, nor any known language; as long as you can nod, wink, grunt, or flip a tendril, they'll take your bet. And your shirt.

No, I shouldn't have been surprised. Clark heads straight for money the way ions head for an electrode. Now I knew where he had ducked out to the first night and where he had been most of the time since.

I went up and tapped him on the shoulder. He didn't look around at once but a man popped up out of the rug like a genie from a lamp and had me by the arm. Clark said to the dealer, "Hit me," and looked around. "Hi, Sis. It's all right, Joe, she's my sister."

"Okay?" the man said doubtfully, still holding my arm.

"Sure, sure. She's harmless. Sis, this is Josie Mendoza, company cop, on lease to me for tonight. Hi, Girdie!" Clark's voice was suddenly enthusiastic. But he remembered to say, "Joe, slip into my seat and watch the stuff. Girdie, this is swell! You gonna play black jack? You can have my seat."

(It must be love, dears. Or a high fever.)

She explained that she was about to play roulette. "Want me to come help?" he said eagerly. "I'm pretty good on the wheel, too."

She explained to him gently that she did not want help because she was working on a system, and promised to see him later in the evening. Girdie is unbelievably patient with Clark. I would have—

Come to think of it, she's unbelievably patient with me.

If Girdie has a system for roulette, it didn't show.

We found two stools together and she tried to give me a few chips. I didn't want to gamble and told her so, and she explained that I would have to stand up if I didn't. Considering what 84 percent gee does to my poor feet I bought a few chips of my own and did just what she did, which was to place minimum bets on the colors, or on odd or even. This way you don't win, you don't lose—except that once in a long while the little ball lands on zero and you lose a chip permanently (that "house percentage" the sign warned against).

The croupier could see what we were doing but we actually were gambling and inside the rules; he didn't object. I discovered almost at once that the trays of food circulating and the drinks were absolutely free—to anyone who was gambling. Girdie had a glass of wine. I don't touch alcoholic drinks even on birthdays—and I certainly wasn't going to drink Hi-Ho, after that obnoxious ad!—but I ate two or three sandwiches and asked for, and got—they had to go get it—a glass of milk. I tipped the amount I saw Girdie tip.

We had been there over an hour and I was maybe three or four chips ahead when I happened to sit up straight—and knocked a glass out of the hand of a man standing behind me, all over him, some over me.

"Oh, dear!" I said, jumping down from my stool and trying to dab off the wet spots on him with my kerchief. "I'm terribly sorry!"

He bowed. "No harm done to me. Merely soda water. But I fear my clumsiness has ruined milady's gown."

Out of one corner of her mouth Girdie said, "Watch it, kid!" but I answered, "This dress? Huh uh! If that was just water, there won't be a wrinkle or a spot in ten minutes. Travel clothes."

"You are a visitor to our city? Then permit me to introduce myself less informally than by soaking you to the skin." He whipped out a card. Girdie was looking grim but I rather liked his looks. Actually not impossibly older than I am (I guessed at twelve Mars years, or say thirty-six of his own—and it turned out he was only thirty-two). He was dressed in the very elegant Venus evening wear, with cape and stick and formal ruff . . . and the cutest little waxed mustaches.

The card read:

DEXTER KURT CUNHA, STK.

I read it, then reread it, then said, "Dexter *Kurt* Cunha— Are you any relation to—"

"My father."

"Why, I know your father!"—and put out my hand.

Ever had your hand kissed? It makes chill bumps that race up your arm, across your shoulders, and down the other arm—and of course nobody would ever do it on Mars. This is a distinct shortcoming in our planet and one I intend to correct, even if I have to bribe Clark to institute the custom.

By the time we had names straight, Dexter was urging us to share a bite of supper and some dancing with him in the roof garden. But Girdie was balky. "Mr. Cunha," she said, "that is a very handsome calling card. But I am responsible for Podkayne to her uncle—and I would rather see your I.D."

For a split second he looked chilly. Then he smiled warmly at her and said, "I can do better," and held up one hand.

The most imposing old gentleman I have ever seen hurried over. From the medals on his chest I would say that he had won every spelling contest from first grade on. His bearing was kingly and his costume unbelievable. "Yes, Stockholder?"

"Dom Pedro, will you please identify me to these ladies?"

"With pleasure, sir." So Dexter was really Dexter and I got my hand kissed again. Dom Pedro does it with great flourish but it didn't have quite the same effect— I don't think he puts his heart into it the way Dexter does.

Girdie insisted on stopping to collect Clark—and Clark suffered an awful moment of spontaneous schizophrenia, for he was still winning. But love won out and Girdie went up on Clark's arm, with Josie trailing us with the loot. I must say I admire my brother in some ways; spending cash money to protect his winnings must have caused even deeper conflict in his soul, if any, than leaving the game while he was winning.

The roof garden is the Brasilia Room and is even more magnificent than the casino proper, with a night-sky roof to match its name, stars and the Milky Way and the Southern Cross such as nobody ever in history actually saw from anywhere on Venus. Tourists were lined up behind a velvet rope waiting to get in—but not us. It was, "This way, if you please, Stockholder," to an elevated table right by the floor and across from the orchestra and a perfect view of the floor show.

We danced and we ate foods I've never heard of and I let a glass of champagne be poured for me but didn't try to drink it because the bubbles go up my nose—and wished for a glass of milk or at least a glass of water because some of the food was quite spicy, but didn't ask for it.

But Dexter leaned over me and said, "Poddy, my spies tell me that you like milk."

"I do!"

"So do I. But I'm too shy to order it unless I have somebody to back me up." He raised a finger and two glasses of milk appeared instantly.

But I noticed that he hardly touched his.

However, I did not realize I had been hoaxed until later. A singer, part of the floor show, a tall handsome dark girl dressed as a gypsy—if gypsies did ever dress that way, which I doubt, but she was billed as "Romany Rose"—toured the ringside tables singing topical verses to a popular song.

She stopped in front of us, looked right at me and smiled, struck a couple of chords and sang:

> *"Poddy Fries-uh came to town,*
> *Pretty, winsome Poddy—*
> *Silver shoes and sky blue gown,*
> *Lovely darling Podkayne—*
>
> *"She has sailed the starry sea,*
> *Pour another toddy!*
> *Lucky Dexter, lucky we!*
> *Drink a toast to Poddy!"*

And everybody clapped and Clark pounded on the table and Romany Rose curtsied to me and I started to cry and covered my face with my hands and suddenly remembered that I mustn't cry because of my makeup and dabbed at my eyes with my napkin and hoped I hadn't ruined it, and suddenly silver buckets with champagne appeared all over that big room and everybody *did* drink a toast to me, standing up when Dexter stood up in a sudden silence brought on by a roll of drums and a crashing chord from the orchestra.

I was speechless and just barely knew enough to stay seated myself and nod and try to smile when he looked at me—

—and he broke his glass, just like story tapes, and everybody imitated him and for a while there was crash and tinkle all over the room, and I felt like Ozma just after she stops being Tip and is Ozma again and I had to remember my makeup very hard indeed!

Later on, after I had gulped my stomach back into place and could stand up without trembling, I danced with Dexter again. He is a dreamy dancer—a firm, sure lead without ever turning it into a wrestling match. During a slow waltz I said, "Dexter? *You* spilled that glass of soda water. On purpose."

"Yes. How did you know?"

"Because it *is* a sky-blue dress—or the color that is called 'sky-blue,' for Earth, although I've never seen a sky this color. And my shoes *are* silvered. So it couldn't have been an accident. Any of it."

He just grinned, not a bit ashamed. "Only a little of it. I went first to your hilton—and it took almost half an hour to find out who had taken you where and I was furious, because Papa would have been most vexed. But I found you."

I chewed that over and didn't like the taste. "Then you did it because your daddy told you to. Told you to entertain me because I'm Uncle Tom's niece."

"No, Poddy."

"Huh? Better check through the circuits again. That's how the numbers read."

"No, Poddy. Papa would never order me to entertain a lady—other than formally, at our cottage—lady on my arm at dinner, that sort of thing. What he did do was show me a picture of you and ask me if I wanted to. And I decided I did want to. But it wasn't a very good picture of you, didn't do you justice—just one snapped by one of the servants of the Tannhäuser when you didn't know it."

(I decided I had to find some way to get rid of Maria and Maria, a girl needs privacy. Although this hadn't turned out too dry.)

But he was still talking. ". . . and when I did find you I almost didn't recognize you, you were so much more dazzling than the photograph. I almost shied off from introducing myself. Then I got the wonderful idea of turning it into an accident. I stood behind you with that glass of soda water almost against your elbow for so long the bubbles all went out of it—and when you did move, you bumped me so gently I had to slop it over myself to make it enough of an accident to let me be properly apologetic." He grinned most disarmingly.

"I see," I said. "But look, Dexter, the photograph was probably a very good one. This isn't my own face." I explained what Girdie had done.

He shrugged. "Then someday wash it for me and let me look at the real Poddy. I'll bet I'll recognize her. Look, dear, the accident was only half fake, too. We're even."

"What do you mean?"

"They named me 'Dexter' for my maternal grand-father, before they found out I was left-handed. Then it was a case of either renaming me 'Sinister,' which doesn't sound too well—or changing me over to right-handed. But that didn't work out either; it just made me the clumsiest man on three planets." (This while twirling me through a figure eight!)

"I'm always spilling things, knocking things over. You can follow me by the sound of fractured frangi-bles. The problem was not to cause an accident, but to keep from spilling that water until the right instant." He grinned that impish grin. "I feel very triumphant about it. But forcing me out of left-handedness did something else to me too. It's made me a rebel—and I think you are one, too."

"Uh ... maybe."

"I certainly am. I am expected to be Chairman of the Board someday, like my papa and my grandpapa. But I shan't. I'm going to space!"

"Oh! So am I!" We stopped dancing and chattered

about spacing. Dexter intends to be an explorer captain, just like me—only I didn't quite admit that my plans for spacing included pilot and master; it is never well in dealing with a male to let him know that you think *you* can do whatever it is he can do best or wants to do most. But Dexter intends to go to Cambridge and study paramagnetics and Davis mechanics and be ready when the first true starships are ready. Goodness!

"Poddy, maybe we'll even do it together. Lots of billets for women in starships."

I agreed that that was so.

"But let's talk about you. Poddy, it wasn't that you looked so much better than your picture."

"No?" (I felt vaguely disappointed.)

"No. Look. I know your background, I know you've lived all your life in Marsopolis. Me, I've been everywhere. Sent to Earth for school, took the Grand Tour while I was there, been to Luna, of course, and all over Venus—and to Mars. When you were a little girl and I wish I had met you then."

"Thank you." (I was beginning to feel like a poor relation.)

"So I know exactly what a honky-tonk town Venusberg is ... and what a shock it is to people the first time. Especially anyone reared in a gentle and civilized place like Marsopolis. Oh, I love my hometown but I know what it is— I've been other places. Poddy? Look at me, Poddy. The thing that impressed me about you was your aplomb."

"Me?"

"Your amazing and perfect savoir-faire ... under conditions I *knew* were strange to you. Your uncle has been everywhere—and Girdie, I take it, has been, too. But lots of strangers here, older women, become quite giddy when first exposed to the fleshpots of Venusberg and behave frightfully. But you carry yourself like a queen. Savoir-faire."

(This man I liked! Definitely. After years and years of "Beat it, runt!" it does something to a woman to be told she has savoir-faire. I didn't even stop to wonder if he told all the girls that— I didn't want to!)

We didn't stay much longer; Girdie made it plain that I had to get my "beauty sleep." So Clark went back to his game (Josie appeared out of nowhere at the right time—and I thought of telling Clark he had better git fer home too, but I decided that wasn't "savoir-faire" and anyhow he wouldn't have listened) and Dexter took us to the Tannhäuser in his papa's Rolls (or maybe his own, I don't know) and bowed over our hands and kissed them as he left us.

I was wondering if he would try to kiss me good night and had made up my mind to be cooperative about it. But he didn't try. Maybe it's not a Venusberg custom, I don't know.

Girdie went up with me because I wanted to chatter. I bounced myself on a couch and said, "Oh, Girdie, it's been the most wonderful night of my life!"

"It hasn't been a bad night for me," she said quietly. "It certainly can't hurt me to have met the son of the Chairman of the Board." It was then that she told me that she was staying on Venus.

"But, Girdie—*why?*"

"Because I'm broke, dear. I need a job."

"You? But you're *rich*. Everybody knows that."

She smiled. "I *was* rich, dear. But my last husband went through it all. He was an optimistic man and excellent company. But not nearly the businessman he thought he was. So now Girdie must gird her loins and get to work. Venusberg is better than Earth for that. Back home I could either be a parasite on my old friends until they got sick of me—the chronic house guest—or get one of them to give me a job that would really be charity, since I don't know anything. Or disappear into the lower depths and change my name. Here, nobody cares and there is always work for anyone who wants to work. I don't drink and I don't gamble—Venusberg is made to order for me."

"But what will you *do*?" It was hard to imagine her as anything but the rich society girl whose parties and pranks were known even on Mars.

"Croupier, I hope. They make the highest wages . . . and I've been studying it. But I've been practicing dealing, too—for black jack, or faro, or chemin de fer. But I'll probably have to start as a change girl."

"*Change girl?* Girdie—would you dress that way?"

She shrugged. "My figure is still good . . . and I'm quite quick at counting money. It's honest work, Poddy—it has to be. Those change girls often have as much as ten thousand on their trays."

I decided I had fubbed and shut up. I guess you can take the girl out of Marsopolis but you can't quite take Marsopolis out of the girl. Those change girls practically don't wear anything but the trays they carry money on—but it certainly was honest work and Girdie has a figure that had all the junior officers in the *Tricorn* running in circles and dropping one wing. I'm sure she could have married any of the bachelors and insured her old age thereby with no effort.

Isn't it more honest to work? And, if so, why shouldn't she capitalize her assets?

She kissed me good night soon after and ordered me to go right to bed and to sleep. Which I did—all but the sleep. Well, she wouldn't be a change girl long; she'd be a croupier in a beautiful evening gown . . . and saving her wages and her tips . . . and someday she would be a stockholder, one share anyway, which is all anybody needs for old age in the Venus Corporation. And I would come back and visit her when I was famous.

I wondered if I could ask Dexter to put in a word for her to Dom Pedro?

Then I thought about Dexter—

I know that can't be love; I was in love once and it feels entirely different. It hurts.

This just feels grand.

X

I hear that Clark has been negotiating to sell me (black market, of course) to one of the concessionaires who ship wives out to contract colonists in the bush. Or so they say. I do not know the truth. But There Are Rumors.

What infuriates me is that he is said to be offering me at a ridiculously low price!

But in truth it is this very fact that convinces me that it is just a rumor, carefully planted by Clark himself, to annoy me—because, while I would not put it past Clark to sell me into what is tantamount to chattel slavery and a Life of Shame if he could get away with it, nevertheless he would wring out of the sordid transaction every penny the traffic would bear. This is certain.

It is much more likely that he is suffering a severe emotional reaction from having opened up and become almost human with me the other night—and therefore found it necessary to counteract it with this

133

rumor in order to restore our relations to their normal, healthy, cold-war status.

Actually I don't think he could get away with it, even on the black market, because I don't have any contract with the Corporation and even if he forged one, I could always manage to get a message to Dexter, and Clark knows this. Girdie tells me that the black market in wives lies mostly in change girls or clerks or hilton chambermaids who haven't managed to snag husbands in Venusberg (where men are in short supply) and are willing to cooperate in being sold out back (where women are scarce) in order to jump their contracts. They don't squawk and the Corporation overlooks the matter.

Most of the bartered brides, of course, are single women among the immigrants, right off a ship. The concessionaires pay their fare and squeeze whatever cumshaw they can out of the women themselves and the miners or ranchers to whom their contracts are assigned. All Kosher.

Not that I understand it— I don't understand _anything_ about how this planet really works. No laws, just Corporate regulations. Want to get married? Find somebody who claims to be a priest or a preacher and have any ceremony you like—but it hasn't any legal standing because it is not a contract with the Corporation. Want a divorce? Pack your clothes and get out, leaving a note or not as you see fit. Illegitimacy? They've never heard of it. A baby is a baby and the Corporation won't let one want, because that baby will grow up and be an employee and Venus has a chronic labor shortage. Polygamy? Polyandry? Who cares? The Corporation doesn't.

Bodily assault? Don't try it in Venusberg; it is the most thoroughly policed city in the system—violent crime is bad for business. I don't wander around alone in some parts of Marsopolis, couth as my hometown is, because some of the old sand rats are a bit sun-struck and not really responsible. But I'm perfectly safe alone anywhere in Venusberg; the only assault I risk is from super salesmanship.

(The bush is another matter. Not the people so much, but Venus itself is lethal—and there is always a chance of encountering a Venerian who has gotten hold of a grain of happy dust. Even the little wingety fairies are bloodthirsty if they sniff happy dust.)

Murder? This is a *very* serious violation of regula-tions. You'll have your pay checked for years and years and years to offset both that employee's earning power for what would have been his working life . . . and his putative value to the Corporation, all calculated by the company's actuaries who are widely known to have no hearts at all, just liquid helium pumps.

So if you are thinking of killing anybody on Venus, *don't do it!* Lure him to a planet where murder is a social matter and all they do is hang you or something. No future in it on Venus.

There are three classes of people on Venus: stock-holders, employees, and a large middle ground. Stock-holder-employees (Girdie's ambition), enterprise employees (taxi drivers, ranchers, prospectors, some retailers, etc.), and of course future employees, chil-dren still being educated. And there are tourists but tourists aren't people; they have more the status of steers in a cattle pen—valuable assets to be treated with great consideration but no pity.

A person from out-planet can be a tourist for an hour or a lifetime—just as long as his money holds out. No visa, no rules of any sort, everybody welcome. But you must have a return ticket and you can't cash it in until *after* you sign a contract with the Corpora-tion. If you do. I wouldn't.

I still don't understand how the system works even though Uncle Tom has been very patient in explaining.

But he says he doesn't understand it either. He calls it "corporate fascism"—which explains nothing—and says that he can't make up his mind whether it is the grimmest tyranny the human race has ever known . . . or the most perfect democracy in history.

He says that nothing here is as bad in many ways as the conditions over 90 percent of the people on Earth endure, and that it isn't even as bad in creature comforts and standard of living as lots of people on Mars, especially the sand rats, even though we never knowingly let anyone starve or lack medical attention.

I Just Don't Know. I can see now that all my life I have simply taken for granted the way we do things on Mars. Oh, sure, I learned about other systems in school—but it didn't soak in. Now I am beginning to grasp emotionally that There Are Other Ways Than Ours . . . and that people can be happy under them. Take Girdie. I can see why she didn't want to stay on Earth, not the way things had changed for her. But she could have stayed on Mars; she's just the sort of high-class immigrant we want. But Mars didn't tempt her at all.

This bothered me because (as you may have gathered) I think Mars is just about perfect. And I think Girdie is just about perfect.

Yet a horrible place like Venusberg is what she picked. She says it is a Challenge.

Furthermore Uncle Tom says that she is Dead Right; Girdie will have Venusberg eating out of her hand in two shakes and be a stockholder before you can say Extra Dividend.

I guess he's right. I felt awfully sorry for Girdie when I found out she was broke. "I wept that I had no shoes—till I met a man who had no feet." Like that, I mean. I've never been broke, never missed any meals, never worried about the future—yet I used to feel sorry for Poddy when money was a little tight around home and I couldn't have a new party dress. Then I found out that the rich and glamorous Miss FitzSnugglie (I still won't use her right name, it wouldn't be fair) had only her ticket back to Earth and had borrowed the money for that. I was so sorry I hurt.

But now I'm beginning to realize that Girdie has "feet" no matter what—and will always land on them.

She has indeed been a change girl, for two whole nights—and asked me please to see to it that Clark did not go to Dom Pedro Casino those nights. I don't think she cared at all whether or not I saw her . . . but she knows what a horrible case of puppy love Clark has on her and she's just so sweet and good all through that she did not want to risk making it worse and/or shocking him.

But she's a dealer now and taking lessons for croupier—and Clark goes there every night. But she won't let him play at her table. She told him point-blank that he could know her socially or professionally, but not both—and Clark never argues with the inevitable; he plays at some other table and tags her around whenever possible.

Do you suppose that my kid brother actually does possess psionic powers? I know he's not a telepath, else he would have cut my throat long since. But he is still winning.

Dexter assures me that a) the games are absolutely honest, and b) no one can possibly beat them, not in the long run, because the house collects its percentage no matter what. "Certainly you can win, Poddy," he assured me. "One tourist came here last year and took home over half a million. We paid it happily—and advertised it all over Earth—and still made money the very week he struck it rich. Don't you even suspect that we are giving your brother a break. If he keeps it up long enough, we will not only win it all back but take every buck he started with. If he's as smart as you say he is, he'll quit while he's ahead. But most people aren't that smart—and Venus Corporation never gambles on anything but a sure thing."

Again, I don't know. But it was both Girdie and winning that caused Clark to become almost human with me. For a while.

It was last week, the night I met Dexter—and Girdie told me to go to bed and I did but I couldn't sleep and I left my door open so that I could hear Clark come in—or if I didn't, phone somebody and have him chased home because, while Uncle Tom is responsible for both of us, I'm responsible for Clark and always have been. I wanted Clark to be home and in bed before Uncle Tom got up. Habit, I guess.

He did come sneaking in about two hours after I did and I *psst'd* to him and he came into my room.

You never saw a six-year-old boy with so much money!

Josie had seen him to our door, so he said. Don't ask me why he didn't put it in the Tannhäuser's vault—or do ask me: I think he wanted to fondle it.

He certainly wanted to boast. He laid it out in stacks on my bed, counting it and making sure that I knew how much it was. He even shoved a pile toward me. "Need some, Poddy? I won't even charge you interest—plenty more where this came from."

I was breathless. Not the money, I didn't need any money. But the offer. There have been times in the past when Clark has lent me money against my allowance—and charged me exactly 100 percent interest come allowance day. Till Daddy caught on and spanked us both.

So I thanked him most sincerely and hugged him. Then he said, "Sis, how old would you say Girdie is?"

I began to understand his off-the-curve behavior. "I

really couldn't guess," I answered carefully. (Didn't need to guess, I knew.) "Why don't you ask her?"

"I did. She just smiled at me and said that women don't have birthdays."

"Probably an Earth custom," I told him and let it go at that. "Clark, how in the world did you win so much money?"

"Nothing to it," he said. "All those games, somebody wins, somebody loses. I just make sure I'm one who wins."

"But how?"

He just grinned his worst grin.

"How much money did you start with?"

He suddenly looked guarded. But he was still amazingly mellow, for Clark, so I pushed ahead. I said, "Look, if I know you, you can't get all your fun out of it unless *somebody* knows, and you're safer telling me than anyone else. Because I've never told on you yet. Now have I?"

He admitted that this was true by not answering— and it is true. When he was small enough, I used to clip him one occasionally. But I never tattled on him. Lately clipping him has become entirely too dangerous; he can give me a fat lip quicker than I can give him one. But I've never tattled on him. "Loosen up," I urged him. "I'm the only one you dare boast to. How much were you paid to sneak those three kilos into the *Tricorn* in my baggage?"

He looked very smug. "Enough."

"Okay. I won't pry any further about that. But what was it you smuggled? You've had me utterly baffled."

"You would have found it if you hadn't been so silly anxious to explore the ship. Poddy, you're stupid. You know that, don't you? You're as predictable as the law of gravity. I can *always* outguess you."

I didn't get mad. If Clark gets you sore, he's got you.

"Guess maybe," I admitted. "Are you going to tell me what it was? Not happy dust, I hope?"

"Oh, no!" he said and looked shocked. "You know what they do to you for happy dust around here? They turn you over to natives who are hopped up with it, that's what they do—and then they don't even have to bother to cremate you."

I shuddered and returned to the subject. "Going to tell me?"

"*Mmm . . .*"

"I swear by Saint Podkayne Not to Tell." This is my own private oath, nobody else would or could use it.

"Better not," he warned me. "You won't like it."

"By Saint Podkayne!" (And I should have kept my lip zipped.)

"Okay," he said. "But you swore it. A bomb."

"A *what*?"

"Oh, not much of a bomb. Just a little squeezer job. Total destruction not more than a kilometer. Nothing much."

I reswallowed my heart. "Why a bomb? And what did you do with it?"

He shrugged. "They were stupid. They paid me this silly amount, see? Just to sneak this little package aboard. Gave me a lot of north wind about how it was meant to be a surprise for the Captain—and that I should give it to him at the Captain's party, last night out. Gift wrapped and everything. 'Sonny,' this silly zero says to me, 'just keep it out of sight and let him be surprised—because last night out is not only the Captain's party, it's his birthday.'

"Now, Sis, you know I wouldn't swallow anything like that. If it had really been a birthday present they would just have given it to the Purser to hold—no need to bribe me. So I just played stupid and kept jacking up the price. And the idiots paid me. They got real jumpy when time came to shove us through passport clearance and paid all I asked. So I shoved it into your bag while you were yakking to Uncle Tom—then saw to it you didn't get inspected.

"Then the minute we were aboard I went to get it—and got held up by a stewardess spraying your cabin and had to do a fast job and go back to relock your bag because Uncle Tom came back in looking for his pipe. That first night I opened the thing in the dark—and opened it from the bottom; I already had a hunch what it might be."

"Why?"

"Sis, use your brain. Don't just sit there and let it rust out. First they offer me what they probably figured was big money to a kid. When I turn it down, they start to sweat and up the ante. I kept crowding it and the money got important. And more important. They don't even give me a tale about how a man with a flower in his lapel will come aboard at Venus and give me a password. It *has* to be that they don't care what happens to it as long as it gets into the ship. What does that add up to? Logic."

He added, "So I opened it and took it apart. Time bomb. Set for three days after we space. *Blooey!*"

I shivered, thinking about it.

"What a horrible thing to do!"

"It could have turned out pretty dry," he admitted, "if I had been as stupid as they thought I was."

"But why would anybody want to do such a thing?"

"Didn't want the ship to get to Venus."

"But *why*?"

"You figure it out. I have."

"Uh . . . what did you do with it?"

"Oh, I saved it. The essential pieces. Never know when you might need a bomb."

And that's all I got out of him—and here I am stuck with a Saint Podkayne oath. And nineteen questions left unanswered. Was there *really* a bomb? Or was I swindled by my brother's talent for improvising explanations that throw one off the obvious track? If there was *where is it*? Still in the *Tricorn*? Right here in this suite? In an innocent-looking package in the safe of the Tannhäuser? Or parked with his private bodyguard, Josie? Or a thousand other places in this big city? Or is it still more likely that I simply made a mistake of three kilograms in my excitement and that Clark was snooping just to be snooping? (Which he will always do if not busy otherwise.)

No way to tell. So I decided to squeeze what else I could from this Moment of Truth—if it was one. "I'm awful glad you found it," I said. "But the slickest thing you ever did was that dye job on Mrs. Garcia and Mrs. Royer. Girdie admires it, too."

"She does?" he said eagerly.

"She certainly does. But I never let on you did it. So you can still tell her yourself, if you want to."

"*Mmm* . . ." He looked quite happy. "I gave Old Lady Royer a little extra, just for luck. Put a mouse in her bed."

"Clark! Oh, wonderful! But where did you get a mouse?"

"Made a deal with the ship's cat."

I wish I had a nice, normal, slightly stupid family. It would be a lot more comfortable. Still, Clark has his points.

But I haven't had too much time to worry about my brother's High Crimes and Misdemeanors; Venusberg offers too much to divert the adolescent female with a hitherto unsuspected taste for high living. Especially Dexter—

I am no longer a leper; I can now go anywhere, even outside the city, without wearing a filter snout that makes me look like a blue-eyed pig—and dashing, darling Dexter has been most flatteringly eager to escort me everywhere. Even shopping. Using both hands a girl could spend a national debt there on clothes alone. But I am being (almost) sensible and spending only that portion of my cash assets earmarked for Venus. If I were not firm with him, Dexter would buy me anything I admire, just by lifting his finger. (He never carries any money, not even a credit card, and even his tipping is done by some unobvious credit system.) But I haven't let him buy me anything more important than a fancy ice cream sundae; I have no intention of jeopardizing my amateur status for some pretty clothes. But I don't feel too compromised over ice cream and fortunately I do not as yet have to worry about my waistline—I'm hollow clear to my ankles.

So, after a hard day of sweating over the latest Rio styles Dexter takes me to an ice cream parlor—one that bears the same relation to our Plaza Sweet Shoppe that the *Tricorn* does to a sand car—and he sits and toys with café au lait and watches in amazement while I eat. First some little trifle like an everlasting strawberry soda, then more serious work on a sundae composed by a master architect from creams and syrups and imported fruits and nuts of course, and perhaps a couple of tens of scoops of ice cream in various flavors and named "The Taj Mahal" or "The Big Rock Candy Mountain" or such.

(Poor Girdie! She diets like a Stylite every day of the year. Query: Will I ever make that sacrifice to remain svelte and glamorous? Or will I get comfortably fat like Mrs. Grew? Echo Answereth Not and I'm afraid to listen.)

I've had to be firm with him in other ways, too, but much less obviously. Dexter turns out to be a master of seductive logic and is ever anxious to tell me a bedtime story. But I have no intention of being a Maid Betrayed, not at my age. The tragedy about Romeo and Juliet is not that they died so young but that the boy-meets-girl reflex should be so overpowering as to defeat all common sense.

My own reflexes are fine, thank you, and my hormonal balance is just dandy. Dexter's fruitless overtures give me a nice warm feeling at the pit of my stomach and hike up my metabolism. Perhaps I should feel insulted at his dastardly intentions toward me—and possibly I would, at home, but this is Venusberg, where the distinction between a shameful proposition and a formal proposal of honorable marriage lies only in the mind and would strain a semantician to define. For all I know, Dexter already has seven wives at home, numbered for the days of the week. I haven't asked him, as I have no intention of becoming number eight, on any basis.

I talked this over with Girdie and asked why I didn't feel "insulted." Had they left the moral circuits out of my cybernet, as they so obviously did with my brother Clark?

Girdie smiled her sweet and secret smile that always means she is thinking about something she doesn't intend to be fully frank about. Then she said, "Poddy, girls are taught to be 'insulted' at such offers for their own protection—and it is a good idea, quite as good an idea as keeping a fire extinguisher handy even though you don't expect a fire. But you are right; it is not an insult, it is never an insult—it is the one utterly honest tribute to a woman's charm and femininity that a man can offer her. The rest of what they tell us is mostly polite lies . . . but on this one subject a man is nakedly honest. I don't see any reason ever to be insulted if a man is polite and gallant about it."

I thought about it. "Maybe you're right, Girdie. I guess it is a compliment, in a way. But why is it that that is all a boy is ever after? Nine times out of ten anyhow."

"You've got it just backwards, Poddy. Why should

he *ever* be after anything else? Millions of years of evolution is the logic behind every proposition. Just be glad that the dears have learned to approach the matter with handkissing instead of a club. Some of them, anyhow. It gives us more choice in the matter than we've ever had before in all history. It's a woman's world today, dear—enjoy it and be grateful."

I had never thought of it that way. When I've thought of it at all, I've mostly been groused because it is so hard for a girl to break into a "male" profession, such as piloting.

I've been doing some hard thinking about piloting—and have concluded that there are more ways of skinning a cat than buttering it with parsnips. Do I *really* want to be a "famous explorer captain"? Or would I be just as happy to be some member of his crew?

Oh, I want to space, let there be no doubt about that! My one little trip from Mars to Venus makes me certain that travel is for me. I'd rather be a junior stewardess in the *Tricorn* than President of the Republic. Shipboard life is fun; you take your home and your friends along with you while you go to romantic new places—and with Davis-drive starships being built those places are going to be newer and more romantic every year. And Poddy is going to go, somehow. I was born to roam—

But let's not kid ourselves, shall we? Is anybody going to let Poddy captain one of those multimegabuck ships?

Dexter's chances are a hundred times as good as mine. He's as smart as I am, or almost; he'll have the best education for it that money can buy (while I'm loyal to Ares U., I know it is a hick college compared with where he plans to go); and also it is quite possible that his daddy could *buy* him a Star Rover ship. But the clincher is that Dexter is twice as big as I am and male. Even if you leave his father's wealth out of the equation, which one of us gets picked?

But all is not lost. Consider Theodora, consider Catherine the Great. Let a man boss the job . . . then boss that man. I am not opposed to marriage. (But if Dexter wants to marry me—or anything—he'll have to follow me to Marsopolis where we are pretty old-fashioned about such things. None of this lighthearted Venusberg stuff.) Marriage should be every woman's end—but not her finish. I do not regard marriage as a sort of death.

Girdie says always to "be what you are." All right, let's look at ourselves in a mirror, dear, and forget "Captain Podkayne Fries, the famous Explorer" for the nonce. What do we see?

Getting just a touch broad-shouldered in the hips, aren't we, dear? No longer any chance of being mistaken for a boy in a dim light. One might say that we were designed for having babies. And that doesn't seem too bad an idea, now does it? Especially if we could have one as nice as Duncan. Fact is, all babies are pretty nice even when they're not.

Those eighteen miserable hours during the storm in the *Tricorn*—weren't they just about the most fun you ever had in your life? A baby is lots more fun than differential equations.

Every starship has a crèche. So which is better? To study crèche engineering and pediatrics—and be a department head in a starship? Or buck for pilot training and make it . . . and wind up as a female pilot nobody wants to hire?

Well, we don't have to decide now—

I'm getting pretty anxious for us to shape for Earth. Truth is, Venusberg's fleshpots can grow monotonous to one of my wholesome (or should I say "limited") tastes. I haven't any more money for shopping, not if

I am to have any to shop in Paris; I don't think I could ever get addicted to gambling (and don't want to; I'm one of those who lose and thereby offset in part Clark's winning); and the incessant noise and lights are going to put wrinkles where I now have dimples. And I think Dexter is beginning to be just a bit bored with my näve inability to understand what he is driving at.

If there is any one thing I have learned about males in my eight and a half years, it is that one should sign off before he gets bored. I look forward to just one last encounter with Dexter now: a tearful farewell just before I *must* enter the *Tricorn*'s loading tube, with a kiss so grown-up, so utterly passionate and all-out giving, that he will believe the rest of his life that Things Could Have Been Different if Only He Had Played His Cards Right.

I've been outside the city just once, in a sealed tourist bus. Once is more than enough; this ball of smog and swamp should be given back to the natives, only they wouldn't take it. Once a fairy in flight was pointed out, so they said, but I didn't see anything. Just smog.

I'll settle now for just one fairy, in flight or even perched. Dexter says that he knows of a whole colony, a thousand or more, less than two hundred kilometers away, and wants to show it to me in his Rolls. But I'm not warm to that idea; he intends to drive it himself— and that dratted thing has automatic controls. If I can sneak Girdie, or even Clark, into the picnic—well, maybe.

But I have learned a lot on Venus and would not have missed it for anything. The Art of Tipping, especially, and now I feel like an Experienced Traveler. Tipping can be a nuisance but it is not quite the vice Marsmen think it is; it is a necessary lubricant for perfect service.

Let's admit it; service in Marsopolis varies from indifferent to terrible—and I simply had not realized it. A clerk waits on you when he feels like it and goes on gossiping with another clerk, not even able to see you until he does feel like it.

Not like that in Venusberg! However, it is not just the money—and here follows the Great Secret of Happy Travel. I haven't soaked up much Portuguese and not everybody speaks Ortho. But it isn't necessary to be a linguist if you will learn just one word—in as many languages as possible. Just "thank you."

I caught onto this first with Maria and Maria—I say "gobble-gobble" to them a hundred times a day, only the word is actually "obrigado" which sounds like "gobble-gobble" if you say it quickly. A *small* tip is much more savoir-fairish—and gets better, more willing service—when accompanied by "thank you" than a big tip while saying nothing.

So I've learned to say "thank you" in as many languages as possible and I always try to say it in the home language of the person I'm dealing with, if I can guess it, which I usually can. Doesn't matter much if you miss, though; porters and clerks and taxi drivers and such usually know that one word in several languages and can spot it even if you can't talk with them at all in any other way. I've written a lot of them down and memorized them:

> Obrigado
> Donkey shane
> Mare-see
> Key toss
> M'goy
> Graht-see-eh
> Arigato
> Spawseebaw
> Gathee-oss
> Tock

Or "money tock" and Clark says this one means "money talks." But Clark is wrong; he has to tip too high because he won't bother to say "thank you." Oh, yes, Clark tips. It hurts him, but he soon discovered that he couldn't get a taxi and that even automatic vending machines were rude to him if he tried to buck the local system. But it infuriates him so much that he won't be pleasant about it and that costs him.

If you say "tock" instead of "key toss" to a Finn, he still understands it. If you mistake a Japanese for a Cantonese and say "m'goy" instead of "arigato"—well, that is the one word of Cantonese he knows. And "obrigado" everybody understands.

However, if you do guess right and pick their home language, they roll out the red carpet and genuflect, all smiles. I've even had tips refused—and this in a city where Clark's greediness about money is considered only natural.

All those other long, long lists of hints on How to Get Along While Traveling that I studied so carefully before I left turn out not to be necessary; this one rule does it all.

Uncle Tom is dreadfully worried about something. He's absent-minded and, while he will smile at me if I manage to get his attention (not easy), the smile soon fades and the worry lines show again. Maybe it's something here and things will be all right once we leave. I wish we were back in the happy Three-Cornered Hat with next stop Luna City.

XI

Things are really grim. Clark hasn't been home for two nights, and Uncle Tom is almost out of his mind. Besides that, I've had a quarrel with Dexter—which isn't important compared with Brother being missing but I could surely use a shoulder to cry on.

And Uncle Tom has had a real quarrel with Mr. Chairman—which was what led to my quarrel with Dexter because I was on Uncle Tom's side even though I didn't know what was going on and I discovered that Dexter was just as blind in his loyalty to his father as I am to Uncle Tom. I saw only a bit of the quarrel with Mr. Chairman and it was one of those frightening, cold, bitter, formally polite, grown-men quarrels of the sort that used to lead inevitably to pistols at dawn.

I think it almost did. Mr. Chairman arrived at our suite, looking not at all like Santa Claus, and I heard Uncle say coldly, "I would rather your friends had called on me, sir."

But Mr. Chairman ignored that and about then Uncle noticed that I was there—back of the piano, keeping quiet and trying to look small—and he told me to go to my room. Which I did.

But I know what part of it is. I had thought that both Clark and I had been allowed to run around loose in Venusberg—although I have usually had either Girdie or Dexter with me. Not so. Both of us have been guarded night and day, every instant we have been out of the Tannhäuser, by Corporation police. I never suspected this and I'm sure Clark didn't or he would never have hired Josie to watch his boodle. But Uncle did know it and had accepted it as a courtesy from Mr. Chairman, one that left him free to do whatever these things are that have kept him so busy here, without riding herd on two kids, one of them nutty as Christmas cake. (And I don't mean me.)

As near as I can reconstruct it Uncle blames Mr. Chairman for Clark's absence—although this is hardly fair as Clark, if he knew he was being watched, could evade eighteen private eyes, the entire Space Corps, and a pack of slavering bloodhounds. Or is it "wolfhounds"?

But, on top of this, Dexter says that they disagree completely on how to locate Clark. Myself, I think that Clark is missing because Clark wants to be missing because he intends to miss the ship and stay here on Venus where a) Girdie is, and b) where all that lovely money is. Although perhaps I have put them in the wrong order.

I keep telling myself this, but Mr. Chairman says that it is a kidnapping, that it has to be a kidnapping, and that there is only one way to handle a kidnapping on Venus if one ever expects to see the kidnappee alive again.

On Venus, kidnapping is just about the only thing a stockholder is afraid of. In fact they are so afraid of it that they have brought the thing down almost to a ritual. If the kidnapper plays by the rules and doesn't hurt his victim, he not only won't be punished but he had the Corporation's assurance that he can keep any ransom agreed on.

But if he doesn't play by the rules and they do catch him, well, it's pretty grisly. Some of the things Dexter just hinted at. But I understand that the mildest punishment is something called a "four-hour death." He wouldn't give me any details on this, either—except that there is some drug that is just the opposite of anesthesia; it makes pain hurt worse.

Dexter says that Clark is absolutely safe as long as Uncle Tom doesn't insist on meddling with things he doesn't understand. "Old fool" is one term that he used and that was when I slapped him.

Long sigh and a wish for my happy girlhood in Marsopolis, where I understood how things worked. I don't here. All I really know is that I can no longer leave the suite save with Uncle Tom—and must leave it and stay with him when he does and wherever he goes.

Which is how I at last saw the Cunha "cottage"— and would have been much interested if Clark hadn't been missing. A modest little place only slightly smaller than the Tannhäuser but much more lavish. Our President's Rose House would fit into its ballroom. That is where I quarreled with Dexter while Uncle and Mr. Chairman were continuing their worst quarrel elsewhere in that "cottage."

Presently Uncle Tom took me back to the Tannhäuser and I've never seen him look so old—fifty at least, or call it a hundred and fifty of the years they use here. We had dinner in the suite and neither of us ate anything and after dinner I went over and sat by the living window. The view was from Earth, I guess. The Grand Canyon of El Dorado, or El

Colorado, or whatever it is. Grand, certainly. But all I got was acrophobia and tears.

Uncle was just sitting, looking like Prometheus enduring the eagles. I put my hand in his and said, "Uncle Tom? I wish you would spank me."

"Eh?" He shook his head and seemed to see me. "Flicka! Why?"

"Because it's my fault."

"What do you mean, dear?"

"Because I'm responsibu—bul for Clark. I always have been. He hasn't any sense. Why, when he was a baby I must have kept him from falling in the Canal at least a thousand times."

He shook his head, negatively this time. "No, Poddy. It is my responsibility and not yours at all. I am in loco parentis to both of you—which means that your parents were loco ever to trust me with it."

"But I *feel* responsible. He's my Chinese obligation."

He shook his head still again. "No. In sober truth no person can ever be truly responsible for another human being. Each one of us faces up to the universe alone, and the universe is what it is and it doesn't soften the rules for any of us—and eventually, in the long run, the universe always wins and takes all. But that doesn't make it any easier when we *try* to be responsible for another—as you have, as I have—and then look back and see how we could have done it better." He sighed. "I should not have blamed Mr. Cunha. He tried to take care of Clark, too. Of both of you. I knew it."

He paused and added, "It was just that I had a foul suspicion, an unworthy one, that he was using Clark to bring pressure on me. I was wrong. In his way and by his rules, Mr. Cunha is an honorable man—and his rules do not include using a boy for political purposes."

"Political purposes?"

Uncle looked around at me, as if surprised that I

was still in the room. "Poddy, I should have told you more than I have. I keep forgetting that you are now a woman. I always think of you as the baby who used to climb on my knee and ask me to tell her 'The Poddy Story.'" He took a deep breath. "I still won't burden you with all of it. But I owe Mr. Cunha an abject apology—because *I* was using Clark for political purposes. And you, too."

"Huh?"

"As a cover-up, dear. Doddering great-uncle escorts beloved niece and nephew on pleasure tour. I'm sorry, Poddy, but it isn't that way at all. The truth is I am Ambassador Extraordinary and Minister Plenipotentiary for the Republic. To the Three Planets Summit. But it seemed desirable to keep it a secret until I present my credentials."

I didn't answer because I was having a little trouble soaking this in. I mean, I *know* Uncle Tom is pretty special and has done some important things, but all my life he has been somebody who always had time to hold a skein of yarn for me while I wound it and would take serious interest in helping me name paper dolls.

But he was talking. "So I used you, Flicka. You and your brother. Because— Poddy, do you really want to know all the ins and outs and snarls of the politics behind this?"

I did, very much. But I tried to be grown up. "Just whatever you think best to tell me, Uncle Tom."

"All right. Because some of it is sordid and all of it is complex and would take hours to explain—and some of it really isn't mine to tell; some of it involves commitments Bozo—sorry, the President— Some of it has to do with promises he made. Do you know who our Ambassador is now, at Luna City?"

I tried to remember. "Mr. Suslov?"

"No, that was last administration. Artie Finnegan.

Artie isn't too bad a boy ... but he thinks he should have been President and he's certain he knows more about interplanetary affairs and what is good for Mars than the President does. Means well, no doubt."

I didn't comment because the name "Arthur Finnegan" I recognized at once— I had once heard Uncle Tom sound off about him to Daddy when I was supposed to be in bed and asleep. Some of the milder expressions were "a head like a sack of mud," "larceny in his heart," and a "size twelve ego in a size nine soul."

"But even though he means well," Uncle Tom went on, "he doesn't see eye to eye with the President— and myself—on matters that will come before this conference. But unless the President sends a special envoy—me, in this case—the Ambassador in residence automatically speaks for Mars. Poddy, what do you know about Switzerland?"

"Huh? William Tell. The apple."

"That's enough, I guess, although there probably never was an apple. Poddy, Mars is the Switzerland of the solar System—or it isn't anything at all. So the President thinks, and so I think. A small man (and a small country, like Mars or Switzerland) can stand up to bigger, powerful neighbors only by being willing to fight. We've never had a war and I pray we never do, because we would probably lose it. But if we are willing enough, we may never have to fight."

He sighed. "That's the way I see it. But Mr. Finnegan thinks that, because Mars is small and weak, Mars should join up with the Terran Federation. Perhaps he's right and this really is the wave of the future. But I don't think so; I think it would be the end of Mars as an independent country and a free society. Furthermore, I think it is logical that if Mars gives up its independence, it is only a matter of time until Venus goes the same way. I've been spending the time since we got here trying to convince Mr. Cunha of this, cause him to have his Resident Commissioner make a common cause with us against Terra. This could persuade Luna to come in with us too, since both Venus and Mars can sell to Luna cheaper than Terra can. But it wasn't at all easy; the Corporation has such a long-standing policy of never meddling in politics at all. 'Put not your faith in princes'—which means to them that they buy and they sell and they ask no questions.

"But I have been trying to make Mr. Cunha see that if Luna and Mars and Terra (the Jovian moons hardly count), if those three were all under the same rules, in short order Venus Corporation would be no more free than is General Motors or I.G. Farbenindustrie. He got the picture too, I'm sure—until I jumped to conclusions about Clark's disappearance and blew my top at him." He shook his head. "Poddy, I'm a poor excuse for a diplomat."

"You aren't the only one who got sore," I said, and told him about slapping Dexter.

He smiled for the first time. "Oh, Poddy, Poddy, we'll never make a lady out of you. You're as bad as I am."

So I grinned back at him and started picking my teeth with a fingernail. This is an even ruder gesture than you might think—and utterly private between Uncle Tom and myself. We Maori have a very bloodthirsty history and I won't even hint at what it is we are supposed to be picking out of our teeth. Uncle Tom used to use this vulgar pantomime on me when I was a little girl, to tell me I wasn't being lady-like.

Whereupon he really smiled and mussed my hair. "You're the blondest blue-eyed savage I ever saw. But you're a savage, all right. And me, too. Better tell him you're sorry, hon, because, much as I appreciate your gallant defense of me, Dexter was perfectly right. I was an 'old fool.' I'll apologize to his father, doing the last hundred meters on my belly if he wants it that way; a man should admit it in full ·when he's wrong, and make amends. And you kiss and make up with Dexter— Dexter is a fine boy."

"I'll say I'm sorry and make up—but I don't think I'll kiss him. I haven't yet."

He looked surprised. "So? Don't you like him? Or have we brought too much Norse blood into the family?"

"I like Dexter just fine and you're crazy with the smog if you think Svenska blood is any colder than Polynesian. I could go for Dexter in a big way—and that's why I haven't kissed him."

He considered this. "I think you're wise, hon. Better do your practice kisses on boys who don't tend to cause your gauges to swing over into the red. Anyhow, although he's a good lad, he's not nearly good enough for my savage niece."

"Maybe so, maybe not. Uncle ... what *are* you going to do about Clark?"

His halfway happy mood vanished. "Nothing. Nothing at all."

"But we've got to do something!"

"But what, Podkayne?"

There he had me. I had already chased it through all the upper and lower segments of my brain. Tell the police? Mr. Chairman *is* the police—they all work for him. Hire a private detective? If Venus has any (I don't know), then they all are under contract to Mr. Cunha, or rather, the Venus Corporation.

Run ads in newspapers? Question all the taxi drivers? Put Clark's picture in the sollies and offer rewards? It didn't matter what you thought of, *everything* on Venus belongs to Mr. Chairman. Or, rather, to the corporation he heads. Same thing, really, although Uncle Tom tells me that the Cunhas actually own only a fraction of the stock.

"Poddy, I've been over everything I could think of with Mr. Cunha—and he is either already doing it, or he has convinced me that there, under conditions he knows much better than I do, it should not be done."

"Then what do we *do*?"

"We wait. But if you think of anything—*anything*— that you think might help, tell me and if it isn't already being done, we'll call Mr. Cunha and find out if it should be done. If I'm asleep, wake me."

"I will." I doubted if he would be asleep. Or me. But something else had been bothering me. "If time comes for the *Tricorn* to shape for Earth—and Clark isn't back—what do you do then?"

He didn't answer; the lines in his face just got deeper. I knew what the Awful Decision was—and I knew how he had decided it.

But I had a little Awful Decision of my own to make . . . and I had talked to Saint Podkayne about it for quite a while and had decided that Poddy had to break a Saint-Podkayne oath. Maybe this sounds silly but it isn't silly to me. Never in my life had I broken one . . . and never in my life will I be utterly sure about Poddy again.

So I told Uncle all about the smuggled bomb.

Somewhat to my surprise he took it seriously—when I had about persuaded myself that Clark had been pulling my leg just for exercise. Smuggling—oh, sure, I understand that every ship in space has smuggling. But not a bomb. Just something valuable enough that it was worthwhile to bribe a boy to get it aboard . . . and probably Clark had been paid off again when he passed it along to a steward, or a cargo hand, or somebody. If I know Clark—

But Uncle wanted me to describe exactly the person I had seen talking to Clark at Deimos Station.

"Uncle, I can't! I barely glanced at him. A man. Not short, not tall, not especially fat or skinny, not dressed in any way that made me remember—and I'm not sure I looked at his face at all. Uh, yes, I did but I can't call up any picture of it."

"Could it have been one of the passengers?"

I thought hard about that. "No. Or I would have noticed his face later when it was still fresh in my mind. *Mmm* . . . I'm almost certain he didn't queue up with us. I think he headed for the exit, the one that takes you back to the shuttle ship."

"That is likely," he agreed. "Certain—*if* it was a bomb. And not just a product of Clark's remarkable imagination."

"But, Uncle Tom, *why* would it be a bomb?"

And he didn't answer and I already knew why. Why would anybody blow up the *Tricorn* and kill everybody in her, babies and all? Not for insurance like you sometimes find in adventure stories; Lloyd's won't insure a ship for enough to show a profit on that sort of crazy stunt—or at least that's the way it was explained to me in my high school economics class.

Why, then?

To keep the ship from getting to Venus.

But the *Tricorn* had been to Venus tens and tens of times—

To keep somebody in the ship from getting to Venus (or perhaps to Luna) *that trip*.

Who? Not Podkayne Fries. I wasn't important to anybody but me.

For the next couple of hours Uncle Tom and I searched that hilton suite. We didn't find anything, nor did I expect us to. If there was a bomb (which I still didn't fully believe) and if Clark had indeed brought it off the ship and hidden it there (which seemed unlikely with all of the *Tricorn* at one end and all of the city at the other end to choose from), nevertheless

he had had days and days in which to make it look
like anything from a vase of flowers to a—a *anything*.

We searched Clark's room last on the theory that it
was the least likely place. Or rather, we started to
search it together and Uncle had to finish it. Pawing
through Clark's things got to be too much for me and
Uncle sent me back into the salon to lie down.

I was all cried out by the time he gave up; I even
had a suggestion to make. "Maybe if we sent for a
Geiger counter?"

Uncle shook his head and sat down. "We aren't looking for a bomb, honey."

"We aren't?"

"No. If we found it, it would simply confirm that
Clark had told you the truth, and I'm already using
that as least hypothesis. Because . . . well because I
know more about this than the short outline I gave to
you . . . and I know just how deadly serious this is to
some people, how far they might go. Politics is neither
a game nor a bad joke the way some people think it
is. War itself is merely an extension of politics . . . so I
don't find anything surprising about a bomb in politics;
bombs have been used in politics hundreds and even
thousands of times in the past. No, we aren't looking
for a bomb, we are looking for a man—a man you saw
for a few seconds once. And probably not even for
that man but for somebody that man might lead us
back to. Probably somebody inside the President's
office, somebody he trusts."

"Oh, gosh, I wish I had really looked at him!"

"Don't fret about it, hon. You didn't know and there
was no reason to look. But you can bet that Clark
knows what he looks like. If Clark—I mean, *when*
Clark comes back, in time we will have him search the
I.D. files at Marsopolis. And all the visa photographs
for the past ten years, if necessary. The man will be
found. And through him the person the President has

been trusting who should not be trusted." Uncle Tom suddenly looked all Maori and very savage. "And when we do, I may take care of the matter personally. We'll see."

Then he smiled and added, "But right now Poddy is going to bed. You're up way past your bedtime, even with all the dancing and late-sleeping you've been doing lately."

"Uh ... what time is it in Marsopolis?"

He looked at his other watch. "Twenty-seventeen. You weren't thinking of phoning your parents? I hope not."

"Oh, no! I won't say a word to them unless—until Clark is back. And maybe not then. But if it's only twenty-seventeen, it's not late at all, real time, and I don't want to go to bed. Not until you do."

"I may not go to bed."

"I don't care. I want to sit with you."

He blinked at me, then said very gently, "All right, Poddy. Nobody ever grows up without spending at least one night of years."

We just sat then for quite a while, with nothing to say that had not already been said and would just hurt to say over again.

At last I said, "Unka Tom? Tell me the Poddy story—"

"At your age?"

"Please." I crawled up on his knees. "I want to sit in your lap once more and hear it. I need to."

"All right," he said, and put his arm around me. "Once upon a time, long, long ago when the world was young, in a specially favored city there lived a little girl named Poddy. All day long she was busy like a ticking clock. *Tick tick tick* went her heels, *tick tick tick* went her knitting needles, and, most especially, *tick tick tick* went her busy little mind. Her hair was the color of butter blossoms in the spring when the ice leaves canals, her eyes were the changing blue of sunshine playing down through the spring floods, her nose had not yet made up its mind what it would be, and her mouth was shaped like a question mark. She greeted the world as an unopened present and there was no badness in her anywhere.

"One day Poddy—"

I stopped him. "But I'm *not* young any longer ... and I don't think the world was ever young!"

"Here's my hanky," he said. "Blow your nose. I never did tell you the end of it, Poddy; you always fell asleep. It ends with a miracle."

"A truly miracle?"

"Yes. This is the end. Poddy grew up and had another Poddy. And then the world was young again."

"Is that all?"

"That's all there ever is. But it's enough."

XII

I guess Uncle Tom put me to bed, for I woke up with just my shoes off and very rumpled. He was gone but he had left a note saying that I could reach him, if I needed to, on Mr. Chairman's private code. I didn't have any excuse to bother him and didn't want to face anyone, so I chased Maria and Maria out and ate breakfast in bed. Ate quite a lot, too, I must admit—the body goes on ticking anyhow.

Then I dug out my journal for the first time since landing. I don't mean I haven't been keeping it; I mean I've been talking it instead of writing it. The library in our suite has a recorder built into its desk and I discovered how easy it was to keep a diary that way. Well, I had really found out before that, because Mr. Clancy let me use the recorder they use to keep the log on.

The only shortcoming of the recorder in the library was that Clark might drop in most any time. But the first day I went shopping I found the most darling

165

little minirecorder at Venus Macy—only ten-fifty and
it just fits in the palm of your hand and you can talk
into it without even being noticed if you want to and
I just couldn't resist it. I've been carrying it in my
purse ever since.

But now I wanted to look way back in my journal,
the early written part, and see if I had said *anything*
that might remind me of what That Man had looked
like or anything about him.

I hadn't. No clues. But I FOUND A NOTE FROM
CLARK.

It read:

Pod,

If you find this at all, it's time you read it. Because
I'm using 24-hr. ink and I expect to lift this out of
here and you'll never see it.

Girdie is in trouble and I'm going to rescue her.
I haven't told anybody because this is one job that
is all mine and I don't want you or anybody horning
in on it.

However, a smart gambler hedges his bets, if he
can. If I'm gone long enough for you to read this,
it's time to get hold of Uncle Tom and have him
get hold of Chairman Cunha. All I can tell you is
that there is a newsstand right at South Gate. You
buy a copy of the *Daily Merchandiser* and ask if they
carry Everlites. Then say, "Better give me two—it's
quite dark where I'm going."

But don't *you* do this, I don't want it muffed up.

If this turns out dry, you can have my rock
collection.

Count your change. Better use
your fingers.
CLARK

I got all blurry. That last line—I know a holographic

last will and testament when I see one, even though I had never seen one before. Then I straightened up and counted ten seconds backwards including the rude word at the end that discharges nervous tension, for I knew this was no time to be blurry and weak; there was work to be done.

So I called Uncle Tom right away, as I agreed perfectly with Clark on one point: I wasn't going to try to emulate Space Ranger Stalwart, Man of Steel, the way Clark evidently had; I was going to get all the help I could get! With both Clark and Girdie in some sort of pinch I would have welcomed two regiments of Patrol Marines and the entire Martian Legion.

So I called Mr. Chairman's private code—and it didn't answer; it simply referred me to another code. This one answered all right . . . but with a recording. Uncle Tom. And this time all he said was to repeat something he had said in the note, that he expected to be busy all day and that I was not to leave the suite under any circumstances whatever until he got back— only this time he added that I was not to let anyone into the suite, either, not even a repairman, not even a servant except those who were already there, like Maria and Maria.

When the recording started to play back for the third time, I switched off. Then I called Mr. Chairman the public way, through the Corporation offices. A dry deal that was! By pointing out that I was Miss Fries, niece of Senator Fries, Mars Republic, I did get as far as his secretary, or maybe his secretary's secretary.

"Mr. Cunha cannot be reached. I am veree sorree, Miss Fries."

So I demanded that she locate Uncle Tom. "I do not have that information. I am veree sorree, Miss Fries."

Then I demanded to be patched in to Dexter. "Mr.

Dexter is on an inspection trip for Mr. Cunha. I am veree soree."

She either couldn't, or wouldn't, tell me when Dexter was expected back—and wouldn't, or couldn't, find some way for me to call him. Which I just plain didn't believe, because if I owned a planetwide corporation there would be some way to phone every mine, every ranch, every factory, every air boat the company owned. All the time. And I don't even suspect that Mr. Chairman is less smart about how to run such a lash-up than I am.

I told her so, using the colorful rhetoric of sand rats and canal men. I mean I really got mad and used idioms I hadn't known I even remembered. I guess Uncle is right; scratch my Nordic skin and a savage is just underneath. I wanted to pick my teeth at her, only she wouldn't have understood it.

But would you believe it? I might as well have been cussing out a sand gator; it had no effect on her at all. She just repeated, "I'm-veree-sorree-Miss-Fries," and I growled and switched off.

Do you suppose Mr. Chairman uses an androidal Tik-Tok as his phone monitor? I wouldn't put it past him—and any live woman should have shown *some* reaction at some of the implausibilities I showered on her, even if she didn't understand most of the words. (Well, I don't understand some of them myself. But they are not compliments.)

I thought about phoning Daddy; I knew he would accept the charges, even if he had to mortgage his salary. But Mars was eleven minutes away; it said so, right on a dial of the phone. And the relays via Hermes Station and Luna City were even worse. With twenty-two minutes between each remark it would take me most of the day just to tell him what was wrong, even though they don't charge you for the waiting time.

But I still might have called except—well, what

could Daddy *do*, three hundred million kilometers away? All it would do would be to turn his last six hairs white.

It wasn't until then that I steadied down enough to realize that there had been something else amiss about that note written into my journal—besides Clark's childish swashbuckling. Girdie—

It was true that I had not seen Girdie for a couple of days; she was on a shift that caused her to zig while I zagged; newly hired dealers don't get the best shifts. But I had indeed talked to her at a time when Clark was probably already gone even though at the time I had simply assumed that he had gotten up early for some inscrutable reason of his own, rather than not coming home at all that night.

But Uncle Tom had talked to her just before we had gone to the Cunha cottage the day before, asked her specifically if she had seen Clark—and she hadn't. Not as recently as we had.

I didn't have any trouble reaching Dom Pedro—not the Dom Pedro I met the night I met Dexter but the Dom Pedro of that shift. However, by now all the Dom Pedros know who Poddy Fries is; she's the girl that is seen with Mr. Dexter. He told me at once that Girdie had gone off shift half an hour earlier and I should try her hilton. Unless—he stopped and made some inquiries; somebody seemed to think that Girdie had gone shopping.

As may be. I already knew that she was not at the little hilton she had moved to from the stylish (and expensive) Tannhäuser; a message I had already recorded there was guaranteed to fetch a call back in seconds, if and when.

That ended it. There was no one left for me to turn to, nothing at all left for me to do, save wait in the suite until Uncle returned, as he had ordered me to do.

So I grabbed my purse and a coat and left.

And got all of three meters outside the door of the suite. A tall, wide, muscular character got in my way. When I tried to duck around him, he said, "Now, now, Miss Fries. Your uncle left orders."

I scurried the other way and found that he was awfully quick on his feet, for such a big man. So there I was, arrested! Shoved back into our own suite and held in durance vile. You know, I don't think Uncle entirely trusts me.

I went back to my room and closed the door and thought about it. The room was still not made up and still cluttered with dirty dishes because, despite the language barrier, I have made clear to Maria and Maria that Miss Fries becomes quite vexed if *anybody* disturbs my room until I signal that I no longer want privacy by leaving the door open.

The clumsy, two-decker, roll-around table that had fetched my breakfast was still by my bed, looking like a plundered city.

I took everything off the lower shelf, stowed it here and there in my bath, covered the stuff on top of the table with the extra cloth used to shield the tender eyes of cash customers from the sight of dirty dishes.

Then I grabbed the house phone and told them I wanted my breakfast dishes cleared away immediately.

I'm not very big. I mean you can fit forty-nine mass kilos only one hundred fifty-seven centimeters long into a fairly small space if you scrunch a little. That lower shelf was hard but not too cramped. It had some ketchup on it I hadn't noticed.

Uncle's orders (or perhaps Mr. Cunha's) were being followed meticulously, however. Ordinarily a pantry boy comes to remove the food wagon; this time the two Marias took it out the service entrance and as far as the service lift—and in the course of it I learned something interesting but not really surprising. Maria said something in Portuguese; the other Maria answered her in Ortho as glib as mine: "She's probably soaking in the tub, the lazy brat."

I made a note not to remember her on birthdays and at Christmas.

Somebody wheeled me off the lift many levels down and shoved me into a corner. I waited a few moments, then crawled out. A man in a well-spotted apron was looking astonished. I said, "Obrigado!" handed him a deuce note and walked out the service entrance with my nose in the air. Two minutes later I was in a taxi.

I've been catching up on this account while the taxi scoots to South Gate in order not to chew my nails back to the elbows. I must admit that I feel good even though nervous. Action is better than waiting. No amount of bad can stonker me, but not knowing drives me nuts.

The spool is almost finished, so I think I'll change spools and mail this one back to Uncle at South Gate. I should have left a note, I know—but this is better than a note. I hope.

XIII

Well, I can't complain about not having seen fairies. They are every bit as cute as they are supposed to be—but I don't care greatly if I never see another one.

Throwing myself bravely into the fray against fearful odds, by sheer audacity I overcame—

It wasn't that way at all. I fubbed. Completely. So here I am, some nowhere place out in the bush, in a room with no windows, and only one door. That door isn't much use to me as there is a fairy perched over it. She's a cute little thing and the green part of her fur looks exactly like a ballet tutu. She doesn't look quite like a miniature human with wings—but they do say that the longer you stay here the more human they look. Her eyes slant up, like a cat's, and she has a very pretty built-in smile.

I call her "Titania" because I can't pronounce her real name. She speaks a few words of Ortho, not much because those little skulls are only about twice the brain capacity of a cat's skull—actually, she's an idiot studying to be a moron and not studying very hard.

Most of the time she just stays perched and nurses her baby—the size of a kitten and twice as cute. I call it "Ariel" although I'm not sure of its sex. I'm not dead sure of Titania's sex; they say that both males and females do this nursing thing, which is not quite nursing but serves the same purpose; they are not mammalians. Ariel hasn't learned to fly yet, but Titania is teaching it—tosses it into the air and it sort of flops and glides to the floor and then stays there, mewing piteously until she comes to get it and flies back to her perch.

I'm spending most of my time a) thinking, b) bringing this journal up to date, c) trying to persuade Titania to let me hold Ariel (making some progress; she now lets me pick it up and hand it to her—the baby isn't a bit afraid of me), and d) thinking, which seems to be a futile occupation.

Because I can go anywhere in the room and do anything as long as I stay a couple of meters away from that door. Guess why? Give up? Because fairies have very sharp teeth and claws; they're carnivorous. I have a nasty bite and two deep scratches on my left arm to prove it—red and tender and don't seem to want to heal. If I get close to that door, she dives on me.

Completely friendly otherwise— Nor do I have anything physically to complain about. Often enough a native comes in with a tray of really quite good food. But I never watch him come in and I never watch him take it away—because Venerians look entirely too human to start with and the more you look at them the worse it is for your stomach. No doubt you have seen pictures but pictures don't give you the smell and that drooling loose mouth, nor the impression that this *thing* has been dead a long time and is now animated by obscene arts.

I call him "Pinhead" and to him that is a compliment.

No doubt as to its being a "him" either. It's enough to make a girl enter a nunnery.

I eat the food because I feel sure Pinhead didn't cook it. I think I know who does. She would be a good cook.

Let me back up a little. I told the news vendor: "Better give me two—it's quite dark where I'm going." He hesitated and looked at me and I repeated it.

So pretty soon I am in another air car and headed out over the bush. Ever make a wide, sweeping turn in smog? That did it. I haven't the slightest idea where I am, save that it is somewhere within two hours' flight of Venusberg and that there is a small colony of fairies nearby. I saw them flying shortly before we landed and was so terribly interested that I didn't really get a good look at the spot before the car stopped and the door opened. Not that it would have done any good—

I got out and the car lifted at once, mussing me up with its fans . . . and here was an open door to a house and a familiar voice was saying, "Poddy! Come in, dear, come in!"

And I was suddenly so relieved that I threw myself into her arms and hugged her and she hugged me back. It was Mrs. Grew, fat and friendly as ever.

And looked around and here was Clark, just sitting—and he looked at me and said, "Stupid," and looked away. And then I saw Uncle—sitting in another chair and was about to throw myself at him with wild shouts of glee—when Mrs. Grew's arms were suddenly awfully strong and she said soothingly, "No, no, dear, not quite so fast" and held me until somebody (Pinhead, it was) did something to the back of my neck.

Then I had a big comfortable chair all to myself and didn't want it because I couldn't move from my neck down. I felt all right, aside from some odd tingles, but I couldn't stir.

Uncle looked like Mr. Lincoln grieving over the deaths at Waterloo. He didn't say anything.

Mrs. Grew said cheerfully, "Well, now we've got the whole family together. Feel a bit more like discussing things rationally, Senator?"

Uncle shook his head half a centimeter.

She said, "Oh, come now! We do want you to attend the conference. We simply want you to attend it in the right frame of mind. If we can't agree—well, it's hardly possible to let any of you be found again. Isn't that obvious? And that would be such a shame . . . especially for the children."

Uncle said, "Pass the hemlock."

"Oh, I'm sure you don't mean that."

"He certainly does mean it!" Clark said shrilly. "You illegal obscenity! I delete all over your censored!" And I knew he was really worked up, because Clark is contemptuous of vulgar idioms; he says they denote an inferior mind.

Mrs. Grew looked at Clark placidly, even tenderly. Then she called in Pinhead again. "Take him out and keep him awake till he dies." Pinhead picked Clark up and carried him out. But Clark had the last word. "And besides that," he yelled, *"you cheat at solitaire!* I've watched you!"

For a split moment Mrs. Grew looked really annoyed. Then she put her face back into its usual kindly expression and said to Uncle, "Now that I have both of the kids I think I can afford to expend one of them. Especially as you are quite fond of Poddy. Too fond of her, some people would say. Psychiatrists, I mean."

I mulled that over . . . and decided that if I ever got out of this mess, I would make a rug out of her hide and give it to Uncle.

Uncle ignored it. Presently there was a most dreadful racket, metal on resounding metal. Mrs. Grew smiled. "It's crude but it works. It is what used to be a water heater when this was a ranch. Unfortunately it isn't quite big enough either to sit down or stand up in—but a boy that rude really shouldn't expect comfort. The noise comes from pounding on the outside of it with a piece of pipe." She blinked and looked thoughtful. "I don't see how we can talk things over with such a racket going on. I think I should have the tank moved farther away—or perhaps our talk would march even more quickly if I had it brought nearer, so that you could hear the sounds he makes inside the tank, too. What do you think, Senator?"

I cut in. "Mrs. Grew!"

"Yes, dear? Poddy, I'm sorry but I'm really quite busy. Later we'll have a nice cup of tea together. Now, Senator—"

"Mrs. Grew, you don't understand my Uncle Tom at all! You'll never get anything out of him this way."

She considered it. "I think you exaggerate, dear. Wishful thinking."

"No, no, no! There isn't *any* way you could possibly get my Uncle Tom to do anything against Mars. But if you hurt Clark—or me—you'll just make him more adamant. Oh, he loves me and he loves Clark, too. But if you try to budge him by hurting either one of us, you're just wasting your time!" I was talking rapidly and just as sincerely as I know how. I seemed to hear Clark's screams. Not likely, I guess, not over that infernal clanging. But once when he was a baby he fell into a wastebasket ... and screamed something dreadful before I rescued him. I guess I was hearing that in my mind.

Mrs. Grew smiled pleasantly. "Poddy dear, you are only a girl and your head has been filled with nonsense. The Senator is going to do just what I want him to do."

"Not if you kill Clark, he won't!"

"You keep quiet, dear. Do keep quiet and let me explain—or I shall have to slap you a few times to keep you quiet. Poddy, I am not going to kill your brother—"

"But you said—"

"*Quiet!* That native who took your brother away didn't understand what I said; he knows only trade Ortho, a few words, never a full sentence. I said what I did for the benefit of your brother . . . so that, when I *do* have him fetched back in, he'll be groveling, begging your uncle to do anything I want him to do."

She smiled warmly. "One piece of nonsense you've apparently been taught is that patriotism, or something silly like that, will overpower a man's own self-interest. Believe me, I have no slightest fear that an old political hack like your uncle will give any real weight to such a silly abstraction. What *does* worry him is his own political ruin if he does what I want him to do. What he is going to do. Eh, Senator?"

"Madam," Uncle Tom answered tightly, "I see no point in bandying words with you."

"Nor do I. Nor shall we. But you can listen while I explain it to Poddy. Dear, your uncle is a stubborn man and he won't accomplish his own political downfall lightly. I need a string to make him dance—and in *you* I have that string, I'm sure."

"I'm not!"

"Want a slap? Or would you rather be gagged? I like you, dear; don't force me to be forceful. In *you*, I said. Not your brother. Oh, no doubt your uncle goes through the solemn farce of treating his niece and his nephew just alike—Christmas presents and birthday presents and such like pretenses. But it is obvious that no one could love your brother . . . not even his own mother, I venture to say. But the Senator *does* love you—rather more than he wants anyone to suspect. So now I am hurting your brother a little—oh, just a smidgen, at worst he'll be deaf—to let your uncle see what will happen to *you*. Unless he is a good boy and speaks his piece just the way I tell him to."

She looked thoughtfully at Uncle. "Senator, I can't decide which of two methods might work the better on you. You see, I want to keep you reminded—after you agree to cooperate—that you *did* agree. Sometimes a politician doesn't stay bought. After I turn you loose, would it be better for me to send your nephew along with you, to keep you reminded? Or would it be better to keep him here and work on him just a little each day—with his sister watching? So that she would have a clear idea of what happens to her . . . if you try any tricks at Luna City. What's your opinion, sir?"

"Madam, the question does not arise."

"Really, Senator?"

"Because I will not be at Luna City unless both children are with me. Unhurt."

Mrs. Grew chuckled. "Campaign promises, Senator. I'll reason with you later. But now"—she glanced at an antique watch pinned to her gross bosom—"I think I had better put a stop to that dreadful racket, it's giving me a headache. And I doubt if your nephew can hear it any longer, save possibly through his bones." She got up and left, moving with surprising agility and grace for a woman her age and mass.

Suddenly the noise stopped.

It was such a surprise that I would have jumped if anything below my neck could jump. Which it couldn't.

Uncle was looking at me. "Poddy, Poddy—" he said softly.

I said, "Uncle, don't you give in a millimeter to that dreadful woman!"

He said, "Poddy, I *can't* give in to her. Not at all. You understand that? Don't you?"

"I certainly do! But look—you could fake it. Tell her anything. Get loose yourself and take Clark along, as she suggested. Then you can rescue me. I'll hold out. You'll see!"

He looked terribly old. "Poddy . . . Poddy darling . . . I'm very much afraid . . . that this is the end. Be brave, dear."

"Uh, I haven't had very much practice at that. But I'll try to be." I pinched myself, mentally, to see if I was scared—and I wasn't, not really. Somehow I couldn't be scared with Uncle there, even though he was helpless just then. "Uncle, what is it she wants? Is she some kind of a fanatic?"

He didn't answer because we both heard Mrs. Grew's jolly, belly-deep laugh. "'Fanatic'!" she repeated, came over and tweaked my cheek. "Poddy dear, I'm not any sort of fanatic and I don't really care any more about politics than your uncle does. But I learned many years ago when I was just a girl—and quite attractive, too, dear, much more so than you will ever be—that a girl's best friend is cash. No, dear, I'm a paid professional and a good one."

She went on briskly, "Senator, I think the boy is deaf but I can't be sure; he's passed out now. We'll discuss it later, it's time for my nap. Perhaps we had all better rest a little."

And she called in Pinhead and I was carried into the room I am in now. When he picked me up, I really was truly aghast!—and found that I could move my arms and legs just a little bit—pins and needles you wouldn't believe!—and I struggled feebly. Did me no good, I was dumped in here anyhow.

After a while the drug wore off and I felt almost normal, though shaky. Shortly thereafter I discovered that Titania is a very good watchdog indeed and I haven't tried to reach that door since; my arm and shoulder are quite sore and getting stiff.

Instead I inspected the room. Not much in it. A bed with a mattress but no bedclothes, not that you need any in this climate. A sort of a table suspended from one wall and a chair fastened to the floor by it. Glow tubes around the upper corners of the room. I checked all these things at once after learning the hard way that Titania was not just a cutie with gauzy wings. It was quite clear that Mrs. Grew, or whoever had outfitted that room, had no intention of leaving anything in it that could be used as a weapon, against Titania or anybody. And I no longer had even my coat and purse.

I particularly regretted losing my purse, because I always carry a number of useful things in it. A nail file for example—if I had had even my nail file I might have considered taking on that bloodthirsty little fairy. But I didn't waste time thinking about it; my purse was where I had dropped it when I was drugged.

I did find one thing very interesting: this room had been used to prison Clark before I landed in it. One of his two bags was there—and I suppose I should have missed it from his room the night before, only I got upset and left Uncle to finish the search. The bag held a very odd collection for a knight errant venturing forth to rescue a damsel in distress: some clothing—three T-shirts and two pairs of shorts, a spare pair of shoes—a slide rule, and three comic books.

If I had found a flame gun or supplies of mysterious chemicals, I would not have been surprised—more Clarkish. I suppose, when you get right down to it, for all his brilliance Clark is just a little boy.

I worried a bit then about the possibility—or probability—that he was deaf. Then I quit thinking about it. If true, I couldn't help it—and he would miss his ears less than anything, since he hardly ever listens anyhow.

So I lay down on the bed and read his comic books.

I am not a comic-book addict but these were quite entertaining, especially as the heroes were always getting out of predicaments much worse than the one I was in.

After a while I fell asleep and had heroic dreams.

I was awakened by "breakfast" (more like dinner but quite good). Pinhead took the tray away, and light plastic dishes and a plastic spoon offered little in the way of lethal weapons. However, I was delighted to find that he had fetched my purse!

Delighted for all of ten seconds, that is— No nail file. No penknife. Not a darn thing in it more deadly than lipstick and hanky. Mrs. Grew hadn't disturbed any money or my tiny minirecorder but she had taken everything that could conceivably do any good (harm). So I gritted my teeth and ate and then brought this useless journal up to date. That's about all I've done since—just sleep and eat and make friends with Ariel. It reminds me of Duncan. Oh, not alike really—but all babies are sort of alike, don't you think?

I had dozed off from lack of anything better to do when I was awakened. "Poddy, dear—"

"Oh! Hello, Mrs. Grew."

"Now, now, no quick moves," she said chidingly. I wasn't about to make any quick moves; she had a gun pointed at my belly button. I'm very fond of it, it's the only one I have.

"Now be a good girl and turn over and cross your wrists behind you." I did so and in a moment she had them tied, quite firmly. Then she looped the line around my neck and had me on a leash—and if I struggled, all I accomplished was choking myself. So I didn't struggle.

Oh, I'm sure there was at least a moment when she didn't have that gun pointed at me and my wrists were not yet tied. One of those comic-book heroes would have snatched that golden instant, rendered her helpless, tied her with her own rope.

Regrettably, none of those heroes was named "Poddy Fries." My education has encompassed cooking, sewing, quite a lot of math and history and science, and such useful tidbits as freehand drawing and how to dip candles and make soap. But hand-to-hand combat I have learned sketchily if at all from occasional border clashes with Clark. I know that Mother feels that this is a lack (she is skilled in both karate and kill-quick, and can shoot as well as Daddy does) but Daddy has put off sending me to classes—I've gathered the impression that he doesn't really want his "baby girl" to know such things.

I vote with Mother, it's a lack. There must have been a split second when I could have lashed out with a heel, caught Mrs. Grew in her solar plexus, then broken her neck while she was still helpless—and run down the Jolly Roger and run up the Union Jack, just like in *Treasure Island*.

Oppernockity tunes but once—and I wasn't in tune with it.

Instead I was led away like a puppy on a string. Titania eyed us as we went through the door but Mrs. Grew clucked at her and she settled back on her perch and cuddled Ariel to her.

She had me walk in front of her down a hallway, through that living room where I had last seen Uncle Tom and Clark, out another door and a passage and into a large room—

—and I gasped and suppressed a scream!

Mrs. Grew said cheerfully, "Take a good look, dear. He's your new roommate."

Half the room was closed off with heavy steel bars, like a cage in a zoo. Inside was—well, it was Pinhead, that's what it was, though it took me a long moment of fright to realize it. You may have gathered that I do not consider Pinhead handsome. Well, dear, he was Apollo Belvedere before compared with the red-eyed maniacal horror he had become.

Then I was lying on the floor and Mrs. Grew was giving me smelling salts. Yes, sir, Captain Podkayne Fries the Famous Explorer had keeled over like a silly girl. All right, go ahead and laugh; I don't mind. *You* haven't ever been shoved into a room with a thing like that and had it introduced to you as "your new roommate."

Mrs. Grew was chuckling. "Feel better, dear?"

"You're not going to put me in there with him!"

"What? Oh, no, no, that was just my little joke. I'm sure your uncle will never make it necessary actually to do it." She looked at Pinhead thoughtfully—and he was straining one arm through the bars, trying again and again to reach us. "He's had only five milligrams, and for a long-time happy dust addict that's barely enough to make him tempery. If I ever do have to put you—or your brother—in with him, I've promised him at least fifteen. I need your advice, dear. You see, I'm about to send your uncle back to Venusberg so that he can catch his ship. Now which do you think would work best with your uncle? To put your brother in there right now, while your uncle watches? He's watching this, you know; he saw you faint—and that couldn't have been better if you had practiced. Or to wait and—"

"My uncle is watching us?"

"Yes, of course. Or to—"

"*Uncle Tom!*"

"Oh, do keep quiet, Poddy. He can see you but he can't hear you and he can't possibly help you. *Hmm*— You're such a silly billy that I don't think I want your advice. On your feet, now!"

She walked me back to my cell.

* * *

That was only hours ago; it merely seems like years.

But it is long enough. Long enough for Poddy to lose her nerve. Look, I don't have to tell this, nobody knows but me. But I've been truthful all through these memoirs and I'll be truthful now: I have made up my mind that as soon as I get a chance to talk with Uncle I will beg him, plead with him, to do *anything* to keep me from being locked up with a happy-dusted native.

I'm not proud of it. I'm not sure I'll ever be proud of Poddy again. But there it is and you can rub my nose in it. I've come up against something that frightens me so much I've cracked.

I feel a little better about it to have admitted it baldly. I sort of hope that, when the time comes, I won't whimper and I won't plead. But I . . . just . . . don't . . . know.

And then somebody was shoved in with me and it was Clark!

I jumped up off the bed and threw my arms around him and lifted him right off his feet and was blubbering over him. "Oh, Clarkie! Brother, brother, are you hurt? What did they do to you? Speak to me! Are you deaf?"

Right in my ear he said, "Cut out the sloppy stuff, Pod."

So I knew he wasn't too badly hurt, he sounded just like Clark. I repeated, more quietly, "Are you deaf?"

He barely whispered in my ear, "No, but she thinks I am, so we'll go on letting her think so." He untangled himself from me, took a quick look in his bag, then rapidly and very thoroughly went over every bit of the room—giving Titania just wide enough berth to keep her from diving on him.

Then he came back, shoved his face close to mine and said, "Poddy, can you read lips?"

"No. Why?"

"The hell you can't, you just did."

Well, it wasn't quite true; Clark had barely whispered—and I did find that I was "hearing" him as much from watching his mouth as I was from truly hearing him. This is a very funny thing but Clark says that almost everybody reads lips more than they think they do, and he had noticed it and practiced it and can really read lips—only he never told anybody because sometimes it is most useful.

He had me talk so low that I couldn't hear it myself and he didn't talk much louder. He told me, "Look, Pod, I don't know that Old Lady Grew"—he didn't say "Lady"—"has this room wired. I can't find any changes in it since she had me in it before. But there are at least four places and maybe more where a mike could be. So we keep quiet—because it stands to reason she put us together to hear what we have to say to each other. So talk out loud all you want to . . . but just static. How scared you are and how dreadful it is that I can't hear anything and such-like noise."

So we did and I moaned and groaned and wept over my poor baby brother and he complained that he couldn't hear a word I was saying and kept asking me to find a pencil and write what I was saying—and in between we really did talk, important talk that Clark didn't want her to hear.

I wanted to know why he wasn't deaf—had he actually been in that tank? "Oh, sure," he told me, "but I wasn't nearly as limp by then as she thought I was, either. I had some paper in my pocket and I chewed it up into pulp and corked my ears." He looked pained. "A twenty-spot note. Most expensive earplugs anybody ever had, I'll bet. Then I wrapped my shirt around my head and ignored it. But stow that and listen."

He was even more vague about how he had managed to get himself trapped. "Okay, okay, so I got hoaxed. You and Uncle don't look so smart, either—and anyhow, you're responsible."

"I am not either responsible!" I whispered indignantly.

"If you're not responsible, then you're irresponsible, which is worse. Logic. But forget it, we've got important things to do now. Look, Pod, we're going to crush out of here."

"How?" I glanced up at Titania. She was nursing Ariel but she never took her eyes off us.

Clark followed my glance. "I'll take care of that insect when the time comes, forget it. It has to be soon and it has to be at night."

"Why at night?" I was thinking that this smoggy paradise was bad enough when you could see a little, but in pitch-darkness—

"Pod, let that cut in your face heal; you're making a draft. It's got to be while Jojo is locked up."

"Jojo?"

"That set of muscles she has working for her. The native."

"Oh, you mean Pinhead."

"Pinhead, Jojo, Albert Einstein. The happy-duster. He serves supper, then he washes the dishes, then she locks him up and gives him his night's ration of dust. Then he stays locked up until he sleeps it off, because she's as scared of him when he's high as anybody else is. So we make our try for it while he is caged—and maybe she'll be asleep, too. With luck the bloke who drives her sky wagon will be away, too; he doesn't always sleep here. But we can't count on it and it has got to be before the *Tricorn* shapes for Luna. When is that?"

"Twelve-seventeen on the eighth, ship Greenwich."

"Which is?"

"Local? Nine-sixteen Venusberg, Wednesday the twentieth."

"Check," he answered. "On both."

"But why?"

"Shut up." He had taken his slide rule from his bag and was setting it. For the conversion, I assumed, so I asked, "Do you want to know the Venus second for this Terran year?" I was rather proud to have it on the tip of my tongue, like a proper pilot; Mr. Clancy's time hadn't been entirely wasted even though I had never let him get cuddly.

"Nope. I know it." Clark reset the rule, read it and announced, "We both remember both figures the same way and the conversion checks. So check timepieces." We both looked at our wrists. "Mark!"

We agreed, within a few seconds, but that wasn't what I noticed; I was looking at the date hand. "Clark! Today's the nineteenth!"

"Maybe you thought it was Christmas," he said sourly. "And don't yip like that again. I can read you if you don't make a sound."

"But that's tomorrow!" (I did make it soundless.)

"Worse. It's less than seventeen hours from now . . . and we can't make a move until that brute is locked up. We get just one chance, no more."

"Our Uncle Tom doesn't get to the conference."

Clark shrugged. "Maybe so, maybe not. Whether he decides to go—or sticks around and tries to find us— I couldn't care less."

Clark was being very talkative, for Clark. But at best he grudges words and I didn't understand him. "What do you mean—*if he sticks around*?"

Apparently Clark thought he had told me, or that I already knew—but he hadn't and I didn't. Uncle Tom was already gone. I felt suddenly lost and forlorn. "Clark, are you sure?"

"Sure, I'm sure. She darn well saw to it that I saw him go. Jojo loaded him in like a sack of meal and I saw the wagon take off into the smog. Uncle Tom is in Venusberg by now."

I suddenly felt much better. "Then he'll rescue us!"

Clark looked bored. "Pod, don't be stupid squared."

"But he will! Uncle Tom . . . and Mr. Chairman . . . and Dexter—"

He cut me off. "Oh, for Pete's sake, Poddy! Analyze it. You're Uncle Tom, you're in Venusberg, you've got all the help possible. *How do you find this place?*"

"Uh . . ." I stopped. "Uh . . ." I said again. Then I closed my mouth and left it closed.

"*Uh,*" he agreed. "Exactly *Uh.* You don't find it. Oh, in eight or ten years with a few thousand people doing nothing but searching, you could find it by elimination. Fat lot of good that would do. Get this through your little head, Sis: nobody is going to rescue us, nobody can possibly help us. We either break out of here tonight—or we've had it."

"Why tonight? Oh, tonight's all right with me. But if we don't get a chance tonight—"

"Then at nine-sixteen tomorrow," he interrupted, "we're dead."

"Huh? Why?"

"Figure it out yourself, Pod. Put yourself in old Gruesome's place. Tomorrow the *Tricorn* leaves. Figure it both ways: Uncle Tom leaves in it, or Uncle Tom won't leave. Okay, you've got his niece and nephew. What do you do with them? Be logical about it. *Her* sort of logic."

I tried, I really tried. But maybe I've been brought up wrong for that sort of logic; I can't seem to visualize killing somebody just because he or she had become a nuisance to me.

But I could see that Clark was right that far: after ship's departure tomorrow we will simply be nuisances to Mrs. Grew. If Uncle Tom *doesn't* leave, we are most special nuisances—and if he *does* leave and she is counting on his worry about us to keep him in line at Luna City (it wouldn't, of course, but that is what she is counting on anyway), in that case every day she risks the possibility that we might escape and get word to Uncle.

All right, maybe I can't imagine just plain murder; it's outside my experience. But suppose both Clark and I came down with green pox and died— That would certainly be convenient for Mrs. Grew—now, wouldn't it?

"I scan it," I agreed.

"Good," he said. "I'll teach you a thing or four yet, Pod. Either we make it tonight . . . or just past nine tomorrow she chills us both . . . and she chills Jojo, too, and sets fire to the place."

"Why Jojo? I mean Pinhead."

"That's the real tipoff, Pod. The happy-duster. This is Venus . . . and yet she let us see that she was supplying dust to a duster. She won't leave any witnesses."

"Uncle Tom is a witness, too."

"What if he is? She's counting on his keeping his lip zipped until the conference is over . . . and by then she's back on Earth and has lost herself among eight billion people. Hang around here and risk being caught? Pod, she's going to wait here only long enough to find out whether or not Uncle Tom catches the *Tricorn*. Then she'll carry out either Plan A, or Plan B—but both plans cancel us out. Get that through your fuzzy head."

I shivered. "All right. I've got it."

He grinned. "But *we* don't wait. We execute our own plan—my plan—first." He looked unbearably smug and added, "You fubbed utterly and came out here without doing any of the things I told you to . . . and Uncle Tom fubbed just about as badly, thinking he could make a straight payoff . . . but I came out here prepared!"

"You did? With what? Your slide rule? Or maybe those comic books?"

Clark said, "Pod, you know I never read comic books; they were just protective coloration."

(And this is true, so far as I know— I thought I had uncovered his Secret Vice.)

"Then what?" I demanded.

"Just compose your soul in patience, Sister dear. All in good time." He moved his bag back of the bed, then added, "Move around here where you can watch down the hallway. If Lady Macbeth shows up, I'm reading comic books."

I did as he told me to but asked him one more question—on another subject, as quizzing Clark when he doesn't want to answer is as futile as slicing water. "Clark? You figure Mrs. Grew is part of the gang that smuggled the bomb?"

He blinked and looked stupid. "What bomb?"

"The one they paid you to sneak aboard the *Tricorn*, of course! *What bomb* indeed!"

"Oh, that. Golly, Poddy, you believe everything you're told. When you get to Terra, don't let anybody sell you the Pyramids—they're not for sale." He went on working and I smothered my annoyance.

Presently he said, "She couldn't possibly know anything about any bombs in the *Tricorn*, or she wouldn't have been a passenger in it herself."

Clark can always make me feel stupid. This was so obvious (after he pointed it out) that I refrained from comment. "How do you figure it, then?"

"Well, she could have been hired by the same people and not have known that they were just using her as a reserve."

My mind raced and another answer came up. "In which case there could be still a third plot to get Uncle Tom between here and Luna!"

"Could be. Certainly a lot of people are taking an

interest in him. But I figure it for two groups. One group—almost certainly from Mars—doesn't want Uncle Tom to be there at all. Another group—from Earth probably, at least old Gruesome actually did come from Earth—wants him to be there but wants him to sing their song. Otherwise when she had Uncle Tom, she would never have turned him loose; she would just have had Jojo shove him into a soft spot and wait for the bubbles to stop coming up." Clark dug out something and looked at it. "Pod, repeat this back and don't make a sound. You are exactly twenty-three kilometers from South Gate and almost due south of it—south seven degrees west."

I repeated it. "How do you know?"

He held up a small black object about as big as two packs of cigarettes. "Inertial tracker, infantry model. You can buy them anywhere here, anybody who ever goes out into the bush carries one." He handed it to me.

I looked at it with interest; I had never seen one that small. Sand rats use them, of course, but they use bigger, more accurate ones mounted in their sand buggies—and anyhow, on Mars you can always see either the stars or the Sun. Not like this gloomy place! I even knew how it worked, more or less, because inertial astrogation is a commonplace for spaceships and guided missiles—vector integration of accelerations and times. But whereas the *Tricorn's* inertial tracker is supposed to be good for one part in a million, this little gadget probably couldn't be read closer than one in a thousand.

But it improved our chances at least a thousand to one!

"Clark! Did Uncle Tom have one of these? 'Cause if he did—"

He shook his head. "If he did, he never got a chance to read it. I figure they gassed him at once; he was

limp when they lifted him out of the air wagon. And
I never had a chance to tell him where this dump is
because this has been my first chance to look at mine.
Now put it in your purse; you're going to use it to get
back to Venusberg."

"Uh ... it'll be bulky in my purse, it'll show. You
better hide it wherever you had it. You won't lose me,
I'm going to hang onto your hand every step of the
way."

"No."

"Why not?"

"In the first place I'm not going to drag this bag
with me and that's where it was hidden; I built a false
bottom into it. In the second place we aren't going
back together—"

"What? Why not? We certainly are! Clark, I'm
responsible for you."

"That's a matter of opinion. Your opinion. Look,
Poddy, I'm going to get you out of this silly mess. But
don't try to use your head, it leaks. Just your memory.
Listen to what I say and then do it exactly the way I
tell you to—and you'll be all right."

"But—"

"Do *you* have a plan to get us out?"

"No."

"Then shut up. You start pulling your Big Sister act
now and you'll get us both killed."

I shut up. And I must confess that his plan made
considerable sense. According to Clark there is nobody
in this house but us, Mrs. Grew, Titania and Ariel,
Pinhead—and sometimes her driver. I certainly haven't
seen or heard any evidences of anybody else and I
suppose that Mrs. Grew has been doing it with an
absolute minimum of witnesses—I know I would if I
were (God forbid!) ever engaged in anything so out-
rageously criminal.

I've never seen the driver's face and neither has

Clark—on purpose, I'm sure. But Clark says that the driver sometimes stays overnight, so we must be prepared to cope with him.

Okay, assume that we cope. As soon as we are out of the house we split up; I go east, he goes west, for a couple of kilometers, in straight lines as near as bogs and swamps permit, which may be not very.

Then we both turn north—and Clark says that the ring road around the city is just three kilometers north of us; he drew me a sketch from memory of a map he had studied before he set out to "rescue Girdie."

At the ring road I go right, he goes left—and we each make use of the first hitchhike transportation, ranch house phone, or whatever, to reach Uncle Tom and/or Chairman Cunha and get lots of reinforcements in a hurry!

The idea of splitting up is the most elementary of tactics, to make sure that at least one of us gets through and gets help. Mrs. Grew is so fat she couldn't chase anybody on a race track, much less a swamp. We plan to do it when she doesn't dare unlock Pinhead for fear of her own life. If we are chased, it will probably be the driver—and he can't chase two directions at once. Maybe there are other natives she can call on for help, but even so, splitting up doubles our chances.

So I get the inertial tracker because Clark doesn't think I can maneuver in the bush without one, even if I wait for it to get light. He's probably right. But he claims that he can steer well enough to find that road using just his watch, a wet finger for the breeze, and polarized spectacles—which, so help me, he has with him.

I shouldn't have sneered at his comic books; he actually did come prepared, quite a lot of ways. If they hadn't gassed him while he was still locked in the passenger compartment of Mrs. Grew's air buggy, I think he could have given them a very busy, bad time. A flame gun in his bag, a Remington pistol hidden on his person, knives, stun bombs—even a *second* inertial tracker, openly in the bag along with his clothes and comic books and slide rule.

I asked him why, and he put on his best superior look. "If anything went wrong and they grabbed me, they would expect me to have one. So I had one—and it hadn't even been started . . . poor little tenderfoot who doesn't even know enough to switch the thing on when he leaves his base position. Old Gruesome got a fine chuckle out of that." He sneered. "She thinks I'm half-witted and I've done my best to help the idea along."

So they did the same thing with his bag that they did with my purse—cleaned everything out of it that looked even faintly useful for mayhem and murder, let him keep what was left.

And most of what was left was concealed by a false bottom so beautifully faked that the manufacturer wouldn't have noticed it.

Except, possibly, for the weight—I asked Clark about that. He shrugged. "Calculated risk," he said. "If you don't bet, you can't win. Jojo carried it in here still packed and she searched it in here—and didn't pick it up afterwards; she had both arms full of junk I didn't mind her confiscating."

(And suppose she had picked it up and noticed? Well, Brother would still have had his brain and his hands—and I think he could take a sewing machine apart and put it back together as a piece of artillery. Clark is a trial to me—but I have great confidence in him.)

I'm going to get some sleep now—or try to—as Pinhead has just fetched in our supper and we have a busy time ahead of us, later. But first I'm going to backtrack this tape and copy it; I have one fresh spool left in my purse. I'm going to give the copy to Clark to give to Uncle, just in case. Just in case Poddy turns out to be bubbles in a swamp, I mean. But I'm not worried about that; it's a much nicer prospect than being Pinhead's roommate. In fact I'm not worried about anything; Clark has the situation well in hand.

But he warned me very strongly about one thing; "Tell them to get here well before nine-sixteen . . . or don't bother to come at all."

"Why?" I wanted to know.

"Just do it."

"Clark, you know perfectly well that two grown men won't pay any attention unless I can give them a sound reason for it."

He blinked. "All right. There is a very sound reason. A half-a-kiloton bomb isn't very much . . . but it still isn't healthy to be around when it goes off. Unless they can get in here and disarm it before that time— up she goes!"

He has it. I've *seen* it. Snugly fitted into that false bottom. That same three kilograms of excess mass I couldn't account for at Deimos. Clark showed me the timing mechanism and how the shaped charges were nestled around it to produce the implosion squeeze.

But he did not show me how to disarm it. I ran into his blankest, most stubborn wall. He expects to escape, yes—and he expects to come back here with plenty of help and in plenty of time and disarm the thing. But he is utterly convinced that Mrs. Grew intends to kill us, and if anything goes wrong and we don't break out of here, or die trying, or anything . . . well, he intends to take her with us.

I told him it was wrong, I said that he mustn't take the law in his own hands. "What law!" he said. "There isn't any law here. And you aren't being logical, Pod. Anything that is right for a group to do is right for one person to do."

That one was too slippery for me to answer so I tried

simply pleading with him and he got sore. "Maybe you would rather be in the cage with Jojo?"

"Well . . . no."

"Then shut up about it. Look, Pod, I planned all this out when she had me in that tank, trying to beat my ears in, make me deaf. I kept my sanity by ignoring what was being done to me and concentrating on when and how I would blow her to bits."

I wondered if he had indeed kept his sanity but I kept my doubts to myself and shut up. Besides I'm not sure that he's wrong; it may be that I'm just squeamish about blood-shed. "Anything that is moral for a group to do is moral for one person to do." There must be a flaw in that, since I've always been taught that it is wrong to take the law in your own hands. But I can't find the flaw and it sounds axiomatic, self-evident. Switch it around. If something is wrong for one person to do, can it possibly be made *right* by having a lot of people (a government) agree to do it together? Even unanimously?

If a thing is wrong, it is wrong—and vox populi can't change it.

Just the same, I'm not sure I can nap with an atom bomb under my bed.

Postlude

I guess I had better finish this.

My sister got right to sleep after I rehearsed her in what we were going to do. I stretched out on the floor but didn't go right to sleep. I'm a worrier, she isn't. I reviewed my plans, trying to make them tighter. Then slept.

I've got one of those built-in alarm clocks and I woke just when I planned to, an hour before dawn. Any later and there would be too much chance that Jojo might be loose, any earlier and there would be too much time in the dark. The Venus bush is chancy even when you can see well; I didn't want Poddy to step into something sticky, or step on something that would turn and bite her leg off. Nor me, either.

But we had to risk the bush, or stay and let old Gruesome kill us at her convenience. The first was a sporting chance; the latter was a dead certainty, even though I had a terrible time convincing Poddy that Mrs. Grew would kill us. Poddy's greatest weakness— the really soft place in her head, she's not too stupid otherwise—is her almost total inability to grasp that some people are as bad as they are. Evil. Poddy never has understood evil. Naughtiness is about as far as her imagination reaches.

But I understand evil, I can get right inside the skull of a person like Mrs. Grew and understand how she thinks.

Perhaps you infer from this that I am evil, or partly so. All right, want to make something of it? Whatever *I* am, I knew Mrs. Grew was evil before we ever left the *Tricorn* ... when Poddy (and even Girdie!) thought the slob was just too darling for words.

I don't trust a person who laughs when there is nothing to laugh about. Or is good-natured no matter what happens. If it's that perfect, it's an act, a phony. So I watched her ... and cheating at solitaire wasn't the only giveaway.

So between the bush and Mrs. Grew, I chose the bush, both for me and my sister.

Unless the air car was there and we could swipe it. This would be a mixed blessing, as it would mean two of them to cope with, them armed and us not. (I don't count a bomb as an arm, you can't point it at a person's head.)

Before I woke Poddy I took care of that alate pseudosimian, that "fairy." Vicious little beast. I didn't have a gun. But I didn't really want one at that point; they understand about guns and are hard to hit, they'll dive on you at once.

Instead I had shoe trees in my spare shoes, elastic bands around my spare clothes, and more elastic bands in my pockets, and several two-centimeter steel ball bearings.

Shift two wing nuts, and the long parts of the shoe trees become a steel fork. Add elastic bands and you have a slingshot. And don't laugh at a slingshot; many a sand rat has kept himself fed with only a slingshot. They are silent and you usually get your ammo back.

I aimed almost three times as high as I would at home, to allow for the local gravity, and got it right on the sternum, knocked it off its perch—crushed the skull with my heel and gave it an extra twist for the nasty bite on Poddy's arm. The young one started to whine, so I pushed the carcass over in the corner, somewhat out of sight, and put the cub on it. It shut up. I took care of all this before I woke Poddy because I knew she had sentimental fancies about these "fairies" and I didn't want her jittering and maybe grabbing my elbow. As it was—clean and fast.

She was still snoring, so I slipped off my shoes and made a fast reconnoiter.

Not so good— Our local witch was already up and reaching for her broom; in a few minutes she would be unlocking Jojo if she hadn't already. I didn't have a chance to see if the sky car was outside; I did well not to get caught. I hurried back and woke Poddy.

"Pod!" I whispered. "You awake?"

"Yes."

"Wide awake? You've got to do your act, right now. Make it loud and make it good."

"Check."

"Help me up on the perch. Can your sore arm take it?"

She nodded, slid quickly off the bed and took position at the door, hands ready. I grabbed her hands, bounced to her shoulders, steadied, and she grabbed my calves as I let go her hands—and then I was up on the perch, over the door. I waved her on.

Poddy went running out the door, screaming, "Mrs. Grew! *Mrs. Grew!* Help, help! My brother!" She did make it good.

And came running back in almost at once with Mrs. Grew puffing after her.

I landed on Gruesome's shoulders, knocking her to the floor and knocking her gun out of her hand. I twisted and snapped her neck before she could catch her breath.

Pod was right on the ball, I have to give her credit. She had that gun before it stopped sliding. Then she held it, looking dazed.

I took it carefully from her. "Grab your purse. We go, right now! Stick close behind me."

Jojo *was* loose, I had cut it too fine. He was in the living room, looking, I guess, to see what the noise was about. I shot him.

Then I looked for the air car while keeping the gun ready for the driver. No sign of either one—and I didn't know whether to groan or cheer. I was all keyed up to shoot him but maybe he would have shot me first. But a car would have been mighty welcome compared with heading into the bush.

I almost changed my plan at that point and maybe I should have. Kept together, I mean, and headed straight north for the ring road.

It was the gun that decided me. Poddy could protect herself with it—and I would just be darn careful what I stepped on or in. I handed it to her and told her to move slowly and carefully until there was more light—but get going!

She was wobbling the gun around. "But, Brother, I've never shot anybody!"

"Well, you can if you have to."

"I guess so."

"Nothing to it. Just point it at 'em and press the button. Better use both hands. And don't shoot unless you really need to."

"All right."

I smacked her behind. "Now get going. See you later."

And I got going. I looked behind once, but she was

already vanished in the smog. I put a little distance between me and the house, just in case, then concentrated on approximating course west.

And I got lost. That's all. I needed that tracker but I had figured I could get along without it and Pod had to have it. I got hopelessly lost. There wasn't breeze enough for me to tell anything by wetting my finger and that polarized light trick for finding the Sun is harder than you would think. Hours after I should have reached the ring road I was still skirting boggy places and open water and trying to keep from being somebody's lunch.

And suddenly there was the most dazzling light possible and I went down flat and stayed there with my eyes buried in my arm and started to count.

I wasn't hurt at all. The blast wave covered me with mud and the noise was pretty rough but I was well outside the real trouble. Maybe half an hour later I was picked up by a cop car.

Certainly, I should have disarmed that bomb. I had intended to, if everything went well; it was just meant to be a "Samson in the Temple" stunt if things turned out dry. A last resort.

Maybe I should have stopped to disarm it as soon as I broke old Gruesome's neck—and maybe Jojo would have caught both of us if I had and him still with a happy-dust hangover. Anyhow I didn't and then I was very busy shooting Jojo and deciding what to do and telling Poddy how to use that gun and getting her started. I didn't think about the bomb until I was several hundred meters from the house—and I certainly didn't want to go back then, even if I could have found it again in the smog, which is doubtful.

But apparently Poddy did just that. Went back to the house, I mean. She was found later that day, about a kilometer from the house, outside the circle of total destruction—but caught by the blast.

With a live baby fairy in her arms—her body had protected it; it doesn't appear to have been hurt at all.

That's why I think she went back to the house. I don't *know* that this baby fairy is the one she called "Ariel." It might have been one that she picked up in the bush. But that doesn't seem at all likely; a wild one would have clawed her and its parents would have torn her to pieces.

I think she intended to save that baby fairy all along and decided not to mention it to me. It is just the kind of sentimental stunt that Poddy would do. She knew I was going to have to kill the adult—and she never said a word against that; Pod could always be sensible when absolutely necessary.

Then in the excitement of breaking out she forgot to grab it, just as I forgot to disarm the bomb after we no longer needed it. So she went back for it.

And lost the inertial tracker, somehow. At least it wasn't found on her or near her. Between the gun and her purse and the baby fairy and the tracker she must have dropped it in a bog. Must be, because she had plenty of time to go back and still get far away from the house. She should have been ten kilometers away by then, so she must have lost the tracker fairly soon and walked in a circle.

I told Uncle Tom all about it and was ready to tell the Corporation people, Mr. Cunha and so forth, and take my medicine. But Uncle told me to keep my mouth shut. He agreed that I had fubbed it, mighty dry indeed—but so had he—and so had everybody. He was gentle with me. I wish he had hit me.

I'm sorry about Poddy. She gave me some trouble from time to time, with her bossy ways and her illogical ideas—but just the same I'm sorry.

I wish I knew how to cry.

Her little recorder was still in her purse and part of the tape could be read. Doesn't mean much, though;

she doesn't tell what she did, she was babbling, sort of:

". . . very dark where I'm going. No man is an island, complete in himself. Remember that, Clarkie. Oh, I'm sorry I fubbed it but remember that; it's important. They all have to be cuddled sometimes. My shoulder— Saint Podkayne! Saint Podkayne, are you listening? Unka Tom, Mother, Daddy—is anybody listening? Do listen, please, because this is important. I love—"

It cuts off there. So we don't know whom she loved. Everybody maybe.

Mr. Cunha made them hold the *Tricorn* and now Uncle Tom and I are on our way again. The baby fairy is still alive and Dr. Torland says it doesn't have radiation sickness. I call it "Ariel" and I guess I'll be taking care of it a long time; they say these fairies live as long as we do. It is taking to shipboard life all right but it gets lonely and has to be held and cuddled or it cries.

she doesn't tell what she did that was habit-forming, so?

... very dark where I'm going. No sun. An island complex in Japan? Robots there, then. Thanks. Oh, I know where I think, it, but remember that it's important. They all have to be told. Sanctuaries. My daughter—family togetherness. Saint Tailayon and you. Someday I think you, Andrew Darby—is anybody listening? Do listen please, because this is important. I repeat—

I could tell them you wanted James Bond and loved Livingood movie.

Mrs. Castevet made them all the biscuits and she was unable to manage them at all, try again. This man they both have and I'm. Zealand as I'd drawn as leaving radiation sanctum. I tell them. In all places I'm looking over one of it, a good note. Fairy say they turned the to let as and while talking at an important-like all right as if it gets harder and I'm at to be told and watched to it cries.

Appendix

Appendix

Postlude

(As Originally Published)

I guess I had better finish this.

My sister got right to sleep after I rehearsed her in what we were going to do. I stretched out on the floor but didn't go right to sleep. I'm a worrier, she isn't. I reviewed my plans, trying to make them tighter. Then I slept.

I've got one of those built-in alarm clocks and I woke just when I planned to, an hour before dawn. Any later and there would be too much chance that Jojo might be loose, any earlier and there would be too much time in the dark. The Venus bush is chancy even when you see well; I didn't want Poddy to step into something sticky, or step on something that would turn and bite her leg off. Nor me, either.

But we had to risk the bush, or stay and let old Gruesome kill us at her convenience. The first was a sporting chance; the latter was a dead certainty, even though I had a terrible time convincing Poddy that Mrs. Grew would kill us. Poddy's greatest weakness—the really soft place in her head, she's not too stupid

209

otherwise—is her almost total inability to grasp that some people are as bad as they are. Evil. Poddy never has understood evil. Naughtiness is about as far as her imagination reaches.

But I understand evil, I can get right inside the skull of a person like Mrs. Grew and understand how she thinks.

Perhaps you infer from this that I am evil, or partly so. All right, want to make something of it? Whatever *I* am, I knew Mrs. Grew was evil before we ever left the *Tricorn* ... when Poddy (and even Girdie!) thought the slob was just too darling for words.

I don't trust a person who laughs when there is nothing to laugh about. Or is good-natured no matter what happens. If it's that perfect, it's an act, a phony. So I watched her ... and cheating at solitaire wasn't the only giveaway.

So between the bush and Mrs. Grew, I chose the bush, both for me and my sister.

Unless the air car was there and we could swipe it. This would be a mixed blessing, as it would mean two of them to cope with, them armed and us not. (I don't count a bomb as an arm, you can't point it at a person's head.)

Before I woke Poddy I took care of that alate pseudosimian, that "fairy." Vicious little beast. I didn't have a gun. But I didn't really want one at that point; they understand about guns and are hard to hit, they'll dive on you at once.

Instead I had shoe trees in my spare shoes, elastic bands around my spare clothes, and more elastic bands in my pockets, and several two-centimeter steel ball bearings.

Shift two wing nuts, and the long parts of the shoe trees become a steel fork. Add elastic bands and you have a slingshot. And don't laugh at a slingshot; many a sand rat has kept himself fed with only a slingshot. They are silent and you usually get your ammo back.

I aimed almost three times as high as I would at home, to allow for the local gravity, and got it right on the sternum, knocked it off its perch—crushed the skull with my heel and gave it an extra twist for the nasty bite on Poddy's arm. The young one started to whine, so I pushed the carcass over into the corner, somewhat out of sight, and put the cub on it. It shut up. I took care of all this before I woke Poddy because I knew she had sentimental fancies about these "fairies" and I didn't want her jittering and maybe grabbing my elbow. As it was—clean and fast.

She was still snoring, so I slipped off my shoes and made a fast reconnoiter.

Not so good— Our local witch was already up and reaching for her broom; in a few minutes she would be unlocking Jojo if she hadn't already. I didn't have a chance to see if the sky car was outside; I did well not to get caught. I hurried back and woke Poddy.

"Pod!" I whispered. "You awake?"

"Yes."

"Wide awake? You've got to do your act, right now. Make it loud and make it good."

"Check."

"Help me up onto the perch. Can your sore arm take it?"

She nodded, slid quickly off the bed and took position at the door, hands ready. I grabbed her hands, bounced to her shoulders, steadied, and she grabbed my calves as I let go her hands—and then I was up on the perch, over the door. I waved her on.

Poddy went running out the door, screaming, "Mrs. Grew! *Mrs. Grew!* Help, help! My brother!" She did make it good.

And came running back in almost at once with Mrs. Grew puffing after her.

I landed on Gruesome's shoulders, knocking her to the floor and knocking her gun out of her hand. I twisted and snapped her neck before she could catch her breath.

Pod was right on the ball, I have to give her credit. She had that gun before it stopped sliding. Then she held it, looking dazed.

I took it carefully from her. "Grab your purse. We go right now! Stick close behind me."

Jojo *was* loose, I had cut it too fine. He was in the living room, looking, I guess, to see what the noise was about. I shot him.

Then I looked for the air car while keeping the gun ready for the driver. No sign of either one—and I didn't know whether to groan or cheer. I was all keyed up to shoot him but maybe he would have shot me first. But a car would have been mighty welcome compared with heading into the bush.

I almost changed my plan at that point and maybe I should have. Kept together, I mean, and headed straight north for the ring road.

It was the gun that decided me. Poddy could protect herself with it—and I would just be darn careful what I stepped on or in. I handed it to her and told her to move slowly and carefully until there was more light—but get going!

She was wobbling the gun around. "But, Brother, I've never shot anybody!"

"Well, you can if you have to."

"I guess so."

"Nothing to it. Just point it at 'em and press the button. Better use both hands. And don't shoot unless you really need to."

"All right."

I smacked her behind. "Now get going. See you later."

And I got going. I looked behind once, but she was

already vanished in the smog. I put a little distance between me and the house, just in case, then concentrated on approximating course west.

And I got lost. That's all. I needed that tracker but I had figured I could get along without it and Pod had to have it. I got hopelessly lost. There wasn't breeze enough for me to tell anything by wetting my finger and that polarized light trick for finding the Sun is harder than you would think. Hours after I should have reached the ring road I was still skirting boggy places and open water and trying to keep from being somebody's lunch.

And suddenly there was the most dazzling light possible and I went down flat and stayed there with my eyes buried in my arm and started to count.

I wasn't hurt at all. The blast wave covered me with mud and the noise was pretty rough, but I was well outside the real trouble. Maybe half an hour later I was picked up by a cop car.

Certainly, I should have disarmed that bomb. I had intended to, if everything went well; it was just meant to be a "Samson in the Temple" stunt if things turned out dry. A last resort.

Maybe I should have stopped to disarm it as soon as I broke old Gruesome's neck—and maybe Jojo would have caught both of us if I had and him still with a happy-dust hangover. Anyhow I didn't and then I was very busy deciding what to do and telling Poddy how to use that gun and getting her started. I didn't think about the bomb until I was several hundred meters from the house—and I certainly didn't want to go back then, even if I could have found it again in the smog, which is doubtful.

But apparently Poddy did just that. Went back to the house, I mean. She was found later that day, about a kilometer from the house, outside the circle of total destruction—but caught by the blast.

With a live baby fairy in her arms—her body had protected it; it doesn't appear to have been hurt at all.

That's why I think she went back to the house. I don't *know* that this baby fairy is the one she called "Ariel." It could have been one that she picked up in the bush. But that doesn't seem at all likely; a wild one would have clawed her and its parents would have torn her to pieces.

I think she intended to save that baby fairy all along and decided not to mention it to me. It is just the kind of sentimental stunt that Poddy would pull. She knew I was going to have to kill the adult—and she never said a word against that; Pod could always be sensible when absolutely necessary.

Then in the excitement of breaking out she forgot to grab it, just as I forgot to disarm the bomb after we no longer needed it. So she went back for it.

And lost the inertial tracker, somehow. At least it wasn't found on her or near her. Between the gun and her purse and the baby fairy and the tracker she must have dropped it in the bog. Must be, because she had plenty of time to go back and still get far away from the house. She should have been ten kilometers away by then, so she must have lost the tracker fairly soon and walked in a circle.

I told Uncle Tom all about it and was ready to tell the Corporation people, Mr. Cunha and so forth, and take my medicine. But Uncle told me to keep my mouth shut. He agreed that I had fubbed it, mighty dry indeed—but so had he—and so had everybody. He was gentle with me. I wish he had hit me.

I'm sorry about Poddy. She gave me some trouble from time to time, with her bossy ways and her illogical ideas—but just the same, I'm sorry.

I wish I knew how to cry.

Her little recorder was still in her purse and part of the tape could be read. Doesn't mean much, though;

she doesn't tell what she did, she was babbling, sort of:

"... very dark where I'm going. No man is an island complete in himself. Remember that; it's important. They all have to be cuddled sometimes. My shoulder— Saint Podkayne! Saint Podkayne, are you listening? Unka Tom, Mother, Daddy—is anybody listening? Do listen, please, because this is important. I love—"

It cuts off there. So we don't know whom she loved. Everybody, maybe.

I'm alone here, now. Mr. Cunha made them hold the *Tricorn* until it was certain whether Poddy would die or get well, then Uncle Tom left and left me behind—alone, that is, except for doctors, and nurses, and Dexter Cunha hanging around all the time, and a whole platoon of guards. I can't go anywhere without one. I can't go to the casinos at all any more—not that I want to, much.

I heard part of what Uncle Tom told Dad about it. Not all of it, as a phone conversation with a bounce time of over twenty minutes is episodic. I heard none of what Dad said and only one monologue of Uncle's:

"Nonsense, sir! I am not dodging my own load of guilt; it will be with me always. Nor can I wait here until you arrive and you know it and you know why— and both children will be safer in Mr. Cunha's hands and *not* close to me ... and you know *that*, too! But I have a message for you, sir, one that you should pass on to your wife. Just this: people who will not take the trouble to raise children should not have them. You with your nose always in a book, your wife gallivanting off God knows where—between you, your daughter was almost killed. No credit to either of you that she wasn't. Just blind luck. You should tell your wife, sir, that building bridges and space stations and such gadgets is all very well ... but that a woman has more important work to do. I tried to suggest this to you years ago ... and was told to mind my own business. Now I am saying it. Your daughter will get well, no thanks to either of you. But I have my doubts about Clark. With him it may be too late. God may give you a second chance if you hurry. Ending transmission!"

I faded into the woodwork then and didn't get caught. But what did Uncle Tom mean by that—trying to scare Dad about *me*? I wasn't hurt at all and he knows it. I just got a load of mud on me, not even a burn ... whereas Poddy still looks like a corpse and they've got her piped and wired like a crèche.

I don't see what he was driving at.

I'm taking care of that baby fairy because Poddy will want to see it when she gets well enough to notice things again; she's always been a sentimentalist. It needs a lot of attention because it gets lonely and has to be held and cuddled, or it cries.

So I'm up a lot in the night—I guess it thinks I'm its mother. I don't mind, I don't have much else to do.

It seems to like me.

We Created a Monster

Ours is the dilemma of the Sorcerer's Apprentice. What started out as a whimsical sales tool, an essay contest based on the question: "Shall Poddy Live or Die?" has become a valedictory to RAH. As you will see as you read the essays, Heinlein more perhaps than any other author our field has ever seen was loved by his readers. Because the essays, even those that did not mention the author per se, made this so abundantly clear, frankly, we have found the response rather overwhelming. Did we call that forth? Well, on the evidence, yes, we did, and now we must do justice to it, or try.

It is said that one can infer a great deal about an author from the nature of the stories he chooses to write and the characters he chooses to write about. What then can we infer about Robert A. Heinlein from the nature of that part of his audience that cares enough to respond to a challenge such as that posed in this contest? They are thoughtful, life-affirming, logical, sentimental in the finest sense but not the least bit sappy, filled with altruism but nobody's fools—they are in fact a mirror image of the author himself.

The question for us became how to be properly respectful toward the outpouring of love and respect from RAH's readers? Well, for one thing, though the contest rules call for one $500 prize and nine $50 prizes, we are instead printing twenty-five essays. The additional printed essays will also garner for their authors a $50 prize.

The next question that arose was how to pick a winner from so many winners. Impossible. There were several of such equal quality that choosing between them would have been no better than coin flipping.

I was surprised to discover that while I started out a confirmed Poddy-killer, as I read their special pleadings I found myself drifting toward the other camp. Despite the fact that both logic and the author's intent spoke to that end, the naked emotional appeal of the other side became nearly overwhelming. The essay that came closest to finishing me off was the one that pointed out that RAH, for whatever reasons, had written a book for youngsters, many of whom simply would not understand the need for Poddy to die and would be much saddened by it and feel betrayed. And yet the other side had the logic of it, the artistry of it, and Heinlein's wishes too: a fatal combination. What to do, what to do ... I was becoming a "wet" against my will. Finally, the answer appeared, again from one of the essays. Of that more anon. . . .

Fortunately there was one entry, perhaps not the "best," that this publisher knows for certain would have been Robert's favorite. The question became how to jigger the results so that favoritism would have its way. Long renowned for our political correctness, the answer to that problem at least was obvious to us:

norming! Not by race, or gender—odious criteria, those—but by age. So our winner is—

Dana L.M. Boltuch

who is nine years old and writes like she's, well, that age and half again.

But every essay herein is a winner, and a fitting tribute to the one who left us here when he went on to other things. We dare to hope that RAH would have been pleased.

—Jim Baen

Heinlein on *Podkayne*

From a letter dated March 10, 1962 to the author's agent, Lurton Blassingame:

Is *Poddy* a juvenile? I didn't think of it as such and I suggest that it violates numerous taboos for the juvenile market. It seems to me that it is what the Swedes call a "cadet" book—upper teenage, plus such adults and juveniles as may enjoy it—and the American trade book market does not recognize such a category. But possibly it might be well to let [Putnam] have this story at once and see what happens.

Lurton, for several years now I have been writing just stories, with no eye on the market, and have been writing them with no criterion save the fixed belief that a story which interests me, and the solution of which satisfies me, will interest and satisfy a sufficient percentage of readers to make the story commercially usable. Maybe I'm wrong about this—maybe I should study the market and try like hell to tailor something which fits the current styles. But it seems to me that, if I am to turn out work of (fairly) permanent value, my own taste (checked by yours and by Ginny's) is what I must follow. Of course, this may result in my losing the market entirely—but I hope that it will result in better stories than if I tried to compound the "mixture as before."

I know that the ending of *Poddy* comes as rather a shock. However, that is the ending that seemed to fit— to me. The story follows a definite progression: a girl child with no worries at all and a preposterous ambition ... then, step by step, she grows up and discovers that the real world is more complex and not nearly as sweet as she had thought ... and that the only basic standard for an adult is the welfare of the young.

Oh, I could revise that last chapter to a "happy" ending in about two hours—let Poddy live through it, injured but promised a full recovery and with the implication that she will eventually marry this rich and handsome bloke who can take her with him to the stars ... and still give her brat kid brother a comeuppance and his lumps (and it is possible that I will at least consider doing this if no editor will risk publishing it as it is). But I don't want to do this; I think it would ruin the story—something like revising *Romeo and Juliet* to let the young lovers "live happily ever after."

But it took the deaths of Romeo and Juliet to show the families Montague and Capulet what damned fools they were being. Poddy's death (it seems to me) is similarly indispensable to this story. The true tragedy in this story lies in the character of the mother, the highly successful career woman who wouldn't take time to raise her own kids—and thereby let her son grow up an infantile monster, no real part of the human race and indifferent to the wellbeing of others ... until the death of his sister, under circumstances which lay on him a guilt he can never shake off, gives some prospect that he is now going to grow up.

I could state that the theme of the story is that death is the only destination for all of us and that the only long-range hope for any adult lies in the young—and that this double realization constitutes growing up, ceasing to be a child and putting away childish things. But I can't say it that baldly, not in fiction, and it seemed to me that I needed Poddy's death to say it at all. If Poddy gets to have her cake and eat it too (both marriage and star-roving), if that little monster, her brother, gets off unscathed to continue his clever but asocial career, if their mother gets away with neglecting her children's rearing without having it backfire on her—then the story is just a series of mildly adventurous incidents, strung together.

—Robert A. Heinlein

The Winners

John Avelis Jr.

This is not so much an essay defending one ending or another to *Podkayne of Mars*; as Julien Gracq said in the 1960s, after refusing the principal accolade of the French literary establishment—the Prix Goncourt—for his novel *Les Rivages des Syrtes*, "in art, there are no rules, there are only examples." The only possible ending for the book is the one Robert Heinlein himself intended for it.

This "essay" is actually a letter, a letter I kept promising myself I would take the time to write before Heinlein died in 1988, and one that I keep promising myself I will write to Virginia Heinlein, "just as soon as I find her address."

As a twelve-year-old, one who would not have known the meaning of the words "science fiction" taken together, I happened to pull a book off the fiction shelves in our local public library, took it home, and insofar as memory serves, did not put it down until I finished it. It was *Red Planet*. Within a week, I had exhausted everything in Terre Haute, Indiana, that remotely pertained to Robert A. Heinlein. As the years passed, I encountered more of his books. Of all the masters of science fiction I have encountered since, though, Heinlein remains the common thread, THE master, the *leitmotif* that runs through the planets and galaxies of my imagination.

For quite some time, I assumed the reason Heinlein was my favorite was that he was the first. As I grew older, I realized that there was something else: as good as Heinlein's stories were, it was his characters, the human individual rising above himself or herself, that indomitable spirit in however different a time or place, rising above whatever peril might present itself to the body or spirit, unyielding in its morality or willingness to risk all for genuinely held belief.

That is the genius of Robert A. Heinlein. I have read little enough of the critical nonsense about the man, about his supposed neuroses and fixations, inevitably written by persons who would not have been fit to carry his typewriter. There is a poisonous spirit abroad in some "professionals" of literature that holds that no author means what he says, and that it is for those who have gathered Ph.D's unto themselves to tell the great unwashed—the rest of us—what the author "really" meant, the better for these folks to justify their chairs in comparative literature, their grants, their wholly unearned (and, one suspects, minute) audience.

Long after anyone reads Joyce's *Ulysses* (or even cares about what he may have meant), people will still be reading and enjoying Raymond Chandler's *The Long Goodbye* and *The Big Sleep*, just as they will still read *Starship Troopers*, *The Moon is a Harsh Mistress*, and *Stranger in a Strange Land*—and, I am sure, *Podkayne of Mars*.

Let the author speak. The author, and not Putnam's—or Macmillan, or Knopf—knows what was intended when the book was written, and wrote it, well or badly. In the case of Robert Heinlein, he wrote surpassingly well indeed. His words should speak for themselves.

Requiescat in pace.

In Memoriam R.A.H.

Patrick Hannan

Podkayne of Mars, R.I.P.

Podkayne must die, and originally she did. She was
supposed to die. She had to die. Why? Because her
death validates her brother Clark's guilt and his hoped-
for transformation. It is the only way her brother Clark
can grow up and grow out of his asocial behavior.
Being a product of his mother's neglect, due to her
highly successful career, Clark has no hope of ever
growing up. Being unchecked, Clark's infantile antisocial behavior and his indifference of social customs and
of people in general, will only grow into a true element
of evil. Poddy Fries epitomizes goodness with a surprising touch of inner innocence; while her brother
Clark's character is highly questionable, and is developing in a totally opposite direction. As the story
opens, we are already made aware that Clark's asocial
behavior has gone on unchecked for too long—it is
now developing beyond mere attitude—it is developing
into a way of life. A very bad way, for Clark has no
true human feeling for other people. His only saving
grace is that he admits to understanding evil, but still
this is not enough. To merely understand evil does not
stop evil, for evil can still fester and grow—as it has
indeed been growing in Clark, due to his mother's
neglect in raising him. The only way to bring Clark
back in line and change his asocial behavior, is for him
to experience a shock—a shock so devastating that he
cannot dodge it or hide behind it. And for it to be a
true shock, it must entail a loss of something which is
personally close to him. And the only thing which is

personally close to Clark is his adoring older sister Poddy Fries; for even though he opposes her, he looks up to her. Poddy is Clark's only true contract with the rest of the outside world, for she has taken over the child rearing duties which his mother has abdicated in place of a career.

Yes, Poddy Fries must die. She must die in order to save her brother from a worse fate, so that he does not grow into the character of Mrs. Grew. The shock of her death truly changes him. When he tells us, at the end of the story, that he is sorry for her death and wishes he knew how to cry, we believe him. If Poddy survives, there's no way to believe him—for what would he have to be sorry about? Nothing. Therefore, in order for Clark to survive, Poddy must die. Her death is sad and shocking, as it has to be. But her spirit lives on in the baby fairy, which her brother Clark calls "Ariel," and which he has to now take care of and hold in order to keep it from crying. And thus goodness conquers evil and survives.

Kathy Pulver

My vote is to return to Heinlein's original ending for *Podkayne of Mars*. I have felt this way ever since I learned there was an original ending and I admit that a large part of my reason for returning to the original ending is literary purity. Having read the book and then both endings, it is obvious that the whole book leads up to having Podkayne die. Having her miraculously survive the explosion at the end of the book is a great disappointment and left me thinking I'd misread the end. I mean, for pity's sake, the girl was a practically ground zero for a bomb blast. By all rights, she should be dead, possibly in several pieces, not recovering nicely in some hospital room on Venus.

It's easy to blame the "revised" ending on the taboos of the time. Unfortunately, it's too easy. I believe part of the reason why the original publishers wanted to change the ending is because they didn't realize who the book is really about. It's not about Poddy, or Uncle Tom, or Mom or Dad or the Triplets. It's about Clark.

From almost the beginning of the book, Clark is lurking in the shadows, occasionally popping up and doing something strange. Thanks to Poddy's naivete, we don't realize just how dangerous Clark is until after she's injured/killed in the explosion. It's only in the last chapter that we get a true glimpse of Clark's mind. Throughout the book, Poddy's inability to think of anyone as truly evil has led us to think of Clark as a highly intelligent but morally stunted eleven-year-old boy. In the final chapter, we find out that Clark is much worse than this, we find out that Clark is a sociopath.

The difference in the endings is in the redemption of Clark. In the published ending, the "nice" version,

Clark realizes he's done something wrong, he understands it and grasps it, but I truly doubt he feels all that sorry. And what does he have to feel sorry about? Poddy lived. Clark may have screwed up, but nothing really terrible happened. Sure the bad guys died, but they were supposed to.

In the original ending, Clark not only realizes he's done something wrong, but he also seems to feel the first glimmerings of guilt. There's no way he can ever forget what he's done. Not only is Poddy dead, but he has Ariel, the infant fairy to constantly remind him that he was responsible for his sister's death.

So, in conclusion, keep the original ending, it's cleaner, it's better and it plays fair with the readers instead of building to a nonexistent conclusion.

Christina L. Ball

I began the reading of this edition of *Podkayne of Mars* with the decision to be made concerning the endings firmly in mind. Actually, *my* mind was already made up—I trusted Robert Heinlein's judgment, and if he had wanted the original, well, so did I. I wasn't concerned with the content difference (though I was familiar with it) or the relative literary merits of the two endings, I simply had faith in the author.

As I got into the story, however, I began to have second thoughts. I found Poddy to be an engaging character, and I felt for her as she faced her various challenges—I didn't want to watch her die! The closer I came to the denouement, the greater the ferocity with which my emotions warred ... would I be able to stick with my choice of the original, or would my sentimental regard for Poddy outweigh my support for the author and force me to choose the revision?

In the end the decision was astonishingly simple. In fact, there was no real decision to be made at all—it seemed very obvious to me that the original was the true ending of this story. I was surprised by the fact that despite all my inner turmoil prior to reading the endings, neither my feelings for Poddy nor for Heinlein had anything to do with my final decision. The revision simply did not fit this rest of the story, and for that reason I wholeheartedly support the original ending.

Robert Heinlein was trying to make several moral points with this work. Poddy's death, the circumstances and consequences of her death, seem critical to both the logical culmination of the plot and to the smooth relaying of the message. Disallowed the opportunity to conclude his story the way he saw fit, the author tried to retain the morals without the plot to support them. His revised ending came across sounding distressingly preachy, since he was forced to make his points both more overt and less justifiable. After all, Poddy was hurt, but she still had a bright future ahead of her—on reading the end one wondered what all the fuss was about. Perhaps if Heinlein had chosen to tone down the lessons of the story and gone for more of a straight adventure, or if he had rewritten the entire work to incorporate his message more subtly, he could have let Poddy live and still have had an interesting and cohesive book. Such speculation is pointless, however—he did neither of those things. He did, however, leave us an interesting and cohesive book in the original. Surely we are mature enough, more than 30 years after the writing of this story, to deal with it in the way that Heinlein intended, the way it works best.

Alan Brown, Jr.

I Like Heinlein (his ending, too)

Hello Mr. (or Mrs.) Judge, let's get right to the meat of it. Poddy is a nice person, but I agree with Mr. Heinlein: she should die.

Don't get me wrong, I'm not sexist or anything but when you think about it she should die.

Let's look at it from a technical viewpoint. Poddy was found 1 kilometer from the house's remains, O.K. The bomb's radius is 10 kilometers, again O.K. Now this bomb is one such that it can eradicate a passenger ship. But the ship takes heavy solar bombardment and is still in decent shape, so come on, she's gone. You could blow up Manhattan with a bomb like that.

O.K. nonbelievers, you say the bomb wasn't that powerful. Fine. Well let's think about this. Poddy is found with a vicious little baby fairy. Heinlein doesn't say what her body looks like. She's been knocked out by the blast. Consider this: her little friend gets the munchies. Even if it wasn't the fairy there are plenty of other dangers referred to that could of gotten her. She's dead, get on with your lives happy people.

Uh oh? What about those poor troubled kiddies, hmm?

SO WHAT!

I'm sorry I got a little over-emotional. But look at the world the way it's portrayed by the media. Death, mayhem, and decapitating. If a parent wants to shelter their kid, let them. But you can't shelter them forever. Anyway, you can't tell if a person likes surprise endings, so don't reject a person's opportunity to be exposed to them.

Now ... her ... BROTHER. Look at how he is portrayed in the editor's version. You get the feeling that he is a trained psychopath. And at the ripe old age of, is this right, 11? Why the heck is the 11-year-old being made into Charles Manson? I mean come on, give him a break, Heinlein did.

So to paraphrase the immortal words of Oliver Hazard Perry, "We have met the ending, and she is toast."

Brian & Carol Maranta

After reading the postlude to the book *Podkayne of Mars* as originally published, one is struck with a certain feeling of dissatisfaction; that the book was in some way not quite finished. The questions that remain as to what becomes of Podkayne, the changes in the character of Podkayne's brother, and the behaviour of Podkayne's Uncle Tom, give the story a distinctly "Un-Heinlein-Like" flavour.

An example would be in Podkayne's brother Clark. There is insufficient tragedy in the story to account for the significant change in his character. The book starts off with Clark being an almost inhuman monster, whose immoral genius is sure to lead him to inevitable retribution by the society he so greatly scorns. In the originally published postlude, he has developed into a caring, thoughtful person. However, one cannot escape the feeling that, if Podkayne had lived through their adventure, Clark would merely shrug off the entire incident, confident that his intellect had once again triumphed.

Another example would be in Uncle Tom's behaviour in the postlude as originally published. It is inconsistent with his character in the rest of the story. He expresses his opinion of the situation in his phone call to Mars and chastises Podkayne's parents about their methods for raising both Podkayne and her brother Clark. It would seem that, since Heinlein could not make his point through the death of Podkayne, he attempted an ulterior method that leaves the reader confused as to why Uncle Tom would intervene now when he chose not to earlier.

When Heinlein wrote *Podkayne of Mars*, he did so in accordance with his particular style of writing;

1) Create a group of interesting characters and let the reader get to know them.

2) Put the characters through a significant, challenging and entertaining adventure.

3) Have them work through their problem and, in doing so, learn an important lesson that imparts upon them a change in nature.

Obviously, Mr. Heinlein felt that his original ending was necessary for the changes to occur in the characters. Unfortunately, due to the concerns of his publishers, Heinlein agreed to change the ending in order to have the book printed. We feel we should respect Heinlein's work, trust in his skills as an author to determine the correct ending to his story, and allow his original postlude to stand.

In conclusion, we feel that the postlude, as originally *written* by Heinlein, is, in all important respects, superior to the one originally published and it should be the one to end the story. Although it is tragic, it is the only way that the book makes sense. We do not mean to be fanatically proclaiming that "PODKAYNE MUST DIE!", her character is endearing and her death is heart-rending in the extreme, but *it is necessary to the story*.

Timothy H. Willis

re: Podkayne; how the story should end . . .

Strangely enough, I actually remember quite distinctly when I first read *Podkayne of Mars*. I'd borrowed it from my junior high school library in Ferguson, Missouri during first period, and I ignored my classes for the rest of the day while reading it—hidden behind my loose-leaf folder. By the time school was out I had the last two chapters left, which I read while lying on the floor in front of the TV set, ignoring the "Early Show" movie—some WW-2 flick with Wallace Beery which was set in the Philippines during the Japanese invasion.

Now, I'd been reading Robert Heinlein's books since early grade school—I was already reading before kindergarten, and read my first SF book (Andre Norton's *Star Man's Son*) shortly after Sputnik went into orbit in '57. Today there are few books from that period which I will re-read, most all of them being his. *Podkayne* has been one of my favorites . . . although I always felt the ending was sort of vague, or disconnected, or incomplete, or ???

Dredging deep into the dusty recesses of my memory I do recollect that I was sure Poddy had been killed, until I re-read it a few months later. Then I was actually surprised to discover that she was just really messed up and would be hospitalized for quite a while. It didn't feel right, though.

Finally, something over a year after Robert's passing, I read *his* ending (I consider the one I had first read the publisher's) in *Grumbles from the Grave*. At last, the story felt right and complete—if a bit of a bummer. But looking at Podkayne's personality it really fits that she would not have survived. A shame, really. Something of a loss, and it would have been nice to "watch" her grow up in following books. Also, twelve-year-old that I was when I first read her tale, I developed a case of the hots for her anyway. (Not like Star in *Glory Road*, but that's another story.)

Then again, sometimes the hero dies gloriously, or more realistically, *in*gloriously. But if I had lobbied for reality in science fiction back then—particularly with one of my teachers, who thought it was all a waste of time—I would have lost miserably.

I believe Robert's originally intended ending is the only proper one. Not just because *he* intended it that way—though that is a perfectly acceptable reason so far as many, if not most, Heinlein fen are concerned. My feeling is based on the fact that the ending I had been familiar with since '63 never felt quite right, somehow.

Looking back at how I believed she had not survived that first time I read it tells me Robert's original intent came through regardless of how the publisher and editor wished to change it. This also tells me volumes on how his writing grabbed me and built real worlds and people.

I remember clearly the time I received word of his passing; appropriately enough, I was at a used book store. A friend came in while I was having coffee with the owner, tears running down her cheeks. She said, simply, "Heinlein's gone." There were three others, besides the owner and her thirteen-year-old daughter in the store, and we all had a good cry together.

But in a real way that even a hard-core atheist could agree with, his spirit is still with us . . . and shall be for who knows how many hundreds of years. I know that his stories, perspectives, and impressions will remain alive in me.

Then there are his letter in *Grumbles* ... and "unedited" versions of *Red Planet*, *Stranger in a Strange Land*, and *Puppet Masters* (three of my all-time favorites, too). New stuff—well, things I hadn't read before. I want to see it all, without censorship or publishers unwarranted concerns.

As for *Podkayne of Mars* ... I firmly believe there will be an overwhelming response from readers that Robert's originally intended ending should be the one and only ending—except in old printings, of course. It's what he created, and we want ... plus, it feels *right*.

Joe Mullins

The Postlude Debate

Should Podkayne Fries die? The Answer, by gut instinct, is always a firm "NO!" Poddy is such a delightful young lady that no one could possibly think it best for her to die. The reader feels outrage enough over Poddy's injuries. Let somebody else die—Clark, maybe, or that oily Dexter character. Not Poddy!

Such is the emotional argument against Mr. Heinlein's original ending. Poddy certainly is too sweet to die, and her death is enough to force tears and a bewildered sense of loss from the reader. The professional clown, however, must make us cry as well as laugh. *Podkayne of Mars* is a tragedy; in order to make its point the ending must be painful. The ending in which Podkayne survives is not painful; it provides a sense of relief, not tragedy. The entire story loses its direction and becomes, as Mr. Heinlein said in *Grumbles from the Grave*, "... a series of mildly adventurous incidents, strung together."

Some may argue that *Podkayne of Mars* need not be a tragedy at all, therefore the originally published ending is quite sufficient. Not true! Mr. Heinlein set out to make a point, specifically: People who won't take time to raise children shouldn't have them in the first place. Mr. Heinlein laid out the entire story to lead to this one inescapable conclusion. The softer ending simply does not provide the necessary impact to make the point.

In an effort to get this idea across anyway, Mr. Heinlein is forced, in the originally published ending, to resort to a lengthy speech by Uncle Tom. The speech simply smacks the reader in the face with the story's purpose. Apart from being preachy, obvious, and contrived, this speech changes things. The idea previously expressed by a lengthy, well-planned story has been crammed into a soliloquy by a character whose wisdom in such matters is suspect at best. After one considers his bachelor status and questionable judgment in taking the children on this political mission, Uncle Tom's opinions simply don't carry much weight. Perhaps if the character of Uncle Tom had been developed differently earlier in the book, the speech would work. as it stands, however, Uncle Tom's speech is simply clear evidence that it is impossible to change the ending without changing the story throughout.

This is not intended, however, to blame Mr. Heinlein for the poor way the originally published ending fits the story. His hand was forced, as recounted in *Grumbles from the Grave*, by his agent and his publisher. Surely it is part of a writer's job to revise his work when necessary, and Mr. Heinlein had done so before. Changing *Podkayne of Mars*, however, was not the same as the cuts required to force *Stranger in a Strange Land* down to a manageable size, or even the same as the censorship imposed on *Red Planet* by Alice Dalgliesh. The changes in these novels removed minor scenes and dialogue and, in the case of *Red Planet*, affected ideas not integral to the story. The change to *Podkayne* is the ending, and therefore the whole book.

Unfortunately, it must be admitted that the originally published ending to *Podkayne of Mars* is ineffective and somewhat weak. The reader comes to a Heinlein story looking for the special blend of hard-boiled pragmatism and high ideals that marks it as a true Heinlein work. The originally published ending, in attempting to shield the reader from the harsh consequences of the parents' behavior, instead presents the reader with the "watered scotch" that Jubal Harshaw would not deign to taste. The revised ending waters down the story, and gives the reader something less than true Heinlein. Mr. Heinlein brought Podkayne to life for a single purpose. Sadly, in order to serve that purpose well, Podkayne must die.

Holly M. Weis

Podkayne of Mars is a captivating, enlivening novel, and it is Podkayne Fries that gives the book its life and buoyancy. Before making any decision about which ending was the better one, we have to ask the question: would Poddy Fries live like that? Poddy carried out everything she did to extremes—would she settle for being weak and barely half alive, unable to finish her own story? Or would her first adventure be her last?

The original published ending, where Podkayne lived, albeit barely, struck me as strange. I simply could not believe that Poddy would exit the story feeble and barely clinging to life. Such an ending was not strong enough for her character. Poddy was vibrant and animated, and I as a reader was incapable of viewing her in any other manner. I certainly did not want Poddy to die, for the finality of death is overwhelming—you cannot imagine a sequel or try to picture Poddy fulfilling her dreams. But the uncertainty of an obscure ending leaves you with an unsettled feeling. Although someone can create a character, the character does not always obey its creator. Once you establish the character's identity, there are some things that it just will not do. And one of these things, for Podkayne Fries, is to exist without life.

Although I was disappointed that Podkayne died, I would give Heinlein's original ending my vote. That is because simply being alive is not enough for Poddy. She needs the quality of life that forms her character. And if she cannot have the same quality and spirit, what is life worth for her? To a person who thrives on excitement, at such a time death would be more of an adventure than the life that was left.

I did not only prefer Heinlein's original ending because I could picture Poddy in that situation. I preferred knowing what had happened. The original published ending left me with a feeling of uncertainty. Would Poddy survive? Would she live as a frail cripple or would she recover? These questions left me feeling uncomfortable, as if there should be an epilogue to inform me of what occurred later. Heinlein's ending left me with the answers, and I therefore felt much more satisfied reading it. And I truly believe that if Podkayne could choose her own ending, she too would pick death over uncertain life, and finality over an unfinished story.

Aaron B. Einzig

It is not uncommon for a publisher to require of an author certain changes in a manuscript in order to make the piece more presentable and therefore more salable. This sort of correction may entail nothing more than removing or rewriting a small passage because the publisher senses that in some way that part of the story may detract from the effectiveness of the whole tale or it could involve the conviction on the publisher's behalf that a certain piece of the story will strike the reader as unpalatable. The latter was the case when G.P. Putnam's Sons obliged Robert Anson Heinlein to compose an alternate ending to *Podkayne of Mars*.

In the original version of *Podkayne*, Poddy Fries is killed at the close of the story. Putnam's, presuming that this ending would have unfavorable impact on its readers, requested a new ending for Poddy, a new postlude to *Podkayne of Mars* in which Poddy survives the deadly blast in which she gets caught. Heinlein made the change and Putnam's published *Podkayne* with its new finish.

As is true with the work of any great author, a book is a whole, constructed of interlocking parts, which, just as in engineering, must fit together in a precise way in which each part complements the rest and the result is a fully functioning efficient machine. Now, as often happens, just as in engineering, parts may be jury rigged, and the machine will still function, albeit not as well as when all the parts fit into an integrated design. When a portion of a story is not as it was intended, does not flow with the current, it is noticeable.

Robert Heinlein was always trying to endow his readers with an understanding of the Truths he had gathered in his experience-rich life. One of these, a recurring theme of his literature, was "Natural laws have no pity." It is an important lesson that nature sees everyone in relation to his ability to survive, and many of the qualities which we admire, have little to do with brute survival, regardless of how important or valuable those qualities may be to us as human beings. Poddy Fries was intelligent, she was pretty, and she was very, very innocent. So innocent that she embodied sweetness. This, of course, makes it very difficult to accept or defend Heinlein's original ending because, **"How dare he?"** How could he kill off such a wonderful person? But the answer is: it happens. It has become a truism—"only the good die young"—that we never consider the meaning of. Heinlein's original ending makes that idea felt.

But there is also another, more present truth in this story that is very easy to lose with the reworked ending to Poddy's story. This is the lesson that Heinlein was trying to impart with his development of Clark. That is that sweetness and caring **are** very important to living **as a human being** and Poddy's death was to be the impulse and catalyst for Clark's entry into the human race—Poddy's tragic death was intended to touch Clark more deeply than he had ever been before.

Podkayne of Mars is, on the surface, the story of a lovely, ambitious, and extraordinarily intelligent young female Mars colonial. But in reality, under the surface, it is the story of a young boy whose brilliance has made him grow up so fast that he has left human sentiments by the wayside, and of his growth as a human being through his connection and eventual loss of connection, with his older sister. This idea is made less poignant and is trivialized by the originally published version. Therefore, though Poddy's death **hurts**, Heinlein's originally written version is the better.

Peggy E. Davis

A Tale of Two Endings

One of the wonders of childhood is the certainty that death will never touch us or ours; that life will continue on in the same vein as we begin it, with never a false step or disappointed wish.

That belief is one that must, sadly, be destroyed in order for us all to become, eventually, functional and productive adults. How much better to become first introduced to it by our favorite authors, with characters we care about and with whom we can empathize.

I have chafed for years over the "happily ever after" ending to Poddy Fries, Space Ship Captain. I much prefer the gentle introduction to human mortality in Heinlein's original ending. One of Heinlein's vast strengths was his expertise at handling the unpleasant side of life and even of characters we care about, while making it seem perfectly normal and acceptable. Let the lesson in his original be revived and allowed to stand. We need it more now than ever as we struggle to face our own humanity.

Heinlein dealt with this idea in its myriad forms in several of his novels, most blatantly *Time For the Stars*, *Have Space-Suit Will Travel*, *Glory Road*, *The Moon is a Harsh Mistress*, *Tunnel in the Sky* and *The Door into Summer*. In all of those, death as a natural, integral part of the life experience was explored from all angles, in as many contexts as possible. In none of them was the message diluted and negated as it was in the sanitized version of *Podkayne of Mars*.

His secondary point of parental guidance but not

control is made more clearly here than in any of his other works. Training without breaking is vital in any advanced society, a point Heinlein made over and over again.

The violence inherent in the human animal can only be counterbalanced by its gallant disregard of self that is evidenced by Poddy's gesture of "rescuing" the innocent baby. Mother had to be eliminated for survival's sake, but innocence should never be destroyed unnecessarily. The recognition of that is all that separates us from the creatures of the forest. Poddy had that, in spades. Clark had it only in its untrained, rudimentary form.

Which was Heinlein's whole point. Which was totally lost in the doctored, as-published version. Give The Grand Master back his point, however late and after the fact. Restore the original ending.

Virginia L. Galloway

Robert A. Heinlein's *Podkayne of Mars* was first published in 1963. I read it shortly after it came out, when I was still quite young. Even as a girlchild living in a repressive, Southern Baptist corner of Southeast Texas, I felt very impatient with Poddy, whom I considered silly, icky, and profoundly dim. I did not understand then, and I do not understand now how a 16-year-old (Earth years) with an IQ of 145 could be such a fuzzy-thinking ninny.

Through the years, Poddy has remained the same age, while I have grown older. I have re-read her story many times during many different phases of my life. It is clearer to me with each reading that with this character, Heinlein has violated his own policy concerning his protagonists: They can be innocent, naive, ignorant, prejudiced, contrary, muleheaded, or—especially his female characters—obsessed with breeding children, but, with the exception of Poddy, they are not stupid.

Poddy, however, is stupid. Worse, she is gushily sentimental. It is precisely that odious blend of stupidity and sentimentality that makes Heinlein's original ending more appropriate and more in keeping with the narrative integrity of the book. This is pointedly illustrated in the last scenes: Poddy's mushy thought processes cause her, during a terrifying, life-threatening imprisonment, to coo over and seek to befriend a Venusian alate pseudosimian cub (a baby "fairy"). Even if it can be assumed that her behavior is a way of coping with her fear, that does not explain why, when given the means of escape by her brother Clark—the most lucid and interesting character in the book, one in the great tradition of Heinleinian individualists—she goes back into enemy territory *and* she loses the inertial tracker that could have guided her, with the baby fairy, to safety. She knew that Clark had set the bomb to detonate and she knew that her best chance of survival lay in getting as far away as possible, but she did not, apparently, use any of her alleged intelligence or even basic common sense in order to go on living.

Had Poddy survived, she would have needed a caretaker to lead her by the hand through the rest of her life. Heinlein was correct in writing the ending so that Poddy died, because he made her too stupid to live.

Robin Siddique

On the End of *Podkayne of Mars*

Is the end of *Podkayne of Mars* truly the end of Poddy Fries, or has her career just begun? Many purists would argue that Podkayne must meet her demise as Heinlein first wrote for the simple reason that such was his original ending. Yet there are more compelling arguments as to why the end of the book must coincide with the end of Podkayne's life.

Sentimentality may argue that our heroine must go on to fulfill her dreams and achieve the impossible; yet that same quality in Podkayne herself is the reason why this could never be. She had sold herself short on the long-time dream—to become the first female starship captain—that defined who Poddy Fries really was. Part of her had died when she relinquished that aspiration. In the same vein, it seems more merciful to allow Podkayne to die than to live knowing that she had let her vision slip away without a struggle. Perhaps it was even as she intended; knowing that her life was not going to be as she had long desired, she ended it as a heroine and mother, fulfilling her vision in the only way open to her. To have done any less would have betrayed the character of Podkayne Fries.

Then there is the matter of her call to St. Podkayne, her Martian patron(ess). What was it that Poddy was asking for? It did not seem a cry for deliverance—she seemed resigned to her fate for many reasons (her relinquished dreams, her mysteriously lost tracker, etc.). It may be that Podkayne was requesting help not for herself, but for her brother Clark. Just before calling the Saint, Poddy admonished Clark to remember that no man is an island. On that principle she sacrificed herself to save the fairy child, whom Clark later found and would take care of for all of his life. Podkayne's death achieved what she could not manage in life—she taught Clark to look beyond himself, openly care for another, and perhaps even feel remorse. Had she lived, the fairy would have returned to her care, and Clark would have forgotten the lesson.

Finally, the ending originally published by Putnam's lacks the cohesion that is the hallmark of good writing. Uncle Tom's final diatribe against Podkayne's parents is out of character, especially the vindictive flavor of his comments on the un-womanly mother. Nothing in the story truly points to their supposed uncaring and neglect, and it seems unlike Tom to try to shift all the blame to another's shoulders so unfairly. The "place of the woman is in the home" attitude flies in the face of all that Podkayne aspired to in her short life, and cheapens the whole story into a moral homily suited for 1950s America. In short, this revised ending rings false, weakens the story's impact, and runs contrary to the tone and style of Heinlein. Only the original ending as written by Heinlein does justice to the story.

Dane Ford

Sometimes a surgeon has to remove a limb to save a life; sometimes you have to kill a character to save a book.

For almost thirty years, *Podkayne of Mars* has taken a bum rap as being a weak, fluffy book and Poddy has become a cliche for a weak female character. I read an article on women characters and science fiction that warned the writer not to use "Podkayne of Mars" style characters. I believe this reputation is unfair and undeserved. At least it is for the book and character as they stood with the original unedited ending. With the edited ending, it goes along fine, until the last chapter.

Podkayne of Mars is about more than a young girl's pleasure cruise through the Solar System with her beloved uncle and crazy brother. Or at least it was until Putnam changed the ending. Instead of creating a more realistic novel with some character depth, the editors created a cheap dime novel adventure where everybody but the bad guys gets away unscathed, or scathed but scheduled to fully recover sometime soon and live happily ever after. The published ending is a TV-style quick and easy wrap-up, since the reader is led to believe everything is going to be hunky-dory around the Fries household once Uncle Tom and the kids get back to Mars. Mom and Dad have seen the light and will instantly become better parents who spend more "quality time" with all their kids (but especially Clark since he's the psychotic one) and everything will be okay.

Nobody deserves a literary fate like this, especially not Podkayne Fries, a decent and likable character. Kill her.

Alan Brown, Sr.

The Author or the Editor

Well, there's no use avoiding the inevitable, I might as well gather my courage and say it.

The editor was right.

I can hear it now. Derision, scorn, gasps. Critics and fans, reviewers and writers joined in common cause. The wisdom of the Grand Master must be obeyed. Artists must follow their muses without question.

Bull.

Editing is a vital part of the creative process.[1] The wealth of ego that helps fuel the writer's creativity often lapses into self-indulgence. Editors keep that self-indulgence in check. Art, to be successful, must connect with the audience. And the editor's job is to insure the connection takes place.

I grew up reading Robert Heinlein's works. He had a profound effect on my view of the world, my value systems. But he did have a tendency to preach. And as his career went on, and he gained the power to present his unedited work, my enjoyment decreased. Recent reissues of some of his books in their original, unedited form are fuller, but no better. And his later works, looping in upon themselves in an incestuous fashion, actually tarnished my appreciation of earlier works. He would evoke memories of *The Moon is a*

---

[1] Of course, before any editors get swelled heads, let me point out that necessity does not imply any lofty status. For example, regular elimination of bodily waste is a vital part of human existence, but nothing people brag about.

Harsh Mistress, of *Glory Road*, and then, oops, here come Lazarus Long's interdimensional gadabouts. And for all of you that think it a crime to question the Master's work, I have a question: what would a champion of individuality like Heinlein think of a person who indulges in slavish devotion?

Podkayne was born in Heinlein's prime. Her adventures were filled with strange wonders, but at the same time, plenty of the trappings of ordinary life for an adolescent to identify with. When I was twelve or thirteen, and first finished the book, I ached to think of the pain Poddy ended up in. Her injuries were more than I wanted to think about. Without remembering the details, for years I remembered *Podkayne* as Heinlein's most depressing work. It's hard to imagine how depressed I might have been had she died, leaving the reader without even a ray of hope. And in reading Heinlein's version, I found myself robbed of the irony of Clark (bomb smuggler and child cynic) wondering why anyone would think it was too late for him.

In fact, I think the moral of *Podkayne of Mars*, as Heinlein invented it, misses its target. Poddy's death drives home the point that children need to be nurtured, and need attention. A good point. But a moral for adults is out of place in a juvenile. So leave the original ending alone, and let Poddy live on in her hospital bed. The point is made, the child sees and feels pain, but is spared the worst of it. The cynics can still imagine her funeral if they wish. And the romantics among us can still imagine Captain Fries going out to find her destiny.

Tandra Ford

My vote: kill Poddy.

The original ending was the ending Heinlein wanted. The published ending is a hastily assembled Frankenstein's monster of an ending designed to please the editors he didn't agree with and it shows. With either ending, the whole book leads up to Poddy's eventual demise thanks to the scheming of her brother Clark. The sudden flip-flop in the published last chapter left me cold and angry with Heinlein. It wasn't until I found out the truth that I knew who I should really be mad at: the editors at Putnam.

I realize that back in the Sixties it was considered wrong to have a child die, especially when that child was a sweet, personable sixteen-year-old girl who was also the title character of the book and the first-person narrator of almost the whole thing. It would have been like having Nancy Drew or the Hardy Boys gunned down or the Bobbsey Twins killed by a drunk driver. But the fact remains that this was Heinlein's book, not the editor's and Heinlein's words should stand, not the cowardly decision of an editor thirty years ago.

Baen Books and the science fiction community have the chance to fix a wrong and create the first new Heinlein book in five years. Sure, we've all read the first part, but wouldn't it be nice to be able to add to your collection the original, uncensored *Podkayne*? To know that for once, the writer won in an editorial decision like this?

It would be a fitting tribute to a great man to have the real ending continue for the rest of time.

NOTE: *This essay was accompanied by a photograph of a dog.*

Liza Kimball

Clap Your Hands for Tinkerbell and Podkayne

I pushed in the front door and escaped the damp chill of a March evening.

"There's a puppy," my mother said, smiling.

My Gramma's dog was in the basement, introducing puppies to the world. I had been promised the privilege of keeping one.

The new dog resembled a black and white rat, with a pushed-in nose and a bent tail.

We checked the next morning, and there weren't any more puppies. The rat-thing was an Only Puppy.

I would name a male dog "Max"—after plucky Maximilian Jones, of *Starman Jones*, by Robert Heinlein. "Podkayne" was the name of choice for a female, after the heroine of Heinlein's *Podkayne of Mars*. I described Poddy in Expository Composition: "A Marsgirl of superior intelligence and kindness, who aspired to be a space explorer, but got into 'hot water' on Venus." (My teacher wrote "Martian," not "Marsgirl." But we know better.)

Well, what do I know about sexing animals? Months after his birth, I found I had made a Grave Mistake. Max was Podkayne.

I was aghast. It was too late to change his—her—
name.

I felt a Major Debt to Podkayne.

Now I will pay it.

Killing Poddy is a Beastly Idea, even if conceived
by the Grand Master himself. (Mumbling, rumbling,
Grumbling from the Grave?)

What purpose does Poddy's death have? What
enlightenment do we receive? Even a story with a
tragic course needs a purpose, a lesson. Apparently
Heinlein intended one moral involving parental
neglect, though this wasn't altogether apparent, as the
character of the parents was inadequately developed.
The other theme evidently deals with the reality of
growing up: discovering a complicated, less-than-per-
fect world.

Unfortunately, Podkayne wouldn't fully realize the
lesson if she dies. Is the lesson for Clark? He's anything but naive. Is it for the reader? We know the
bad news.

I believe Poddy's death is purposeless, melodra-
matic. Her death achieves no more than do her life-
threatening injuries; we learn nothing more. The political ruthlessness and near-death are sufficient. The
human experience is displayed.

Heinlein thought the death "indispensable." But is
this version more realistic? Not necessarily. The death
doesn't appear to be a necessary consequence of any
action in the book. Pod doesn't "dig persistently the
pit of her own destruction" (Phyllis Whitney), and her
distance from the explosion allows possible survival.
And Pod's survival does not imply an unrealistic
"happy ever after" life.

The death-ending simply shows the "inevitable"
triumph of Evil over Hope, Innocence and Good.
Nobody wants to read that book. Kindness as weakness.

Meaningful Wisdom is given us by Uncle Tom, about the "Poddy Story":

... I never did tell you the end of it, Poddy; you always fell asleep. It ends with a miracle. [Podkayne: A truly miracle?] Yes. This is the end. Poddy grew up and had another Poddy. And then the world was young again.

Should we kill the object of this proverb?
The end of Podkayne.
The world will never be young again.

J.J. Minor

Memories of Podkayne

More than anything else about *Podkayne of Mars*, I remember the sadness I felt upon its conclusion. It was like when I was eight years old and saw Bambi's mother die, or heard the terrible sound of that rifle being shot in *The Yearling*. Dad would say, "It was just a movie, just a made up story. They didn't really die." It helped a little, but not much.

I was just a few years older, twelve to be exact, when I picked up a slightly faded copy of *Podkayne of Mars* in a used book shop. I bought it because it was small; it didn't have that overwhelming thickness that most of the other books on the shelf had. Besides, I liked the monochrome red painting of the giant spaceship on the cover. This was my first real science fiction book and I was going to read it while at summer camp.

It was a small book; I read a little each day. I liked reading about Clark; he got into the kind of trouble that I could only dream about. So far this story, written by the guy whose name I didn't know how to pronounce, was good. I made a point of reading some of the more interesting passages to my cabin-mates. They weren't much for science fiction, but seemed to enjoy listening to the highlights. By the end of the fourth week, they all wanted to know how it ended.

I didn't want to tell them.

You're probably saying, "But why? It had a happy ending. Podkayne lived." Because, I didn't read it clearly enough! I thought she had died! I hadn't really understood that the line: "... Poddy still looks like a corpse ..." meant anything other than that she was a corpse. I suppose I was so saddened by Poddy's assumed death that I didn't go back and reread what had actually been written. So you see, for me there has always been only one ending: the one in which poor Podkayne dies.

Nineteen years ago, I remember having to tell the other guys that Podkayne had died saving the baby fairy's life. None of us could really appreciate what that ending was all about, what it was trying to show us. It took me three years after that before I picked up another Heinlein book; I didn't want to read another sad story. It was one thing to have woodland creatures die, but kids? No, I didn't like it; it was too real for me at the age of twelve.

After Robert A. Heinlein died, the book *Grumbles from the Grave* was published. I bought it immediately. Although my first experience with Mr. Heinlein's writing had not been an altogether pleasant one, over the years he had become my favorite author. Finding a book with stories in it that I hadn't read before was like receiving a gift from heaven. Needless to say, I was a bit surprised to discover that Podkayne *had not* died, at least not in the copy I had read.

I found my old yellowing paperback, compared the endings and felt ... well, I felt kind of dumb. Nineteen years ago I had felt terrible. You mean she's been alive all these years and if I had just read it correctly I wouldn't have had to suffer that needless loss? It seemed so.

This brings me to the vote for the official ending for Podkayne of Mars. For me she had always died to save that baby fairy, giving her life for something she loved. I read it the way it was written originally (kind of), as if my mind had purposefully ignored the part about Podkayne being hooked up to life support equipment. And I feel lucky now, after all these years, to have read it that way.

I just reread *Podkayne of Mars*, comparing the two endings. Now with an adult's perspective, I can see why she had to die, appreciate the true importance of what happened and what it means. And I now know, as unfortunate as it is to lose someone, especially a young person, that her death makes for a much stronger ending to the story.

While alive, Podkayne shows us that there are things worth risking our life for. She shows us what kind of power love can have, how being courageous and selfless is worth emulating. With Podkayne's death we are reminded with brutal clarity how life must be savored that much more, how it could all end so quickly. Through her demise, we are able to feel a loss and know that without death we can not possibly be aware of the true joy of being alive.

The true *Podkayne of Mars* doesn't have a sugar-coated happy ending. It isn't *just* a movie, or *just* a story; it's real and it hurts. But that's the point, isn't it: without the hurt, life really wouldn't be worth living. Thank you, Mr. Heinlein, for making that a little plainer for me to see.

William D. McGuire

Forgive me Father Heinlein, for I am about to SIN.

For six months I've put off writing this. I've been trying to come up with a way to defend your ending of *Podkayne*. Can't do it. Sure Podkayne isn't the heroine or genius-grade of D.T. Burroughs, Hilda Corners, Maureen Johnson, Minerva, Anne or Gwen Novak/Hazel Stone—crap—the list is Long, but how many young hooligans studied math, physics, engineering with a hope somewhere in their heads to crew that starship for Captain Fries? I wanted to be her Navigator. She should have the chance somewhen.

The whole point of the story was to illustrate the consequences of a mother who was too busy to tend to the rearing of her children. (And didn't I recently read some idiot who claimed Podkayne was "dated"? Sounds like right now in River City to me.) SO WHAT?! You taught me that big hairy men were put on this planet to protect little girls.

Mr. Heinlein, the part of me concerned with Honor, Duty and protecting women and children (political correctness be damned) are all due to you. It *hurts* to criticize any part of your work. But let me tell you—I have earned my franchise and my vote is for Poddy.

Dana L.M. Boltuch

I like the ending of *Podkayne of Mars* as it was originally published because most of the book is told from Poddy's point of view, and you really get to like her and get a feeling for her. You understand how she feels and reacts and thinks. And then, when you read Heinlein's original ending, and Poddy dies, it is really sad. You feel kind of like you would if a pet that you really loved a lot had died or run away. I like how the endings are told from Clark's point of view. Poddy thinks of him as a six-year-old (Marsmen years) genius, who does weird things. But if you know Clark, you know why he did them—sort of. Then at the end, when things are told from Clark's point of view, you fully understand the reasoning for them. Clark explains the reasoning for his actions—and it makes perfect sense. When you switch the main character, it gives you a better understanding of what is being stated. I am a nine-year-old girl, and this is the first book I have ever read by Robert Heinlein. My father recommended this book (and many others by Robert Heinlein) to me. He enjoys them very much and thinks I will, too. I did enjoy *Podkayne of Mars* very much.

David Majors

Podkayne Lives

Whether readers vote Podkayne to death or not, she will still live. All true characters live on after their stories have been read. Their books are alive and can be read again and again. Some of Robert Heinlein's stories, such as *Number of the Beast* or *Job*, tell us that every choice leads to alternate worlds. Podkayne might be dead in some worlds, but in others she continues to live. We need her alive. We need her alive in our world. We need to know she has the chance to face her choices and make them. We need innocent Marsmen who love everyone.

Thirty years ago when she was first presented to the public we listened to her adolescent dreams and fears. Does she want to be a famous explorer star ship captain if she must be all alone? Today, her problem still faces society. Women, men, girls and boys struggle to make the same choices. How do you choose between a career and a family? Must you choose or can you have it all? If Podkayne sacrifices herself to save one baby she makes a choice. A choice that honors her heroism. She fights for the rightness of what she believes in. She wades in to defend her uncle, her brother, or her planet. Hers is the courage needed to make choices. Not one choice that ends in death, but a lifetime of choices that builds a complete human being. A human being built of love and dreams. We need Podkayne alive.

James Kahle

To Croak or Not to Croak,
That is the Question

A few years ago, DC Comics, Inc. held a telephone survey, asking their readers to decide the final fate of Robin, the Batman's sidekick. Between the callers with a surprisingly morbid streak within them and those who thought that the brat had it coming, the survey ended with the Boy Wonder in a body bag

Now history repeats itself with Robert A. Heinlein's *Podkayne of Mars*, and I find myself arguing for the Postlude as originally published, but for reasons other than just saving Poddy's butt.

Thanks to Mrs. Heinlein's inclusion of the original ending in *Grumbles from the Grave* (her biography of Robert Heinlein), I already knew about the other ending. However, I was astonished upon discovering that the only changes Heinlein made to the original Postlude was in the last paragraph. Initially, the last paragraph simply wrapped up the story, sending Clark and Uncle Tom back to the *Tricorn* with the baby fairy.

In the published version, that paragraph is extended into an additional page. This allowed us to hear Uncle Tom arguing with Podkayne's parents over the phone, mostly berating them for caring more about their careers than their children, but also warning them of Clark's twisted morals, as well as resurrecting Podkayne in a hospital bed.

Let us also consider Clark. In both versions, he acts exceedingly ruthless (Ex: killing Mrs. Grew and the guard fairy). This would be the usual way for a tough-as-nails generic adventure hero, but in a smegging 11-year-old? At least, in the published version, we get to hear Uncle Tom say how he really feels about Clark's attitude.

As for Heinlein's own essay defending his original ending, I'd like to know when he wrote it. Why do I ask? Go read the last chapter of Heinlein's 1980 book *The Number of the Beast*, where Heinlein had a family reunion of sorts, uniting characters from some of his best books, including the casts of *Stranger in a Strange Land*, Baen's own *Glory Road*, as well as a somewhat older and wiser Podkayne Fries (who never became the first female starship captain, instead opting to become a "therapy empathist," whatever that is). Anyone can change his mind, even stodgy old science fiction writers.

Well, that about wraps up my argument for the second ending. Just consider the original ending a first draft. Being forced to change the ending allowed Heinlein to add material previously ignored, which is thus a good thing. As for saving Podkayne, consider that icing on the cake.

Incidentally, I voted to save Robin, too.

Barbara Whitmore

One of the main factors in choosing which Postlude to use, whether one agrees with Heinlein's basic premise or not, is which one better conveys the point of the story and is better for the book.

In *Grumbles from the Grave* he wrote to a reader,

". . . I write for the following reasons—
1. To support myself and my family;
2. To entertain my readers;
3. And, if possible, to cause my readers to *think*."

He also wrote that "The third reason is more complex. A writer can afford to indulge only if he clears the first two hurdles." The Originally Written Postlude tried to achieve the third at the expense of the first two. An ending that is, as one might say, a "downer" would not be popular with the group the story was intended for, namely juveniles. Word of mouth alone would decrease sales. Also, it would be less likely to be reread, which would mean that the meaning of the story would have less chance to "sink in" to a reader.

Another factor is that in the Originally Written Postlude the point of the story (namely that the adults did not raise Podkayne and Clark very well—as stated in *Grumbles from the Grave*) is only *implied* in it, and so can be missed by the reader. But in the Originally Published Postlude, that point is *stated* by Uncle Tom in his conversation to the children's father that Clark overhears. It is not missed by the reader. In the implied version, the blame might be placed on Clark's forgetfulness and Podkayne's clumsiness in losing the tracker, instead of on the adults for not raising them correctly and for not protecting them enough, which is in the stated version.

Heinlein seemed to think that the Published version's ending was too "happy." That she would recover, marry Dexter, and sail off into space. However, one may not see it that way. One wonders if she would ever fully recover from the bomb blast. One may also doubt that she would marry Dexter because she would never be sure if he were asking because of politics or guilt instead of love.

Also, in the Published version, once gets a better view of the problems with Clark because of his puzzlement at what Uncle Tom said to his father about him. And the last sentence is both chilling and poignant in its insight into Clark. The story would suffer without it.

The Originally Written ending is also too abrupt. Its timing is off, rather like a play in which the actors have rushed through the last act.

An editor may want a book changed for reasons that will harm a book (as chronicled in *Grumbles*), or for reasons that will help a book. In this case, an editor had the objectivity to see what changes were needed to help him to get the point of the story across. The Originally Published Postlude should stand.

Matthew Haun

Does Podkayne Live or Die?

To begin with, I must admit to certain prejudices in this matter: For one thing, I've always believed that if critics and publishers have such penetrating wisdom on how a book should be written, then they should sit down and write it themselves. Moreover, Heinlein tended to favor pat, happy endings. It's almost refreshing to encounter a truly tragic ending. Nonetheless, I must favor the *Postlude* as originally published, my prejudices not withstanding.

The key lies in Uncle Tom's aggravated conversation with the folks back on Mars, wherein he warns them that, regardless of Poddy's fate, it is Clark they need to worry about. This conversation could just as well have taken place in the *Postlude* where Poddy dies; yet it did not. I look forward to reading Heinlein's defense of the original, to see if he recognized any significance in this conversation.

Uncle Tom's concern about Clark is indeed valid. He would, as Poddy notes, blow up the universe just to hear the bang. And yet Clark, despite his phenomenal (if malicious) savvy, can't imagine what Uncle Tom is talking about. He just doesn't get it. Poddy herself is prone to wondering if she shouldn't lower her sights from commanding a starship to something more modest. Whether or not she realizes that ambition, I submit that Podkayne has a far greater destiny in coaching the demented genius of her erstwhile kid brother into some semblance of humanity—and a far more challenging vocation as well! She had already pushed Clark

towards this goal when she shanghaied the junior nihilist into nursery duty aboard the *Tricorn*. He balked;
but he picked it up. Then, ensnaring him in her own
final (?), desperate human gesture, she left him in
charge of the baby fairy.

That baby fairy counts. I mean, I feel the weight of
a tremendous hubris in attempting to gainsay this
author, or his characters (or even, God forbid, his publishers!). But hey, if it turns out dry, we all know Clark
can take care of himself. The trouble is he will also
be taking care of the baby fairy. Surely a creature with
such a pronounced innate capacity for mauling and
biting needs a better role model than Clark Fries.
Surely . . .

G. David Nordley

Heinlein's original ending was right for its times. We were living in a fool's paradise in the fifties, most of us. Things were nice and set. To prosper you kept your nose and your gray flannel suit clean and didn't look closely to see all the problems hidden under the rug by the experts. We needed shocks then, needed to know the sacrifices on which our comfortable time was built, needed to know that when fools run rampant, even precious young women might pay the price of being a heroine.

But that was then.

Now, after Pol Pot and The Shining Path; after Jim Jones and David Koresh; after Tamils and Serbs; after an unending stream of art imitating life imitating art in a charnel house; after so many bad-is-good revolutions that those words even resemble their opposites in this dialect or that; after all of that, killing Poddy would mean just one more plop in the literary privy.

What we desperately need to know now is that sometimes things do work out; that sometimes pluck and decency survive. We need to know that while you might not succeed in everything, the ones that do succeed are chosen from the ones that at least try. Perhaps the master knew that when he cast some of his last bread on the water and gave us Friday.

Today, in 1993, we need to believe that Poddy lives.

Karen E. Walch

"Poddy grew up and had another Poddy. And then the world was young again," Heinlein writes, adding, "That's all there ever is. But it's enough."

Aren't the author's own words answer enough? How can Heinlein's insistence on Poddy's death stand up against them? In many ways, Poddy's fate becomes a symbol for all the future as a whole. If this young, vibrant, hopeful woman dies, a needless casualty of her own best intentions, what hope is there for anyone in the book? Can the aging delegate of a small world really hope to overturn the arguments of his planet's own ambassador and save three worlds from tyranny? Can a young psychopath really change his colors—especially after he has recovered from the shock of his sister's death and his normal, selfish instincts have a chance to resurface? In a book whose message is the importance of protecting and caring for the young, what hope is there if the one person who best represents youth is killed off?

Poddy's death wasn't even good literature. Having it reported after the fact, without any preparation or even a glimpse of Poddy's decision to risk her life, makes it a passive event. After seeing Poddy develop and learn throughout the book, depriving her of strength at the climax rings false. It might have worked if Clark's fate was the most important thing in the book. Then having the arrogant, amoral genius brought up short by another's tragedy might work. But Clark is only supporting cast, not the lead.

Sometimes, authors make mistakes. Some of the greatest writers in history started a story in one direction only to have it take off on its own and go some-

273

where else. Shaw could never admit that Liza Doolittle should marry Professor Higgins instead of the spineless Freddy. Dickens never could decide which ending he preferred for *Great Expectations*. Chaucer thought his masterpiece, *The Canterbury Tales*, should be burned. One mistake doesn't put Heinlein in a bad crowd, and that is what his ending to *Podkayne* was, a wrong choice that was a disservice to the fine book he wrote and to all those who will always love this novel.

Harry Lewis Crumpacker

Years ago there lived a certain type of teenager. They played in band, had thick glasses with ugly plastic frames and wore pocket protectors stuffed with pens and mechanical pencils. They got good grades, but were invariably last to be picked for the athletic events their schoolmates relished so. In this day and age they would probably be computer nerds, but they had no computers. Computers in those days cost millions of dollars and took up entire rooms. No, these youthful dweebs probably had a slide rule. But they knew damn well what computers were. Because they **READ SCIENCE FICTION**!

What does the name Robert A. Heinlein mean to them? Quite a bit, oh yes indeed, quite a bit.

So picking which ending is the proper one for *Podkayne of Mars* is largely moot, at least to those faithful few. There can be only one answer to a question offering such a choice.

Both, of course.

Many scholars of the genre, with high falutin' degrees and credentials, could write entire dissertations on the relative merits of either choice. But it seems to me that such an analysis—the picking apart of phases of the grand old curmudgeon's work—misses the point. Whether *Podkayne of Mars* falls into his juvenile phase, or was one of the first of what has been termed the "Glory Years," and how that affects which ending is more fitting are questions better left to the learned. Not the lovers.

For us it doesn't matter a hoot. We *are* the juveniles RAH was supposedly writing for, and we didn't care about such abstracts. All we knew was that we wanted to read more about Scar Gordon and Thorby Baslim. D.D. Harriman and Rhysling the Blind Singer—that was what was important. Anything with the RAH name would do. We were not even allowed to submit science fiction novels as book reports in school, so what did we care for critics and scholars? It wasn't important then and it isn't now.

So give us both. *And* the RAH essay. Sure it will take up a few more pages, maybe cost another penny or two. But if that spark still lingers, Mr. Baen, if you remember the hardbacks in the library with the little rocketship emblem, or Ace doubles, or any of those glorious days when the world was gentler somehow and the stars seemed close enough to touch—if you ever dreamed of being an M.I. or joining the Patrol with Ezra Dahlquist—give us both.

After all, we would probably read anything the old fellow wrote.

Even his laundry list.

A Final Word . . .

Having been brought to the spirit of the thing by judging the essay entrants, I have spent no little time musing on the merits of the two positions. The Poddy killers, among whom I am forced to number myself for much the reasons given in the essays, won all right—by about two to one in votes, and perhaps the same in reasoning—but the folks who tossed logic to the winds and leaped to the defense of a sixteen-year-old girl were following a deeper logic, and that logic should not be disregarded. Furthermore, and this is the nub of it, *Podkayne of Mars* was intended as a book for children, and has been, over the years, read by a very great number of them.

Now it may be that adults don't want overt messages getting in the way of their stories, and they surely did not give the writer a license to preach at them when they plunked down their money for an entertainment, but kids are different. When the lessons a story illustrates are hard ones, for children an explanation may very well be in order. So in the spirit of an uncle trying to explain God's ways to an eleven-year-old at his sister's funeral, I offer the following revision to the ending for the Putnam edition as a postlude to RAH's story. And, hey, maybe Uncle Tom knew Clark was listening . . . and that was part of the lesson, too.

Who knows? If enough people want to, perhaps we might persuade Virginia Heinlein to let us add this edited postlude from the first edition to RAH's original ending. But that is for you and Ginny to decide.

—Jim Baen

Postlude

I'm alone now. Uncle Tom left and left me behind—alone, that is, except for a whole platoon of guards. I can't go anywhere without one. I can't go to the casinos at all any more—not that I want to, much.

I heard part of what Uncle Tom told Dad about it. Not all of it, as a phone conversation with a bounce time of over twenty minutes is episodic. I heard none of what Dad said and only one monologue of Uncle's:

"Nonsense, sir! I am not dodging my own load of guilt; it will be with me always. Indeed, when my present task is finished, I think I may die of it. Nor can I wait here until you arrive and you know it and you know why—and Clark will be safer in Mr. Cunha's hands and *not* close to me and you know *that*, too! But I have a message for you, sir, one that you should pass on to your wife. Just this: people who will not take the trouble to raise children should not have them. You with your nose always in a book, your wife gallivanting off God knows where—You should tell your wife, sir, that building bridges and space stations and such gadgets is all very well ... but that a woman has more important work to do. I tried to suggest this to you years ago ... and was told to mind my own business.

279

Now I am saying it. Your daughter is beyond our help, but Clark, perhaps, is not. With him it *may* be too late, but God may give you a second chance if you hurry. Ending transmission!"

I faded into the woodwork then and didn't get caught. I'm sure the world would have ended if Uncle Tom had caught me watching him cry— But what did Uncle Tom mean by that—trying to scare Dad about *me*? I wasn't hurt at all and he knows it. I just got a load of mud on me, not even a burn . . . whereas *Poddy is dead*.

I don't see what he was driving at.

I'm taking care of that baby fairy. Poddy would have wanted me to; she's always been a sentimentalist. It needs a lot of attention because it gets lonely and has to be held and cuddled, or it cries.

So I'm up a lot in the night—I guess it thinks I'm its mother. I don't mind, I don't have much else to do.

It seems to like me.

Here is the same text, but with additions noted by underlining and deletions noted by strikethroughs, so that you may judge if we have limited ourselves to necessary changes.

Postlude

I'm alone ~~with her~~ now. ~~Mr. Cunha made them hold the *Tricorn* until it was certain whether Poddy would die or get well, then~~ Uncle Tom left and left me behind—alone, that is, except for ~~doctors, and nurses, and Dexter Cunha hanging around all the time, and~~ a whole platoon of guards. I can't go anywhere without one. I can't go to the casinos at all any more—not that I want to, much.

I heard part of what Uncle Tom told Dad about it. Not all of it, as a phone conversation with a bounce time of over twenty minutes is episodic. I heard none of what Dad said and only one monologue of Uncle's:

"Nonsense, sir! I am not dodging my own load of guilt; it will be with me always. <u>Indeed, when my present task is finished, I think I may die of it.</u> Nor can I wait here until you arrive and you know it and you know why—and Clark ~~both children~~ will be safer in Mr. Cunha's hands and *not* close to me ... and you know *that*, too! But I have a message for you, sir, one that you should pass on to your wife. Just this: people who will not take the trouble to raise children should not have them. You with your nose always in a book, your wife gallivanting off God knows where—~~between~~

281

you, your daughter was almost killed. No credit to either of you that she wasn't. Just blind luck. You should tell your wife, sir, that building bridges and space stations and such gadgets is all very well ... but that a woman has more important work to do. I tried to suggest this to you years ago ... and was told to mind my own business. Now I am saying it. Your daughter is beyond our help, will get well, no thanks to either of you. But I have my doubts about Clark but Clark, perhaps, is not. With him it *may* be too late, but God may give you a second chance if you hurry. Ending transmission!"

I faded into the woodwork then and didn't get caught.—I'm sure the world would have ended if Uncle Tom had caught me watching him cry—But what did Uncle Tom mean by that—trying to scare Dad about *me*? I wasn't hurt at all and he knows it. I just got a load of mud on me, not even a burn ... whereas Poddy is *dead*. still looks like a corpse and they've got her piped and wired like a creche.

I don't see what he was driving at.

I'm taking care of that baby fairy. Poddy would have wanted me to; she's always been a sentimentalist. Because Poddy will want to see it when she gets well enough to notice things again. It needs a lot of attention because it gets lonely and has to be held and cuddled, or it cries.

So I'm up a lot in the night—I guess it thinks I'm its mother. I don't mind, I don't have much else to do.

It seems to like me.